SORCHA
THE HIGHLAND CLAN BOOK 8
Published by Keira Montclair
Copyright © 2017 by Keira Montclair

Cover Design and Interior Format
© KILLION
GROUP, INC.

Sorcha

THE HIGHLAND CLAN — EIGHT

KEIRA MONTCLAIR

BESTSELLING AUTHOR

TO THE READER

EACH OF THE NOVELS IN The Highland Clan is a stand-alone novel. However, for the richest experience, I would recommend starting with the first novel: Loki.

You'll see there is an extensive list of characters, ones you will grow to love if you start at the beginning.

The Clan Grant Series is the series in which the parents were introduced.

The series can be read separately, but many characters appear in both.

THE GRANTS AND RAMSAYS IN 1280S

GRANTS

LAIRD ALEXANDER GRANT and wife, MADDIE
John (Jake) and wife, Aline
James (Jamie) and wife, Gracie
Kyla
Connor
Elizabeth
Maeve

BRENNA GRANT and husband, QUADE RAMSAY
Torrian (Quade's son from his first marriage) and wife, Heather—
Nellie and son, Lachlan
Lily (Quade's daughter from his first marriage) and husband,
Kyle—twin daughters, Lise and Liliana
Bethia
Gregor
Jennet

ROBBIE GRANT and wife, CARALYN
Ashlyn (Caralyn's daughter from a previous relationship) and husband, Magnus
Gracie (Caralyn's daughter from a previous relationship) and husband, Jamie
Rodric (Roddy)
Padraig

BRODIE GRANT and wife, CELESTINA
Loki (adopted) and wife, Arabella—sons, Kenzie and Lucas
Braden
Catriona
Alison

JENNIE GRANT and husband, AEDAN CAMERON
Riley
Tara
Brin

RAMSAYS

QUADE RAMSAY and wife, BRENNA GRANT (see above)

LOGAN RAMSAY and wife, GWYNETH
Molly (adopted) and husband, Tormod
Maggie (adopted)
Sorcha
Gavin
Brigid

MICHEIL RAMSAY and wife, DIANA
David
Daniel

AVELINA RAMSAY and DREW MENZIE
Elyse
Tad
Tomag
Maitland

CHAPTER ONE

᠊ᢊ

Highlands of Scotland, 1280s

THEY WERE SUPPOSED TO BE hunting.
Instead, they had become the hunted.

Sorcha Ramsay screamed as an arrow sluiced through the air, embedding in a nearby tree with a loud thwack. The three men hunting with her gathered in around her horse, sending her dearest friend into a fit of irritation.

"Get your head down, Sorcha!" Cailean MacAdam yelled.

Get my head down? "And how am I supposed to see where I'm going with you three circled around me and my head down?"

"Bend over your horse," Cailean's brother, Alan, bellowed at her.

Another arrow whizzed through the air, missing them all.

Frang, the third member of their group, pointed off to the side. "It came from over there." He motioned toward Alan and the two rode off in that direction.

Sorcha, intending to make her escape, went in the opposite direction—only to hear a third arrow swish even closer to her. The danger made her gasp, but what happened next infuriated her.

Cailean growled and rode his horse up next to hers. Then, without saying a word, he leaned over to scoop her off her horse and onto his lap with a plunk.

Sorcha sat the horse sideways. As soon as she balanced herself, she swung at the lout. "What the hell, Cailean? I can ride my own horse. Leave me be." She twisted around in search of her dear horse.

"Must you curse like a reiver?"

"I'll curse however I please. Why the hell do you care?"

"I don't, just thought I'd ask." He rolled his eyes.

She ignored him. True, he was doing his best to help her, but she was too worried about her dear pet to pay him any mind. "Where's Horsie?"

"Could you not have come up with a better name for the animal than Horsie?"

"I was only ten summers when my sire brought her home. He said he'd bought me a horsie, so that's her name." She held a firm grip on him so she could whirl around to look for her horse.

"Settle yourself. We're going back to the keep." He reached for her hip, trying to face her forward.

"Nay." She swung at his shoulder again.

He caught her hand mid-air. "What the blazes are you doin'? I'm trying to help you."

"Nay, you're not. You're keeping me from my horse." She turned around again and finally found her beautiful chestnut-colored horse nosing about some bushes to their left. There was no sign of their attacker, no sign of Alan and Frang. "There. We must go to her. She's wild. I cannot leave her out here alone."

Cailean growled, "We're headed back. I'll not have Logan Ramsay's daughter take an arrow in my presence."

He turned his horse back toward the keep. Sorcha was furious. She'd only convinced the lads to go hunting because her sire was away again. He was always impressed with the hunting parties that brought home big game, and she was eager to do something to make him proud, something to make up for...

Hellfire, she could not bear to think of the evil thing she'd done.

But her horse, her dear Horsie was in danger. She shoved against Cailean's chest and tried to wrangle the reins from him. He was built like a stone wall and her plan failed terribly.

"Woman, unhand the reins," Cailean bellowed. "I'm in control. Not you."

"We need to go back. You don't understand. I'm worried about my horse. I'll never forgive myself if aught happens to her. Give me the reins." She made another grab for them.

"I do not answer to you. This is my horse, and I'd like to stay alive. If you're hurt out here, your father will hang me by my bollocks for all to see."

"But my horse…" She shoved him, trying to force his hand as she fought to keep her tears at bay, but she lost her balance instead. Tumbling off the side of the horse, she took Cailean down with her. She landed hard on a section of soft moss and leaves, fortunately, but the fall knocked the wind out of her lungs, forcing her to scrabble for a deep breath.

Cailean landed next to her, the sheer size of the big brute shaking the ground underneath her. Another arrow whizzed through the air just above them, and Cailean rolled on top of her. Heat rushed through her, but she reached up and pushed his chest as hard as she could. "You big lout…"

He kissed her. The lout was kissing her. Her eyes flew open to glare at him, but he wasn't looking. His warm lips pressed hard against hers, enticing her to part her lips. Before she knew it, his tongue was inside her mouth, caressing every crevice he could find, and her hands fisted in his hair, gripping him closer rather than pushing him away. He made her forget everything—the arrows, Horsie, her sire—and just revel in his taste, in this moment.

Her horse made the worst sound she'd ever heard. Horror washed through her. She'd let Cailean kiss her instead of running to Horsie, and now her friend had been hurt. Pulling away, she shoved at Cailean's chest again and kicked him. "Hellfire. Horsie? Horsie? Are you all right?"

The lout held her down. "She took an arrow, but you must stay down. You'll not put yourself in the path of another arrow."

"Leave me be." She did her best to squirm out from under him, but the man was one of the biggest lads she'd ever met, almost as large as her uncle Alex and his twin sons, Jake and Jamie. The effort had her breathing hard again, her body hot.

"Sorcha, I cannot. Please stop fighting me. When it's safe, I'll let you go again."

"So you can steal another kiss?" The man was making her daft. She pushed and shoved against him with all she had, but he still didn't budge. "*Mo creach*! I need to get to her!"

"I had to kiss you to keep you quiet. An archer is attacking us, Sorcha, and your screams will lead him right to us. You have no sense, lass."

"I do, too! Papa says I have as much sense as any lad in the guards, and that includes you, you big brute. Poor excuse for steal-ing a kiss."

He glanced up and checked the area, then caught her gaze. His green eyes had a glitter in them she didn't like, his sandy brown hair falling forward. "Are you going to lie to me and say you didn't enjoy it?"

"I did not. You tasted like a wet frog. Now get off me." She shoved his shoulder again.

"A wet frog, is it? Is that why your hands grabbed my hair and pulled me closer?" He ran his finger down her jawline and she jerked away from him.

"You have a vivid imagination."

He laughed and she kicked him.

"Ow. Will you stop using your boots on me?"

She finally managed to get out from under him and the sound of horses' hooves reached their ears. A thrill of fear shot through her, but it was only Frang and Alan.

"What did you find?" Cailean yelled as they rode closer.

"He's gone," Frang said. "He was shooting at us from a tree, but we watched him take off on his horse. Could not tell who 'twas."

"Good." Cailean got up and held his hand out to help Sorcha up. Alan was watching them with open curiosity, but if anyone needed to make an explanation, it was *not* her.

Sorcha stood up on her own, brushing off Cailean's hand, and took off at a dead run toward her dear pet. "Horsie?"

She heard some talk behind her, but all she registered was her beautiful horse's pained cries. As she came closer, she gasped in horror. Horsie lay on her side, an arrow in her flank. "Nay!"

Distantly, she could hear the others making their approach. She heard Cailean say, "That's because it's not a fitting name for a fine animal like that. I'll make up my own name for her. Chestnut. That's what I'll call her. She's a beautiful color." How dare he say such a thing when Horsie was injured?

Sorcha fell onto her knees next to the mare. Horsie's raspy breathing was audible, and blood streamed from the wound. "How can this be happening?"

Alan dismounted as soon as he got there, then Frang. Cailean arrived last.

She paid them no mind until Frang pulled out his dagger.

"What are you doing?" she asked. "Put that back." She stood in front of her horse, her hands on her hips, daring him to try to get past her.

"Sorcha, your horse is in pain," Frang said. "I'm going to take her out of her misery. 'Tis the right thing to do. The injury will fester and cause her more pain. Cailean, take Sorcha back to the keep and I'll take care of the horse. Sorry, lass, but there's no choice."

His words bit into her—and yet it couldn't be true. She wouldn't let it be true. Sorcha bit her lower lip and charged him, hitting him full force with both her hands square to his chest, knocking him off his feet. "You mean brute! You'll never touch my horse. Cousin Bethia will save her. You'll see. She's the best with animals. She'll save Horsie."

Frang said, "Cailean, explain to her that this is the right thing to do."

The horse flopped its free front leg three times.

Sorcha hurried back and fell to the ground, wrapping her arms around the horse's neck. "I'll not let him kill you, Horsie. I know he's upset you, but pay him no mind. I'll protect you. Bethia *will* help you."

"Cailean," Alan said. "Take Sorcha back to the castle."

Tears rolled down Sorcha's cheeks. Besides her cousin Bethia, Horsie was the only one she could talk to, of late. Her mother only had time for her younger sister, Brigid, ever since they'd rescued her from the clutches of her kidnapper. Molly had gone off somewhere with her new husband, Tormod, and it was a grand mystery where they'd gone. All Sorcha knew was that they were working for the Crown. Sorcha's next eldest sister, Maggie, was always trying to keep her away from lads—as though Sorcha would desert her the way Molly had, which was ridiculous because no lads dared to come close enough to kiss her. She was Logan Ramsay's daughter, but the difference between her and her sisters was she was the *image* of her father. Her father could strike fear into the best warrior in the lists.

And there was her sire. He was always gone, and he was upset with her more often than not when he *was* home. She'd always been adventurous and free-spirited, riding her dear horse wherever she pleased, but he was no longer as tolerant of it. He didn't care for her habit of keeping company with lads her age or older.

Sorcha hadn't changed. She'd always preferred being outside in the fresh Highland air, playing with the lads, instead of inside with the lassies.

Some called her a flirt, but it wasn't about that—at least not most of the time. She loved being out in nature. She'd spent her youngest days attached to her sire's chest in a folded plaid, moving through the mountains and the valleys of their land. Her mother liked to tell the story of how wee Sorcha used to throw her arms in the air and giggle whenever she was pelted by rain while strapped to her sire's chest, laughing at streaks of lightning illuminating the night sky.

No one understood her. Well, her sire used to, but his attitude had changed ever since she'd gained her woman's body. She wished things could go back to the way they used to be.

"Cailean, please help me get her back? I adore my horse. I cannot lose her."

Then something miraculous happened.

"Put your dagger away, Frang," Cailean said. "Ride back to the keep and send a cart out. I'll get the horse into it if I have to do it myself."

☾

Cailean had just made the most ridiculous promise of his life, but he simply couldn't do it to the lass—especially not after the kiss they'd shared. Hellfire, the lass had fisted his hair like she wanted everything he could give her. If that hadn't made his cock spring to action in a flash...

He'd pined for Sorcha Ramsay for months, dreamed of the different ways he could court her, kiss her, wrap his arms around her glorious curves. But never had he expected it to happen without him even thinking about it. Thank the saints above that he'd thought of a convincing excuse. It wasn't even a lie, not exactly— he *had* been trying to silence her to protect her from the attacker.

What he wouldn't give to have those breasts pushed against him again, her arms wrapped around him as if she'd never let go.

Her sweet voice brought him out of his dreams. "Cailean, you'll do your best not to hurt Horsie when you put her in the cart, will you not?"

Her eyes misted with the tears she wished to shed over her dear horse. She was too strong to let them fall.

He rubbed his jaw, using the rasp of his thumbnail to wake him-self back up, draw himself back to reality. "Sorcha, you know I cannot promise she'll be fine, but I *do* promise to get her back to Bethia. I'll see what we can do."

"My thanks." She leaned over, resting her head near Horsie's neck, just under the horse's jaw. "I would not be able to tolerate losing her. She was a special gift from Papa."

"Where is your sire? I have not seen him about." He paced behind her, his hand near the hilt of his sword in case the horse lost its mind or the archer suddenly appeared in front of them. The sight of her lying in the grass next to her wounded horse brought out a strange protectiveness in him.

"He's off for the Crown again. I never know when he'll be here. I need to speak to him about something important, but he disap-peared after Molly and Tormod married."

"Are you upset about Molly marrying?"

"Nay. Why would I be upset?"

He saw her scowl and decided to change the subject. He must have hit a nerve, and she was already upset about her horse.

"No reason. Did your mother go with him?" He cast a glance toward the castle, hoping his brother wouldn't hurry much. He was actually alone with Sorcha Ramsay, and he had justification for it. He'd often wished to talk to her, but she'd always seemed so unapproachable. Beautiful and fierce, and fiercely guarded by her sire.

"Nay, she stayed behind. She hasn't left Brigid's side since Molly saved her. Brigid was too upset by the whole ordeal." Her hand massaged the coat of her horse, and she whispered sweet words in the mare's ear.

Cailean had half expected the beast would start squirming in pain, hurting Sorcha with a flailing hoof, but the animal was much calmer now that Sorcha lay beside her, stroking her coat, soothing her.

Now if he could just figure out how to get the lass to rub him that way...or talk sweet words to him. How foolish he'd been to fall for Logan Ramsay's daughter. True, Logan had three other daughters—Molly and Maggie, whom Logan and his wife had adopted in Edinburgh, and wee Brigid, but Sorcha was the man's firstborn child. Everyone in the Ramsay clan knew Sorcha was the light of her sire's eyes.

Sorcha was the only daughter who bore Logan Ramsay's image, though her brother was starting to resemble him more and more. You could not look at Sorcha and ignore that she was his daughter, and all the lads in the clan stayed away from her because they all feared the king's famous friend. Logan Ramsay had to be past forty, but he was still solid muscle and a hell of a swordsman and an archer. The only thing he'd lost was speed—and only then because Molly was fast enough to outrun everyone. The man had plenty of cunning; if he wanted to find you, he would. None of the lads dared to go near Sorcha when Logan was at the keep.

The poor lass would probably never marry.

One night, after the Ramsay warriors had spent a long day in the lists trying to please Logan, they'd thought of all the different ways he could hurt a lad. Those visions had never left Cailean. Sweat broke out across his forehead when he realized there could be witnesses to the fact that he'd kissed Ramsay's daughter in the grass, his body sprawled across hers. He wasn't worried about his brother telling anyone—there was no one more loyal than Alan— but he had to wonder about Frang. What would Logan do if he found out?

Alan did not take his time, alas, and he soon came across the field with the cart. Frang rode alongside him, and Kyle Maule, the laird's second, rode ahead of them.

"Cailean," Kyle yelled before he dismounted. "Tell me what you saw of the archer."

Sorcha jumped up from her horse's side and interrupted them. "Kyle, Horsie is hurt. We must help her."

Kyle glanced at the beast and held his hand up to Sorcha. "We'll get your horse back to Bethia. Your life is more important, so I'll deal with the threat to you first."

"But my horse…"

Kyle arched his brow at her, his hands settling on his hips. "So you'd like me to tell your sire that I have no idea why someone was firing arrows at you and the lads? Don't argue with me, Sorcha." Alan had dismounted and Frang came up behind him. Kyle motioned for them to get the ropes and the large hunk of coarse cloth they would maneuver under the animal. Then he turned his attention back to Cailean. "Your version?"

"We were hunting a boar when an arrow came out of nowhere. We surrounded Sorcha, but the arrows continued to fly. I scooped her off her horse and onto mine minutes before Horsie—" he shifted his gaze toward Sorcha, "—took an arrow."

"That was it? Two arrows?"

"Nay, there were two more."

"How did they miss all of you?" Kyle strode toward one of the trees, pulling an arrow out of the bark, checking the tip.

"Sorcha couldn't keep still, and we both fell off the horse."

Kyle stopped in his tracks and asked, "Logan Ramsay's daughter fell off your horse? Do you know you took your life in your hands, MacAdam?"

"She shoved at me, and we both lost our balance."

"And then what?"

"We fell off and two more arrows flew by. I covered her with my body to protect her. Frang and Alan rode after the archer, but they were too far to do aught but watch him go."

Sorcha screeched, "Protected me? You stole a kiss." She spun around and strode directly toward him. When she reached him, her finger managed to land in the center of his chest. "You stole a kiss when I was worried about my sweet mare."

Cailean couldn't believe what he was hearing. The lass must hate him for certain to talk that way. "I kissed you to keep you quiet. You were yelling about your horse, giving away our position." Shite, his bollocks already ached from the pain that would be inflicted on him if Logan Ramsay ever heard her say that. He fought the urge to reach down and cover them.

"Because you wouldn't let me go to her." Tears threatened to spill down her cheeks.

He couldn't decide what was worse, her anger or her tears. Hell, he'd never live this one down in the lists. Kyle's demeanor was serious, but Frang and Alan were both struggling to stop their laughter from erupting.

Kyle held his hand up to Cailean. "Four arrows?"

Cailean nodded, discomfort still churning inside him. That feeling only became keener when Kyle took his arm and pulled him aside. But rather than punish him, Kyle whispered, "She's upset over her horse. There's no need for you to worry."

Then he spun around and gave directions on how he wanted the horse loaded into the cart. "Alan and Frang over there," he said, pointing to the horse's flank. "Cailean and I will lift the upper body."

Before they began, Kyle added, "You'll not repeat any of this. 'Tis my job to pass it on to those that need to know. You understand, Alan and Frang?"

Alan frowned, but he nodded. Frang did the same, although he shot a furtive look at Cailean.

They started moving the horse. Moments later, Cailean grumbled and shouted, "Stop." Everyone stared at him. "I'll protect her flank. You're hurting her, Alan."

Sorcha's face lit up, her hands wringing in front of her. "Thank you, Cailean. She's such a good horse. I know she's heavy, but try not to hurt her. Kyle, my thanks for coming out to help us. You know I'd be devastated if we couldn't get her back to the castle."

The sweet words had such an effect on Cailean, he decided he could lift the animal by himself if it would make Sorcha happy. Damn, but he'd sworn never to let himself fall in love with a lass… ever. He just couldn't allow it.

He was headed for sure disaster.

CHAPTER TWO

꙾

A S SOON AS THEY GOT Horsie into the stables, Sorcha relaxed. Horsie would not be killed. She had been given a chance. "My thanks to all for getting my horse back home. She is verra special to me."

They all nodded in acknowledgment, then Kyle said, "Frang, you belong in the lists. Alan, go to the keep and find Bethia. Tell her 'tis urgent. I'm going to share the tidings with our laird. Cailean, stay with Sorcha until Bethia arrives in case she needs help moving Horsie."

After they all left, Sorcha turned to Cailean, a sheepish expression on her face. "Forgive me. I did not mean to cause any trouble. I did not expect…" She could feel the tears begging to flow in streams down her cheeks, but did her best to contain them.

Cailean leaned one arm against a nearby post. "Sorcha, why were you so eager to go hunting today?"

She sighed loud enough to scare a flock of birds away had there been one near. Crossing her arms, she stared at the ceiling for a moment, then huffed before bringing her gaze back to Cailean. "My sire is gone, and I wished to make him proud. I suppose that sounds foolish to you, but you know how much I adore my father. I thought if I brought a boar or a deer down, he'd be proud of me. I hoped you could help me. I'm not verra good at it on my own."

He scratched the back of his neck, the same thing her sire did when he was upset with her. "You were in danger. Promise me you'll not go out on your own while the unknown archer is still free. I know your mother believes in strong women, and she is the strongest of any I know, but if someone is attacking the clan, you need a strong man to protect you."

She rolled her eyes and swallowed the curse that was begging to be set free from her lips. "My mother would tell you nay. We were raised to protect ourselves."

He chuckled. "Aye, I've no doubt in the truth of that statement. Mayhap your mother would agree with you, but my guess is your sire would agree with *me* after the attack we experienced." He was quiet for a moment as she rubbed Horsie's muzzle. "Why are you worried about pleasing your sire?" he finally asked. "He adores you. Just be yourself, lass."

Her stomach tightened. "I am trying to be myself."

"You are known for being adventurous, Sorcha, but I wasn't aware you had an interest in hunting."

How did the man know so much about her? She shrugged. "I used to hunt with Molly."

"Molly is one of the best hunters in the clan. She also took down one of the wickedest villains the Scots have seen in a long time. You are no' trying to compete with her, are you?"

"Nay, I just thought…I…" She rolled her eyes and sighed again. How to put words to something she couldn't fully express? Until her sire knew all she'd done, she wished to have as many good deeds as possible to hold up against her failure.

"Sigh any louder, lass, and you'll call your mother down from the keep."

She jerked as if he'd slapped her. "Nay, I do not want her here. She's busy…she's taking care of Brigid."

He had the uncanny ability to raise only one brow at her. The door opened, and Bethia entered the stables, her usual calm demeanor in place. Never had Sorcha been more pleased to see someone. "Bethia, my horse was hit by an arrow. Can you fix her, please? You know how I love her."

Her cousin gave her a warm smile. Her brown hair was pulled back in an unusual manner, tied neatly at the base of her neck, much like her mother Brenna often wore her locks. She had the most beautiful smile of any lass in their clan, but Sorcha did not think she'd ever find a lad to marry, since she was too shy by far and too wide in the hip for many. If the lads missed her charms, it was their misfortune. Her cousin had a beautiful soul.

Bethia didn't speak, just knelt next to Horsie, placing herself in the horse's line of vision so the animal wouldn't panic. "Sweet Horsie, what has happened to you?" She continued to speak to the horse as she checked the wound. "Sorcha, I'd like you up here talking to Horsie. Cailean can hold her back legs down while I check the damage."

As Sorcha muttered sweet things to her horse, she also said a silent thank you to Aunt Brenna, renowned as the best healer in the Highlands. Brenna had helped Bethia, who loved animals, build a large supply of herbs and poultices to help heal the clan's vast array of animals. Bethia had a magical touch with all creatures; she'd even cured a squirrel that Sorcha had hurt unintentionally when she was wee.

Bethia assessed the wound carefully and then stood up, brushing the straw from her hands. "I shall return with my poultice and other tools. I need to get that arrowhead out. Mayhap I'll put Horsie to sleep so she won't kick us while I work." She left the stables.

"Cailean?" Sorcha kept her face a short distance from her beloved horse's nose.

He sat at the horse's back haunches, waiting to assist Bethia. He was a handsome brute, she had to admit, with sandy brown-colored hair that was full but not too long, and green eyes that had a way of speaking to her. They were filled with a special glitter again. Was that just for her, too?

"Aye?" he whispered.

"I'm sorry for being a brat." Her tongue darted out to lick her lips. There was something about Cailean MacAdam that she'd never noticed before today. She thought about how his lips had felt on hers. She'd kissed a few lads, enough to know what she liked, and his kiss felt heavenly. She wanted someone strong and dominant, not soft and mushy. A smile crossed her face at the last thought. There was nothing about this man that conjured up the word "mushy."

"You weren't a brat. 'Tis not often someone is shot at by an unknown archer."

"Do you think he was aiming for me?"

"Aye, I believe 'tis possible. You need to be verra careful." He leveled those bright eyes on her. "You never told me why you are so eager to make your sire proud when you know you already do."

She watched his hand as he tenderly brushed her horse in a spot far away from the horse's wound, a movement that Horsie seemed to savor. What type of man was that kind to an animal without consciously thinking about it?

He tipped his head toward her. "Sorcha?"

"What?" *Mo creach*, the man had made her lose track of her thoughts.

"Your sire. Why are you trying so hard to make him proud? He adores you."

She didn't know how to answer that, simply because she didn't wish to tell anyone about what she'd done wrong. Other than her, there were only two people who were aware of her blunder, and she doubted either one would willingly share her worst moment. "I always try to make my sire proud." A true statement, but she knew she'd dodged the heart of the matter.

"I think you should try some other way. Give up on hunting. 'Tis too dangerous. What if we'd hit the boar before the archer started to shoot? Then you would have had to deal with a wild beast squealing through the forest *and* the archer. Have you forgotten the tale of how your uncle nearly died after being gored by a boar? Your sire saw the beast take down his brother. I do not think he would be happy to see the same fate befall his daughter."

She gazed into his green eyes, wondering why he cared. Cailean had always seemed so aloof—well, in the time she'd known him. Up until the last couple of years, he had been invisible to her. He worked hard in the lists, but had done little else. His uncle had suffered a grievous injury long ago, and Cailean had devoted himself to assisting him, making sure he could take care of himself—another noble task. Now, Cailean was everywhere. She'd heard many of the lasses swoon over his looks, but he did not seem to be interested in anyone in particular. In fact, she wondered why he wasn't yet married. "How old are you?"

That one eyebrow lifted at her again. Did the other one go up on its own, too? The thought brought a smile to her lips.

He replied, "One and twenty. Why does that amuse you?"

"It does not. I was just wondering why you aren't married yet." Horsie nickered and she rubbed the animal's chin.

"Because I'm not interested in marriage."

That comment came out so easily, she had to wonder what lay

beneath it. Had he been hurt by a woman? Rejected? She vowed to find out what she could.

Bethia came back into the room, and they moved forward with their task. After Horsie fell asleep from Bethia's potion, Sorcha whispered, "You'll not have to put her asleep forever, will you, Bethia?" She held her breath, afraid to hear her cousin's answer.

"Nay. 'Tis not too deep. So as long as she does not get a bad infection, she should be fine. However, you'll not be riding her for a long time." Bethia used her tool to pull the arrowhead out of the horseflesh, Horsie never once flinching.

Cailean stood up. "I guess you'll not be needing me anymore." He nodded to both of them and left.

Sorcha called out after him, "Many thanks, Cailean."

"Do not go out alone, Sorcha," he warned over his shoulder as he left.

As soon as he left, Sorcha asked, "You've not told anyone, have you, Bethia?"

Bethia gave her a sympathetic look, just as she'd expected. "Nay, and I will not tell anyone. You have naught to worry about. Forget it, I tell you."

How she loved her cousin. A sweeter soul had never walked the Highlands. "My thanks. I know not how I would handle my sire." She stared off in the distance, trying to imagine how angry he would be. Shaking her head, she vowed to stop thinking about it since she certainly had not intended for her plan to cause any harm.

Her plan. Why must she always veer from what she was supposed to do?

"Sorcha, do you have feelings for Cailean?" Her cousin gave her a knowing smile.

"What? Cailean? Nay…I…why would you ask such a thing?" She switched positions so she could help Bethia wash Horsie's leg near the wound. The mare was sound asleep, her warm breath tickling Sorcha's hand before she moved.

"Because I thought I caught a difference in you. As if mayhap you liked him."

Bethia was often interested in hearing about boys. She asked for so little, Sorcha was always inclined to do her bidding.

"Nay. I begged Frang to take me hunting and he talked Cailean and Alan into going along with us. 'Tis all there is about it. There's naught between the two of us. Besides, Cailean told me he's not interested in marriage."

Bethia waggled her eyebrows at her and whispered, "Mayhap he's been waiting for you." She giggled at her own comment.

Sorcha was so taken aback at the thought that she froze. But then she remembered his kiss, and how wonderful it had felt to be wrapped up in his arms.

Was there something there after all?

☾

The following morn, Cailean strode into the cottage he shared with Alan and their uncle Isaac, the same cottage they'd grown up in with their now deceased parents. As soon as he stepped inside, his uncle spoke to him.

"Cailean, where have you been? Have you been sleeping in the warrior camp every eve?" His uncle got up from his chair and carried his bowl over to the counter.

"Aye. With all that's happened these last moons, Maule wants us ready at all times." He moved over to the urn of water, filling the bowl next to it so he could wash the grime from his face.

"I'm not used to it with both you lads gone. 'Tis too quiet here. Enjoy your days of youth. I miss my days in the warrior camp. And while I did not think I would ever miss practicing in the lists or listening to your parents argue, I do." He ran his hand down his injured leg as if he could entice it to return to normal. His uncle had sustained his injury in the battle of the sapphire sword and moved in with them to heal. Their mother had died a few years later in her sleep, and their sire not long after from a festered wound. He loved his uncle, but he wished he could get him to leave home more, to engage with the rest of the clan.

"I do not miss listening to my parents argue." Cailean hated to say it, but it was the truth. So many years had passed, but he still remembered how it had been. The year of his seventh summer, the lists had become a welcome escape from home. In the lists, he had the friendship of the other lads; at home, his mother was always crying, and his sire was always yelling at her.

"They did not argue that much, Cailean," his uncle replied. "They had their good days."

"Why do I not recall those moments?" He did recall happy times from early childhood, moments when his mother would laugh at her two laddies or with her husband, but those memories were so old they had almost been forgotten. His last memories were the most potent—and they were all unhappy.

The fear that he had inherited his sire's temper—and would make his wife miserable—was enough to convince him he should never marry.

Alan came in behind him, stomping his feet at the door. "Kyle Maule was wild today. I think he's upset about what happened with Sorcha."

"What happened?" their uncle asked. "Logan Ramsay will kill any lad who dares to touch her."

That was exactly what Cailean feared.

Uncle Isaac looked back and forth between them, anxious for any tidbit of excitement going on in the clan. His injury pained him enough that he did not leave the house as often as he should.

"Naught you need to worry about, Uncle. Why do you not go visit with the carpenter? You know he's always looking for help." Cailean grabbed a goblet and filled it with ale.

"Aye, but I cannot stand for long. I'd not be much help." He sat down with a plunk that told Cailean how useless he felt.

"The carpenter just lost two men, Uncle. They've decided to join the guards. We hear something else is stirring in the Highlands. He could use your help." He threw back two chugs of his ale. "Do you want to go to the keep to eat or shall we bring you back something?" Silently, he urged his uncle to come.

The older man shook his head. "Nay, bring me back something."

Alan said, "Uncle Isaac, Cailean's right. You should go visit the carpenter on the morrow. We are all supposed to do something to contribute to the clan, and there's naught for you to do here." It was a more direct approach, and thus more likely to work. Cailean gave him a small nod of acknowledgment.

"On the morrow. I'll go on the morrow." Their uncle smiled and waved them on.

Cailean moved toward the door. "Are you coming along?"

His brother nodded and followed him up the hill to the keep. "Word is Logan Ramsay is on his way home. He sent word to Lady Brenna, telling her to get ready."

"Lady Brenna is leaving? Who needs her?" Cailean knew this would upset the entire clan. Their mistress was their rock. She saved lives, delivered bairns, and sewed the warriors' wounds with such skill they barely felt her needles. Fast and efficient, she was a boon to their clan and one of the most beloved members. A strong guard would be sent to protect her on the journey, no doubt.

Alan waited for two men to pass them before he continued. "I know not, but I'm afraid to hear what Ramsay will say when he finds out what happened with Sorcha and Horsie. What do you think he'll do?"

"What can he do?" Cailean replied, clapping his brother on the back. He had reasons of his own to fear Logan's return, but he did not like for Alan to worry. His brother was his rock. "Kyle and Torrian did all they could to try to find the culprit, but they turned up naught."

"He will not be happy we took her hunting." Alan made this comment low enough to be sure they were not overheard.

"She's a seasoned archer, taught by the best. Even if she is not as skilled as her sister or her mother, she still has talent. She could shoot a boar as easily as we could." Cailean glanced around them. "I do not understand why you're so concerned."

"It just bothers me," Alan said. "I cannot explain why, but I do not think he'll be pleased." He twisted his neck back and forth the way he did whenever his worries got the best of him. Cailean had seen him do it many times. As always, he would do aught he could to calm his brother's fears.

"Shite, he'll not be pleased to hear an archer shot at our group, but 'tis not our fault. There's no reason for him to come to us about it other than to seek answers."

"True. You're probably right. I've had nightmares about Logan Ramsay coming after me before. Hellfire, that man scares me." Alan shook his shoulders at the thought.

They arrived at the keep and stopped suddenly. A large group of guards had gathered in the courtyard. Something had happened. Could this be related to the request for Lady Brenna's help?

"What is it?" Cailean asked as he moved into the middle of the group, feeling a sensation of uneasiness travel through the crowd.

Their laird, Torrian, turned toward them. "My uncle returns quickly for my parents."

"What has happened?" Cailean glanced again at the sea of grim faces, not liking what he saw.

"Laird Alexander Grant has been severely injured in a battle with Baron Crichton. They need both my stepmother and Aunt Jennie to help heal him. We're awaiting instructions, but I've chosen this group to escort them to Cameron land. The rest of our guards will be on alert."

Cailean couldn't believe it. Alex Grant was the best swordsman in all the land, and someone had taken him down?

He glanced at Alan, busy twisting his neck again as the warriors in the group all started to talk at once. "No need to worry about Logan Ramsay. He'll have other things on his mind."

CHAPTER THREE

S ORCHA PACED IN FRONT OF the hearth in the Ramsay great hall. Her mother, Gwyneth, sat watching her while her wee sister Brigid and their cousin Jennet played with the laird's newest litter of deerhound pups in the corner.

"Tell me again why you went hunting without talking to me first?" Her mother crossed her long legs in front of her, wearing her favorite outfit of dark green leggings with a blue and green plaid tunic over them. Sorcha had to admit that her mother had aged beautifully, still lean and graceful, her hair arranged in the unusual style she alone wore. She pulled her hair tight back to her crown, then tied it and plaited it or left it wild to swing back and forth. A few streaks of gray peppered her brown locks, but otherwise she was almost as fit as she had ever been. Gwyneth's reputation as one of the best archers in the land was known throughout all of England, and she commanded respect from almost every male in the land of the Scots and beyond.

"Mama, I forgot to ask about your leg? Does it feel completely healed?" She chewed on her lip as she waited to see if her plan would work. Her mother had sustained the injury not long ago on a mission to find Brigid's kidnappers.

"Do not try to distract me from my purpose, daughter. You know my ankle has healed. I only have to practice running again to be back in shape."

"So you've said." Sorcha pursed her lips as a belch escaped her. "I guess I had forgotten. What was your question again?" Her mother was not easily distracted. The tactics that worked on her sire were not effective on her mother.

"You hate to hunt. What prompted this? And will you ever cease that terrible habit of belching around others?"

Her shoulders slumped in resignation. She had tried to stop her belching, but now it seemed to happen whenever she was upset about something. Perhaps honesty would be best. "I wanted to make Papa proud of me. I asked Frang if he would help me bring down a deer or a boar. Alan said he wanted to come along, too."

"And Cailean?"

"He just decided to join us at the last minute." She honestly had no idea why. He didn't usually talk with her the way many other lads did. She'd noticed he'd sprouted tall of late, but the only other thing she could say about him was he took no notice of the attention from the lasses in the clan. Knowing what little she did about lads, Sorcha couldn't help but wonder why.

"Thank goodness he did. According to Kyle, he was the only lad with any sense. The others would have left you atop your horse, an easy target. Enough of that. What did you see?"

"I did not see anyone, Mama. I was too frightened. Cailean grabbed me from my horse, and I was too focused on trying to stay on the horse in front of him…"

Her mother gave her the typical "Gwyneth Ramsay knows when you're lying" look, her head tipped and her brows arched. Sorcha had seen her mother bring men to their knees with that look—the one of exasperation over one's stupidity.

Or a daughter's attempt at lying.

Her mother cleared her throat. "I do not think 'tis how Cailean would tell the story. I imagine *he* was the one trying to stay on his horse because you were so mad he'd plucked you from yours. After all, didn't you then both topple to the ground—which again could have been a disaster but ended up being a blessing?"

The door flew open with a bang, and Sorcha jumped. Only one man could push that heavy oaken door open with such force: her sire. Many others did their best to mimic him, but they all inevitably failed.

Logan Ramsay strode inside, then headed straight for the hearth to give his wife a kiss.

"Papa!" Brigid ran to his side, jumping up and down.

Her sire had saved Sorcha from her mother's inquisition. It was a relief…and yet…she was determined to talk to him this eve or on the morrow about her transgression. Though it was tempting to let the matter rest, she *had* to talk to him about it. Her conscience would not let her rest until she confessed all to him. She had a sinking feeling he knew exactly what she'd done, and that it was the very reason he'd been so unhappy with her of late.

She greeted her father with a kiss on his cheek, but she could see this was not the time for casual conversation. "Papa? What is it?"

"Alex is seriously hurt. Gwynie, get your things. I'll go talk to Brenna. We need her there right away. I'd like you to go with us so Maddie will not be alone while Brenna and Jennie work."

Gwyneth's hands went straight to her chest. "Oh, dearest Lord. Please save him. Poor Maddie. Where?"

"Papa, are we all going?" Sorcha hoped they would all go together. The journey would give her the perfect opportunity to talk to her father. There was no need to worry overmuch about Uncle Alex. Aunt Brenna could cure just about anyone of anything.

"Nay," he took off toward the healer's chamber, yelling over his shoulder. "Maddie and Jamie are bringing him by cart to Cameron land. We need to get Brenna there as soon as possible." He paused and turned around, his hands on his hips, not concerned with who heard the news. "They say he has no more than a day."

Sorcha's stomach lurched as her father spun on his heel and hurried off to Brenna's chamber. "What? Papa? He has no more than a day for what?" In her heart she knew what it meant…but it couldn't be true. Uncle Alex was the strongest man she'd ever met.

Jennet jumped up and answered, "I believe he means until he passes. 'Tis true, Aunt Gwyneth? Is Uncle Alex going to die?" Her cousin's face crumpled, something Sorcha rarely saw. Jennet had a stronger backbone than any horse, proven by her recent kidnapping. She'd unsettled the kidnappers in order to keep Brigid calm and safe.

Brigid started wailing. "Nay, not Uncle Alex. I love him so. Mama, Aunt Brenna must fix him." Her tears continued and Gwyneth tugged her onto her lap.

The Grant and Ramsay clans had become tightly interwoven after Brenna Grant, Alex's sister, married Quade, the former laird of the Ramsays. Even though Alex Grant was not a blood relation to Sorcha and Brigid, he had always felt like an uncle.

Sorcha sat next to her in shock. What was happening?

Her mother looked at her and said, "We're leaving you and Bethia to watch over the lasses. Can you do that for me? No more hunting. You need to stay here."

She nodded, tears brimming over the uncertain fate of her uncle, a larger-than-life man with a soft heart.

Lily came flying in, one twin on each hip. She set them down next to Jennet. "Go, Aunt Gwyneth. We will take care of everyone. Torrian and Kyle are arranging the guards to escort you off our land and another group to follow all the way to Cameron land. Get your things together."

Aunt Brenna emerged from her chamber, her shoulders squared as she headed straight for Jennet. "My sweet, we are leaving you here."

The great hall had become a center of chaos. Sorcha could see how shaken Aunt Brenna and her mother were, though no one else was likely to notice.

"Mama, I'll get your satchel, pack your things." She had to do something. Before she left, she said to the serving girl who had run out of the kitchens, "Pack a quick satchel of food for ten, Emmy."

The girl nodded and ran back into the kitchens.

Sorcha's sire came out of Brenna's chamber, carrying her satchel of tools and poultices. Heather, Torrian's wife, came in the door, so Sorcha said, "Heather, follow me and pack a satchel for Aunt Brenna and Uncle Quade, please."

By the time Sorcha returned with a satchel packed for her mother and a fresh one for her father, all were quiet as Uncle Quade stood on the landing addressing the gathered crowd. "Torrian and Kyle are in charge. Have faith in Brenna and Jennie. I do. They'll fix Alex, but we need to move now. We're counting on you all to handle everything in our absence."

Heather barreled down the staircase with two satchels in her hand.

"I'll go get our things, Gwynie," Logan said with a nod.

Sorcha stopped him and thrust the bags she'd prepared into her sire's hands. "Here is yours, and here is Mama's."

Her sire looked surprised but nodded with appreciation. "Then I'll get food."

Emmy stepped forward with a sack. "Sorcha sent me already, my lord."

"Well done, Sorcha," he said. His look of approval almost brought tears to her eyes. "We must leave now. We cannot slow for aught." He leaned down and gave Sorcha and Brigid kisses, then ushered the travelers outside.

She followed them out, not surprised to see Uncle Quade's horse already in the courtyard along with three others. They mounted as everyone stood blankly watching them, still unable to believe the tidings.

Sorcha stared bleakly over the crowd waving her parents and aunt and uncle off, following them on foot until they reached the gate, where the guards waited to escort them.

Her sire yelled, "Stay inside the gates unless Torrian says otherwise."

Aunt Brenna and Aunt Jennie had to save Uncle Alex.

They just had to.

☾

Cailean trudged up the hill toward the stables. His uncle had made breakfast for him and Alan. Uncle Isaac was still talking about Alex Grant—he'd only stopped for long enough to tell the brothers to enjoy each other's company because he still missed his brother. Alan had stayed back to keep him company for a bit longer, but Cailean had needed to leave.

Uncle Isaac talked about their sire as if he had been a saint, but the man he described was very different from the one they recalled. Cailean still did not understand why his father had changed into such a cruel creature. The last time he remembered seeing—or rather hearing—his parents together, he'd stood outside of their room, listening as his mother sobbed and his father yelled at her to stop it. She'd died not long after, leaving Cailean with many unanswered questions. Lady Brenna had told them her heart had given out. His sire had died several moons later, leaving Cailean and his brother stunned. He'd been nearly eight summers and Alan just past five, too young to understand death. Without their uncle, they would not have made it.

Cailean prayed every day that he would be different from his father. His sire's temper had ruined their family.

Yesterday was one of the worst days the Ramsay clan had seen in a long time. The possibility of Laird Alexander Grant dying was something no one wished to consider. After the traveling party had left in such a hurry, the mood of the clan had turned somber. He could only hope today would be a better day.

An unsettling thought itched at the back of his mind, and he felt compelled to give it his full attention. Wiping the sweat from his brow, he nodded to any clanmates he passed, but his mind was too busy for him to speak. He was counting all the villains the Ramsay and Grant clan had encountered over the last few years.

Ranulf MacNiven—the worst villain in Scottish history

Walrick—MacNiven's second

Bearchun and Shaw—the two Ramsay guards who had kidnapped Jennet and Brigid and delivered them to MacNiven

Baron Gordon Crichton of Duncrub—the man who'd just attacked the Grant Castle

Simon de La Porte—Crichton's hired second

Hew Gordon—the man working with MacNiven

Glen of Buchan and his sons, Dugald and Cormag—the family who had connived with MacNiven to take over the Ramsay Castle and failed.

He forced himself to stop. There were too many. True, some were now dead, but many of the villains were still out there. Bearchun and Shaw had escaped after stealing Jennet and Brigid from beneath the Ramsays' noses. Not even Logan Ramsay could find them.

The Highlands were full of unrest like never before. The news of Alexander Grant's injury would travel through their land as fast as an untended fire through a forest in the middle of a drought.

It could draw out all who wished them harm.

Could they stop it? He needed to talk to Torrian and Kyle, hear their thoughts on the matter.

He stepped inside the stables and stopped instantly. A soft, cooing voice reached his ears—a sweet, dulcet tone that drew him in. He followed the melodic sounds down to the end of the building, and he froze in his tracks when he found the source.

Sorcha lay in the straw in a position that gave him thoughts Logan Ramsay would kill him for entertaining. Flat on her back, dressed in her mother's style of tunic and leggings, which revealed every curve and dip of her body, her head rested not far from Horsie's muzzle, her nimble fingers caressing her horse while her lips parted in a suggestive way. It took every part of his inner will to tamp down what his mind wished to conjure up. He feared the repercussions if he allowed those thoughts to grow.

He glanced away from the beauty in front of him in an attempt to soothe the heat racing through his body, feigning interest in the horse in the next stall, and almost jumped when another voice caught his attention.

Brigid asked, "Sorcha, how does it look?"

Thank the Lord above for the wee favor just granted to him.

"Brigid, you are doing a fine job braiding Horsie's mane." Sorcha studied her sister's work.

"Do you think so?" Brigid's gaze never left her task, her wee fingers weaving a pattern so quickly he could not follow them.

Sorcha bounded up to a standing position as soon as she noticed him, brushing the straw from her clothing. "Greetings, Cailean."

"How does Horsie fare today?"

"She's much better. Bethia thinks she may try to stand tomorrow. She's keeping her a bit sedated today." She moved closer to him, the wrong thing to do.

Now he could hardly avoid inhaling her scent, an unusual mix of flowers and pine with a huge dose of woman. He stifled the urge to grunt with pleasure. "No fever?"

"Nay. I am grateful for your assistance getting her back here so quickly." She finished primping herself, pulling the remaining pieces of straw from her outfit.

He reached over and plucked a lone piece from her hair. "You missed one."

"You have a stalk on your bum still, Sorcha," Brigid said, all innocence.

Cailean stifled a groan when Sorcha turned her curvaceous butt around to face him, pulling her tunic up to reveal the perfectly rounded globes—which surely had been made by the Lord above for the sole purpose of a man's enjoyment—and ran her hand up and down it until she found the offending piece of yellow stubble and tossed it onto the floor.

She glanced up at him, her cheeks turning a light shade of pink. Mayhap she was just now realizing what she'd done in front of him.

He'd beg her to do it again if he could.

Cailean stepped back, deciding it was time for him to move on before he said or did something he'd regret. He ran his hand down his face to force his eyes shut for long enough to erase the image of Sorcha's perfect arse from his mind.

The image would not release its hold on him.

"Cailean? Do you think you could run the obstacle course with me?"

Before he could respond—a rousing no—he registered the sound of footsteps behind him. A quick glance behind his shoulder revealed the newcomer was Torrian, who was much closer than he would have expected. Sorcha's tantalizing presence had deafened him to the sound of the laird's approach.

"Nay, he'll not be taking you outside the gates until our sires return to tell us what's happening. We know little of how Uncle Alex was hurt."

Sorcha scowled and crossed her arms. "Can I not practice riding a different horse? The obstacle course is just outside the gates."

"You can prance near the stables. There's enough room for you to get a feel for a new horse there. Or, if you're feeling restless, you can practice archery at the small field inside the gates, the same one you've been using for years." Torrian's gaze narrowed. "Sorcha, what is going on in your mind lately? Why did you ask the lads to go hunting with you? I've never known you to go hunting without Molly."

She lifted her chin and replied, "I'm just trying to help the clan while my parents are away."

"You'll help your clan by not getting into trouble again. We have plenty of meat. Stay inside. That's an order." Torrian grasped Cailean's shoulder and said, "Join Maule and me for a bit?"

Cailean nodded and spun around to head out of the stables, but not before he heard Sorcha grumble, "I liked Torrian better before he was laird."

Brigid said, "He's just trying to protect us, and you cannot go outside. If aught happened to you, I know not what I'd do. Mama and Papa and Molly are all gone. I need you, Sorcha."

He hoped that was enough to sway Sorcha from her stubborn ways, but he doubted it. He, however, would not fall victim to one of her schemes this time. He followed Torrian out into the sunshine and then to an area just outside the lists. Most of the guards were just starting to gather to work on their usual routines.

"Maule," Cailean said in a greeting as soon as he made it to his side. He glanced from Torrian to Kyle to see what they had to offer.

Torrian spoke first. "We've been discussing all that has taken place in the Highlands, wondering what your thoughts are, Cailean."

Kyle stood back, his arms crossed, waiting to hear what he had to offer.

"Might I ask what happened to Laird Grant? How was he injured? How did Baron Crichton gather enough men to attack the Grants?"

Torrian nodded to Kyle, so Kyle was the one who answered him. "We only heard a brief explanation from Logan. Alex's son, Jamie, wed Gracie in a hurry to prevent the king from ordering a match between her and the baron, and the baron did not take it well.

"Simon de La Porte acted as the baron's second. Battle ensued, and Alex was sliced open from someone's sword, although 'tis uncertain who injured him. Jamie was not far away but didn't see who did it. Jamie and Maddie brought Alex to Cameron land in a cart, hoping he'd make it that far."

Torrian added, "It sounds as though his condition is quite serious. We'll not hear any tidings for a couple of days, I'm sure."

"We've heard of de La Porte," Cailean said, rubbing his chin. "Is he not the ruthless knight known all over England for his band of mercenaries? How did he end up in league with Baron Crichton?"

Torrian replied, "No one knows, but he did bring some of his men, and that's what worries me. I doubt they were all taken down. De La Porte is still alive, so where is he now? Duncrub, at least, was taken down by Jamie's sword. If de La Porte sends for the rest of his band, we could be in trouble."

"That must have been a hell of a battle," Cailean added. He'd heard stories of the Grants in battle, but he had yet to witness any firsthand. The laird and his two sons were the largest warriors he'd ever seen. Alex was still taller and broader than Jamie or Jake, but some thought Jake was still growing. "Many of Duncrub's men must have been slain in battle. The Grants are the best-trained in the Highlands. Mayhap only a few of La Porte's mercenaries survived. If so, I'm sure they are regrouping in England. Let's hope they do not return."

Torrian added, "Aye, I imagine, but I'm not allowing anyone to leave the grounds except our warriors. There is too much we do not know about where de La Porte has gone and how many of his men are on the run. I've sent two patrols out to keep us updated on any new presences on our land."

Cailean scratched the back of his neck, thoughts flying through his mind. "Do you think they are related?" he finally said. "The attack in the woods and that battle?"

Torrian said, "I think we must consider the possibility. Everyone in the Highlands knows the Ramsays and Grants are blood clans. Mayhap a few of his guards who escaped decided to make the Ramsays a target, upset by their loss of the battle and hoping to retaliate on anyone related to the Grants. The possibility occurred to both of us, which is one of the reasons we wanted to speak with you. Who exactly was the target of the archer in the woods? Was it a random shooting or a specific person?"

Cailean understood the importance of the question.

"You said there were four arrows," Kyle said. "Did they land haphazardly or around someone specific? Take as much time as you need to think it through."

Cailean scratched his head, wishing to deny what he'd seen, but he could not. His gut had already convinced him of the need to protect Sorcha, and he thought he knew why. "At least three of the arrows appeared to be aimed at Sorcha. The fourth one flew by after Sorcha and I tumbled to the ground. I believe 'twas the one that hit Horsie. Alan and Frang had ridden off in pursuit of the archer. 'Twas almost a wild arrow, so mayhap he'd just noticed the two were coming his way."

Kyle slapped his thigh. "That's exactly what I thought."

Torrian whistled through pursed lips. "And what I feared. We must be careful. Cailean, I'm giving you an important assignment. You are to watch over Sorcha until her sire returns."

Cailean wished to question him, but he could not. "Aye, my laird." Torrian and Quade shared laird duties normally, but with his sire gone, Torrian was completely in charge. A loyal warrior never questioned an order given by his laird.

"I ask you because you did an admirable job of keeping her safe from the archer's attack. Please keep an eye on her. She is more unsettled than I've ever seen her, and I do not trust her when she's unsettled. We all know she shares her sire's tendency to wander. I cannot allow it in his absence. If you need to restrain her, do so. She is not allowed outside the gates until her sire returns."

Cailean nodded. "Her life has been in tumult of late. Her sister and cousin were kidnapped, her mother was injured, her eldest sister was married, and now her uncle's life is in danger. 'Tis reasonable that she's unsettled."

"I cannot argue with you, but my cousin has a remarkable ability to endanger herself when she's unsettled. Stay close to her. If you need to, sit on her."

Kyle barked a laugh at Torrian's last comment, but Cailean did not.

He knew exactly how difficult this assignment would be.

CHAPTER FOUR

ॐ

SORCHA CAME DOWN THE PASSAGEWAY, surprised at the sounds coming from below stairs in the great hall. She turned the corner and headed down, her hand on the railing as she slowed down to assess all that took place below her.

Chaos. Absolute chaos. Her parents and her aunt and uncle had only been gone for a day and chaos already reigned. Peering around from her perch above them all, she searched for a possible source of the chaos and found nothing.

Jennet and Brigid sat in the corner with the Torrian's pups, hugging the squirming bundles of fur, wailing at will. Bethia stood next to them, attempting to calm them in a voice that was too soft to be heard over the chaos. Maggie sat in front of the hearth staring at the bouncing flames, her arms crossed, not speaking to anyone. Lily had the twins propped up on the table. She was trying to feed them porridge, but both of the babes were wailing incessantly, probably because Lily herself was in tears. Heather and her wee daughter were trying to calm the crying babe in Heather's lap.

Torrian and Kyle were nowhere to be seen, undoubtedly busy directing the guards, but Cailean sat in a chair in the corner, his eyes taking in everything.

Sorcha decided they needed someone to take charge, and it was in her nature to take over, just as her mother or sire would do.

She leaned over the railing and bellowed in the loudest voice she could muster, "Enough! Everyone stop crying, and come over in front of the stairs right away." She stood four steps above the landing, waiting for everyone to move, but they all appeared stunned. Even the bairns were staring at her. "I meant now!" She tipped her head to the rafters, hoping to let them know how serious she was about this undertaking.

Finally, she had their attention. Jennet and Brigid each grabbed a puppy and ambled over to the stairs, still sniffling, Bethia and Maggie trailing behind them. Lily was close enough that she didn't have to move with the bairns, but she gave Sorcha her full attention. Even Heather came over to the staircase.

The only one that didn't move was Cailean, a big grin on his face and that familiar glitter in his eyes.

To hell with him.

Once she had their attention, she said, "Now, if Mama and Papa and Aunt and Uncle came in here right now, what would they think of this fuss? Those of us who are older are going to stop crying and help the wee ones to stop as well."

Jennet whispered, "But Uncle Alex…"

"Hush, I said. You will have only positive thoughts about Uncle Alex. Who is the strongest warrior in all the land?"

No one replied.

"I did not hear any answers. Who is the strongest warrior in the land of the Scots? Who fought at the Battle of Largs in a golden helm?"

"Uncle Alex."

"Uncle Alex."

Giggles and a snort reverberated in the cavernous space. "Did he really have a golden helm?" Heather asked.

Four voices yelled, "Aye, he did!"

Sorcha's brother, Gavin, and cousin Gregor came in through the door. At first they looked taken aback by the gathering near the stairs, but they soon joined it.

"He fought like a daft man, they said," Bethia added, "taking down all kinds of Norsemen."

"Aye," Maggie said, warming to the topic. "Uncle Alex drove them back onto their big galley ship. They ran from him."

Gregor and Gavin lit up, clearly pleased with the topic of conversation.

"Have you not seen Uncle Alex swing his sword?" Gregor asked.

There were several affirmative answers, and someone shouted out, "He has a talent like no other!"

"He killed someone who hurt Aunt Maddie. He's her protector," Bethia said. "'Tis so romantic."

"Aye," Sorcha said, smiling. "'Tis much better to talk about how wonderful Uncle Alex is. He's one of the strongest warriors of all, and he'll survive this. Do you not all believe in Aunt Brenna and Aunt Jennie?"

Jennet nodded her head. "Together, Mama and Aunt Jennie are unstoppable. They can cure most anyone."

"Mama cured me *and* she cured Torrian," Lily said. She swiped at her tears and whispered, "You are correct, Sorcha. My mama can save him, especially with Aunt Jennie at her side."

"Now can we all stop crying?" Sorcha asked. "Jennet and Brigid, I would like you to help Lily feed the twins. You know how much they love you two. The puppies are tired out, just leave them near their bedding. Maggie and Bethia, would you find some snacks in the kitchens? We can set them out near the hearth, and once the bairns are all fed, we can listen to stories. In fact, are there any specific tales you'd like to hear?"

"Aye," Heather said. "I'd like to hear the whole story of the Battle of Largs. Is there anyone here who can tell it?"

Sorcha felt a surge of gratitude. It was the perfect story—the tale of the battle in which Uncle Alex had dealt the Norse attackers a crushing defeat. She pointed to the back of the group. "Those two." Her brother and Gregor both smiled. Sorcha continued, "They have listened to every story Uncle Brodie and Uncle Robbie have ever told. Can you tell us all about it in a half hour?" After they nodded, she continued, "Everyone see to their tasks and meet over by the hearth. Gavin and Gregor will tell us all after they gather extra blankets and pillows for all of us."

Brigid bounced up and down. "Sorcha, may we all sleep in the hall together tonight?"

"Aye. All of us together!" Jennet said.

Sorcha recalled the days when she was younger, how they would all huddle around the hearth together, no guards allowed. Her sire would stand guard to make sure the men stayed out. They had loved every moment they'd spent together. With all the chaos, they hadn't done it in a long time. A smile broke out across her face as she glanced at Maggie and Bethia, the closest in age to her. The expressions on their faces told her they had the same memories.

"I'll ask our laird and his second and see if they give their approval," Sorcha said to her wee sister. "Do a good job with Lise and Liliana. You know how Kyle hates to hear his lassies cry."

Brigid and Jennet sprang up with a fervor she hadn't seen in them for a while. Before Sorcha came down the steps, she pointed to her brother and cousin. "Be gentle with your stories, lads. Must be appropriate for the wee ones."

"I'll tell about Loki and his slinger," Gavin said with a grin.

Gregor added, "I'll tell about Uncle Brodie getting cut in his thigh, Loki taking him to the healer, and then Uncle Logan and Nicol throwing him in the river because he smelled so…"

Lily giggled. "Och, 'tis a great one. Do not forget about Uncle Logan punching him in the face to knock him out because he complained so."

"Off you go!" Sorcha threw her arms in the air, and they all scurried in different directions.

Cailean, who'd sat watching the whole scene without partici-pating, sauntered over to her at last. "Well done. I had no idea you possessed such peacemaking skills."

She rolled her eyes. "Someone needs to keep calm. Why could you not do aught to help me?"

"I was busy."

Her hands flew to her hips. "Doing what? You were sitting there in the corner, doing naught that I could see."

"Doing my duty." He was being purposefully vague; she knew it.

Her gaze narrowed as the grin on his face grew. "What duty?" An intensely bad feeling was crawling up the back of her neck.

"Watching you." He grinned, showing her all of his beautiful white teeth. "I must admit 'tis one of my more pleasant duties."

"What? Why are you…? Did my cousin…? Arghhhh…I'll kill him with my bare hands." Her hands fisted at her sides and she climbed down the stairs leading to the door. When she reached it, she stopped abruptly before she opened it, spinning on her heel to face him. "Stop following me," she ground out, trying to keep anyone from overhearing their conversation.

"Cannot do that. I follow my laird's orders." She would have thought his expression innocent had she not known better.

"I'm relieving you of your duties."

"I take orders from the laird and the laird only." He held the door for her, standing close enough that she could feel the heat from his skin. "Would you like to find him? Make sure you stay within the gates." Then he leaned down to whisper in her ear. "I've been granted permission to sit on you, if need be, to keep you from going outside the curtain wall."

The warmth of his breath on her ear sent a shiver down her spine, but the look on his face was what made her tremble. It was downright carnal. Heat spread through her insides, followed by a tingling unlike anything she'd felt before.

The worse thing of all was that she *liked* it. She liked the way he looked at her and how it made her feel. It filled her with a strange sensation of power.

Mo creach, but she had a feeling something had changed inside her forever. This man had the ability to make her insides quiver, and she reveled in it. She couldn't help but wonder if this was what love felt like. As their gazes locked, the air between them crackling with tension, Sorcha made a decision that she would challenge herself to make that smoldering look in his eyes turn to fire. Cailean wanted her and she wanted him, and there was nothing she would enjoy more than to bring the man in front of her to his knees with want and desire. She just had to figure out how to do it—*after* she freed him from his duty. Spinning around, she stood back, allowing him to hold the door. Before she stepped out ahead of him, she leaned over to whisper in his ear.

"Cailean, 'twould be my pleasure to have you sit on me."

She could play his game.

C

If Cailean had been eating something, he would have choked for sure. The saucy temptress had gone beyond his expectations and more. He followed behind her, glad for the darkness of the night to hide his burgeoning erection as he followed the sway of her hips.

Sorcha Ramsay was a sweet morsel he'd wanted to taste for a long time, and she'd just called his bluff. Searching the area, he was surprised to see they were alone. Still, these were somber times, and Torrian was keeping the guards busy. His hand settled on her waist and urged her off to the side, behind the now-empty armorer's building, unable to stop himself. A tree towered over the building, so he maneuvered her underneath it and took her into his arms.

When she spun around to stare up at him, he couldn't help but notice her beautiful breasts standing proudly in front of him. Much as he was tempted, he knew where not to go.

His lips descended on hers, and though he could tell he'd taken her by surprise, she got over it quickly. Her soft curves leaned toward him until she was flush against him, her nipples so taut he could feel their peaks through the layers of their clothes.

He groaned and angled his mouth over hers, teasing her and taunting her until she parted her lips, allowing him to delve deeper, giving him the taste he yearned for. True, they'd kissed before in the woods on the ground, but that had been driven by survival and urgency.

The urgency was different this time. He sensed her passion, her want for more. He left her mouth and trailed a path down her neck to the soft hollow in front, feathering kisses on her skin, tasting the saltiness and sweetness of her all at once. He grabbed her hips, enjoying the feel of her generous curves in his hands, and kissed her again, this one a slow assault that fueled his own needs. He ended the kiss and stepped back, forced to catch her as she lost her balance and fell toward him.

That made him smile, and she swung her hand lightly at him, little effort behind it, as she struggled to stand upright. She frowned and pushed away from him and around him, a befuddled expression on her face. Following the path back, she didn't speak, just continued on toward the gate, presumably looking for their laird, Torrian, to complain about his assignment.

Without warning, she spun around back toward the keep. Staring up at Cailean, she licked her lips and whispered, "Fine, guard me."

He didn't know how to respond to that, so he simply waited for her to move and then followed her back to the keep.

They'd almost made it back to the castle when someone emerged from the blacksmith's building—Baltair, whose sire worked there.

"Greetings, Baltair," Sorcha called out in a melodic tone that Cailean found irrationally irritating.

"Greetings. Any word on your sire yet, Sorcha?" He stopped for a moment to await her answer. Baltair was an average swordsman, average also in appearance, but everyone in the clan knew he was a fine archer. The middle child in a family of five brothers, he was a quiet person, one who was unlikely to cause trouble for anyone. Invisible, many called him.

"Nay, but 'tis early. Mayhap on the morrow."

He nodded and started to move away, but Sorcha called out, "Baltair, would you be willing to help me with my archery skills in the morn?" She smiled and took two steps closer to him.

"Me?" He cleared his throat and glanced at Cailean. "You want *me* to help you?"

"Aye, 'tis said you have fine skills on the archery field. In fact, I'd love for you to take me hunting once my sire returns, but the inner archery field will have to be enough for now. Do you have time?"

He thought for a moment and then spoke, "I was supposed to help my sire, but I'm sure he can free me up for an hour or so."

"Wonderful! Come to the field when you're ready. I'm sure you can help me with my stance."

Baltair glanced at Cailean. "Why do you not help her?"

"Och, do not worry," he said, giving Sorcha a pointed look. "I'll be there, too."

Sorcha giggled, then moved toward the keep, waving over her shoulder. "Until then, Baltair."

Though the man was clearly still muddled and confused, Baltair's gaze followed Sorcha up toward the steps, his eyes not leaving her sweet bottom.

That sweet bottom belonged to *Cailean*—or so he wished to proclaim to anyone with ears. He'd kissed his share of lassies before, but never before had he felt this protective, as if one kiss had staked his claim. Cailean had to run to catch up, just making it in time to open the heavy door for her. He paused intentionally as he leaned over her to grab the handle.

"That was quite a kiss, lass," he whispered.

"Oh, did you think so?" She cast an innocent gaze at him, then flew in through the door and over to the hearth, arriving just in time to listen to the tales of the Battle of Largs.

Apparently, Sorcha was going to play games with him, and he looked forward to it. He'd just have to be persistent about reminding himself she was going to tease him.

He loved games, especially with a beautiful, sultry woman.

Something occurred to him, something he wished to ignore.

He'd sworn never to marry, yet if he had his way, he'd stake his claim on Sorcha Ramsay and kill anyone who dared to touch her. What the hell was happening to him? The lass was ensnaring him in her spell, and he was *enjoying* it.

He couldn't ignore that this new possessiveness was exactly the type of emotion that led to marriage.

Well, he'd not worry about that now. Better to enjoy his time with the lass and consider what it meant later. Of course, he only had until her sire returned to convince Sorcha that she was his.

This would be a challenge.

CHAPTER FIVE

ᕒ

IT TOOK EVERY OUNCE OF strength Sorcha had not to trip as she entered the hall, visions of sprawling head first into the group infiltrating her mind. It would have been an appalling display, but that kiss had been beyond distracting. Hellfire, the man could kiss.

She licked her lips subconsciously, thinking of how the brute compared to the other lads she'd kissed. Granted, her experience was somewhat limited simply because there were few lads in her clan brave enough to steal a kiss from Logan Ramsay's daughter. Had she not taken advantage of unsuspecting lads at the Grant keep or other places they'd traveled as a family, she'd have no experience at all. Her cousin Lily, on the other hand, had managed to get a group of lads to line up for a kiss. Of course that had not been done intentionally.

Offering a few kisses was something she did not regret. How else was a lass to know what she wanted?

Sorcha knew what she wanted—more of Cailean MacAdam.

When she shifted her focus to the group gathered in front of her, she was pleasantly surprised to see how well her instructions were being followed. Maggie and Bethia were hard at work building a lovely grouping near the hearth, plump cushions on the floor, which was padded with plaids and blankets galore. Jennet and Brigid were busy playing with Lise, Liliana, and Lachie, Torrian and Heather's lad. The three bairns giggled at Brigid's antics, a sound that rebounded off the rafters, bringing a smile to everyone's faces. The space that had been filled with sadness so recently now felt bright with joy.

The door opened and Torrian stepped inside, Kyle directly behind him. It only then struck her that she'd forgotten to ask him about the lassies' wish to sleep in the hall tonight. The kiss had erased her memory.

"What's this?" Torrian asked, his eyes widening as he took in the gaiety in the hall.

Kyle hurried over to give a smiling Lily a kiss, then stood back in wonder, watching the now giggling bairns. "Lily? What did you do?"

Jennet and Brigid ran over to Torrian. "Sorcha said if we were good and helped Lily out, we could sleep in the hall tonight."

"And I also said what?" Sorcha added.

"If our laird agrees," Brigid whispered, crinkling her nose. "Do you agree, my laird?" She looked up at him with wide eyes.

"Aye, Torrian. May we, please? We are too upset about Uncle Alex. We would sleep better here." Jennet reached for his hand and tugged on it, bouncing in place on her wee feet.

Torrian glanced around the hall, reaching for his wife as Heather found her way over to him. He leaned down to kiss her.

"Gavin and Gregor have promised to tell us the tale of Uncle Alex at the Battle of Largs," Heather said, staring up at him. "Sorcha set all this up so we could enjoy an eve of storytelling while our parents are gone. What do you think?"

Torrian kissed his wife again, wrapping his arm around her before he peeked over Heather's shoulder to acknowledge his cousin. "Well done, Sorcha." He glanced at the man next to her and said, "You may leave, Cailean. Come back at dawn to resume your duties."

Sorcha was gratified that her plan had worked out as intended, but she felt a little pang at the thought of Cailean leaving.

Then he turned to the group and said, "Since you have food here, Kyle and I will join you for a wee bit. I look forward to hearing your tales, Gavin and Gregor. Find your spots, everyone." The wee ones squealed with joy.

Cheers bounced off the walls and the youngest scrambled for their favorite spots. Their voices were so loud that she almost didn't hear the voice that came from behind her. "Meet me in the kitchens at midnight, lass, and I'll give you another one of those kisses you did not like."

Her body responded in a way that she did not comprehend. By the time she turned around, Cailean was almost to the door. He stopped and glanced over his shoulder at her, giving her a small smile, the gleam in his gaze visible from where she stood.

Then he was gone.

A fluttering feeling filled her belly at the thought of meeting him in the dead of night. Should she go? Did she dare?

Maggie came up to her, whispering in her ear, "I saw that. What was that about?"

Sorcha rolled her eyes at her sister, whose gaze had narrowed to the smallest of slits. "Cailean was assigned to keep watch over me. Torrian thinks I'll run outside the gates without permission."

Maggie snorted. "Torrian knows you well, does he not? And Cailean is probably one of the few who can keep up with you, especially as upset as you are about all that happened."

"What do you mean by that?" Sorcha jerked on her arm as she said it.

"You know what I mean," Maggie said with an arch look, "but I don't think you wish me to explain myself here in front of everyone."

This time the fluttering feeling was one of nerves, not excitement. Sorcha turned toward the group. "Maggie and I will get more food," she announced. "Gavin, go ahead and start. We know the stories." She grabbed her sister by the arm, tugging her into the kitchens with her. Cook was probably already abed, but they still snuck into one of the storage rooms so they could not be heard.

"Explain yourself, sister." Sorcha let go of Maggie's arm as soon as the door closed on the small chamber filled with foodstuffs.

"I know what you're doing. You are dealing with so much guilt that you cannot think clearly. You are trying to come up with all these ways to make Papa proud of you because you think he'll be furious with you when he learns the truth."

"You do not think he will?"

Maggie shrugged her shoulders. "He may get a little upset, but Papa adores you. You've always been his pride and joy. Do not start doing foolish things to get yourself in more trouble."

"And what are you suspecting?"

"Stealing away to be with a guard when Papa is not here will only get you into more trouble. What if he catches Cailean kissing you?"

Sorcha wouldn't have jumped any higher if her sire had just opened the door. "What are you referring to? He'll not catch Cailean kissing me."

Maggie snorted again.

"That sound 'tis most unbecoming of you, sister."

"Worse than your belching?"

Sorcha burped as if on cue. "Sorry, I had been holding that one in around Cailean." She gave her sister an innocent look and the two erupted into giggles. When their laughter finally abated, Sorcha whispered, "What exactly are you implying?"

"I'm quite sure I can guess what you two were doing before you came in the hall. You should have seen your face." She leaned on a shelf and drilled her fingers across the wood.

Sorcha gasped. "We were not…"

"Be careful. You'll wrap yourself so tightly in lies, you'll never get out." Maggie crossed her arms and pursed her lips.

Maggie had always been the quickest of her sisters. She wished to stomp her foot and argue, but hell, they *had* been kissing. So be it if Maggie knew. She doubted the others would suspect anything. Rather than argue, she decided to use distraction. "So what if I want Papa to be proud of me. Why is that so bad?"

"Sorcha, 'tis not bad, but you have taken a small thing and made it much bigger. He will not hate you for your transgression. In fact, if you don't tell him about it, he'll probably never know."

"Mayhap you are correct." She kneaded her hands, her conscience niggling at her. "But I *have* to tell him. I do want him to be proud of me, and well…you know how he's been around me lately. He always seems upset with me. Mayhap he knows what I did and he's waiting for me to confess."

"Or mayhap he's upset by your tendency to ignore everyone's advice and ride off on your own into the forests? Or, worse, spend time alone with the lads. You're getting older, and he worries about your reputation."

"No one understands," Sorcha said glumly. "I like being outdoors, like our mama." Staying inside was too confining, much like this chamber they stood in. She turned away from her sister, searching for something on the shelf to keep her hands busy. There was a sack of oats that had spilled over, and she busied herself with refilling the spilled grain and straightening up the shelf.

"But Mama stays with Papa. Molly stays with Tormod. They do not wander off on their own or ride about with a group of lads. I believe *that* is what infuriates Papa. You should be with lasses now that you're older."

"But lasses don't go out in the forest. Molly was the only one. Who should I go with? And the lads are nice to me. They never try to kiss me."

"Except Cailean, you mean?"

"Before Cailean. They treat me with kindness."

"Because they're all afraid of our sire. 'Tis why. But you'll regret it someday."

She stopped her fussing and leaned her elbow on the shelf. It was no use conforming to what everyone expected of her. "I'll never become an indoor person. 'Tis not me. If Papa were here, *he* would take me hunting." She stared at the floor, knowing her sister was right. When had it all changed? When had talking to lads become a bad thing?

"Do what you must, but you could have been killed by that archer. Stop risking your and others' safety because you are doing things you should not be doing. Promise me not to go outside the gates until Papa returns."

"I promise. I'll stay inside." She chewed on her bottom lip.

"And promise me you'll not sneak out to meet Cailean tonight."

"What?" She stared at her sister in shock, wondering how she'd divined Cailean's exact request. Actually, she wasn't lying. If she decided to keep their meeting, she'd meet him in the kitchens, not outside.

"'Twas easy to guess what he said to you. Be verra careful. You could get burned from all the heat between the two of you." Maggie turned around and opened the door. "Trust me. Cailean is too much for you right now."

Sorcha followed her out, lost in thought. Was Maggie right? Was she worried over much about her sire? Should she stay away from Cailean MacAdam?

It hurt too much to think on it all.

Cailean strode down the hill heading toward his cottage outside the gates. He would stop in to see if Alan was there, but he planned to sleep under the stars with the other guards. There was a small building where they could relax and chat, or sleep protected in the winter, but this was summer. The nights were almost perfect, just a little cool air, enough for him to sleep like a babe in his mama's arms.

He wondered how that had been. He had vague memories of when Alan was born, of how much their mother had doted on his wee brother. His sire had been kind to her then, helping her whenever he could. If their relationship had stayed that way, he wouldn't have such a poor view of marriage. But something had soured between them, and it had infected the whole family.

Now, he found thoughts of a honey-haired beauty were making him question his long-held beliefs. He'd never treat Sorcha the way his sire treated his mother. He'd treasure her, sleep with his arms around her every night.

When he arrived, he stepped inside the darkened cottage. His uncle was sitting in a chair, staring at the tallow on the table in front of him. There was a mournful look in his eyes that Cailean had long since grown accustomed to seeing.

"Uncle Isaac? Is Alan here?" He closed the door behind him.

"Alan left. He went to sleep with the guards. Are you going to leave me, too?"

He moved closer and sat on a nearby stool. "Uncle, these are dangerous times. You know the expectation is for the warriors to sleep together in case we are needed. It would not make much sense if they had to go from cottage to cottage to gather us all, would it? We must be ready for aught that comes our way, especially with Quade and Logan both gone."

His uncle waved his hand in Cailean's direction before he brought it up to rub his forehead, his shoulders slumped. "I know all of that. I just enjoy talking to both of you. I like to know what transpires in the clan." His uncle sighed, clasping his hands together in front of his chest. "But I need to get used to you being gone. Someday, I hope you both marry. We could all live here together, add a couple of chambers off the back."

"I'll never marry," Cailean quickly said, but he saw a flash of Sorcha in his mind, her hair askew, her lips soft and open. "Mayhap

Alan will."

"Why not? Marriage is wonderful. I married the lass of my dreams, and we were as happy as could be until childbirth took her from me. I wish for you and your brother to live full lives—to love a woman and have bairns. Why would you not want that for yourself, Cailean? Can you not see how lonely my life is?"

"Because I cannot wish for the life my parents shared. I hated listening to them argue."

"But that was only near the end, in the year before their deaths. They were not always like that."

"'Tis what I remember best. Papa had a hot temper, and I vow never to treat a woman the way he did." The worry that he would become his father had been his constant companion in life. Gentle Alan had no reason to share that fear.

"Aye, your father did have a temper, but you do not share it."

"Are you certain about that? Lately I find myself getting angry over the smallest things, just like Da. 'Tis better if I never marry, then I'll never treat a woman the way Papa treated Mama."

"Och, Cailean, you do not understand," his uncle said, leaning over the table. "'Twas different than you think."

"How?" He put his elbows on the table and leaned toward his uncle, wishing the man would tell him anything that would change the resolution he'd made years ago. "How am I wrong?"

His uncle just waved his hand at him and turned his head away.

Disappointment washed over him. "I'm sorry about your wife, I can only guess how difficult that must have been for you, but the possibility of losing a wife does not make me more eager to marry."

His uncle snapped his head back around. "She was the light of my life. I accept the pain of losing her because she gave me memories to cherish. Your life will be empty if you push everyone away."

Cailean hopped off his stool. "I cannot discuss this anymore. I'm leaving."

"You do not know everything, I'm telling you. Please think on what I say, Cailean."

The words rang in his ears as he left the cottage and strode down the path to join the other guards. It was best if he left. It was always best to leave if he felt himself losing his temper. He would not be like his father.

Ever.

He strode down to the warriors' quarters, deciding whether or not he should actually sneak into the kitchens at midnight. Would Sorcha show up? He doubted it, but it would be fun to see if she did...

Cailean caught himself smiling, something he shouldn't do before he strolled into the warriors' camp. They'd all think him daft, but he couldn't help it. Sorcha made him go from furious to laughing in a matter of moments. What hold did the lass have on him?

He headed into the small building, stifling his urge to smile. Four men sat at the table in the center of the space. When his eyes adjusted to the low light, he recognized two of them as his brother and Frang. There were serious expressions on all four faces. He strode over, his ears straining to catch what they were discussing, but he was too far away.

Alan shouted out to him, "Cailean, join us."

He sat in the empty chair across from his brother. "What news from the guards?" he asked.

"Naught good." Frang shook his head. "The general feeling is unrest. The baron's friend Simon de la Porte is still about, and he could have any number of men with him. Do you think anyone would dare attack the Grants while their laird is gone?"

Cailean crossed his arms and stared at the floor. He did not wish to admit it, but Frang had the right of it. His friend had put voice to the worries that had taken root in his own mind.

"I hate to say it, but 'tis possible."

The truth was that Clan Grant could be ripe for an attack.

But not more than Clan Ramsay, in his opinion.

CHAPTER SIX

ᛟ

SORCHA BRUSHED HER FINGERS ACROSS her lips, the memory of Cailean's kiss still ripe in her mind. It was almost midnight... Maggie had actually fallen asleep along with all the wee ones, so if Sorcha wanted to sneak into the kitchens, she had her opportunity. No one else knew about Cailean's promise. They would have no reason to suspect her of anything.

She pushed herself up from her spot on the floor, doing her best not to awaken anyone. Then she grabbed a robe and tugged it around her waist, crossing her arms in front of her as she crept to the back of the hall toward the door to the kitchens.

Once inside, she waited for her vision to adjust to the darkness, then scanned the area for Cailean. Cook would not be here at this hour. Her breath caught as soon as she saw him in the back.

His voice carried across the silence of the chamber. "Hell, lass. Did you not know enough to stay away?"

His tone sounded different—deeper, soft and husky—but she knew not why. His body was propped against a tall chest full of dinnerware. He pushed off it and strode toward her, her skin tingling with excitement the closer he came. She shook her head, unable to come up with rational thoughts yet. This man threw her insides into a dither. The closer he came, the faster her heart beat. He stopped in front of her and brushed his thumb across her bottom lip.

"A part of me could not wait for you to come, and another part of me hoped you would never step through that door," he whispered. He smelled of ale and the winds of the Highlands, and all she could think of was that she wanted more of him.

"Why wouldn't you wish for me to come?" She had to ask, thought she wasn't sure she would like his answer.

"I know your sire and what he's capable of." His thumb followed her jawline up to her hair. He reached behind her and undid her plait. "But it seems you've cast a spell over me. I lose my ability to reason whenever I'm around you." He ran his hands through the strands, unwinding them. "Sometimes I'm not sure what color your hair is. It can be brown with strands of red in it, but when the sun shines on you, it is as golden as a wheat field in summer."

"I didn't know if you would come, but I'm glad you did," she whispered before she shivered, wrapping her arms more tightly around her waist.

He rubbed her arms. "Cold, lass? I'd be glad to warm you."

Rather than answer, she leaned into him, her arms still crossed in front. He reached out and enveloped her in the heat of his embrace. After holding her like that for a moment, so close, so warm, he pulled back and chucked her chin delicately so she was staring up at him. She became lost in his green eyes, though she spent some time studying them to decide what shade they were, ultimately dismissing the green of the forest for the green of a freshly budded apple tree.

They stared into each other's eyes for a long moment before his lips descended on hers, a soft kiss that made her moan from somewhere deep inside of her belly. Cailean responded with a chuckle, reaching around for her bottom and tugging her closer.

There was little material between the two of them. It had been a mistake to come in her night rail and robe, though she had not wished to arouse suspicion by staying in her leggings and tunic. Her breasts pressed against his chest in such a way that made her squirm, enjoying the feel of his chest against her taut nipples. But even more tempting was the sensation of his hands caressing the globes of her bottom. She arched against him, feeling his hardness against her belly, savoring the evidence of his attraction to her.

Cailean lifted her and wrapped her legs around his waist, sending a new sensation coursing through her, a desire at her core that screamed to be satisfied. Without thinking, she did what came naturally, rubbing and squirming against him for more friction, more heat, more *everything*. His erection somehow managed to connect with her skin in exactly the right spot, and she involuntarily manipulated her position so the magical stroking continued.

Suddenly, he stopped, setting her down on the floor a few paces away from him.

Her knees buckled when her feet touched the ground. He caught her, settled her, but then immediately removed his hands. "Sorcha, as tempting as you are, I take my life in my hands by acting inappropriately with you."

"What?" She could not think clearly, instead focused on all the feelings flowing through her body. Rubbing her hand in her hair, she did her best to fix the wild strands. "What did I do wrong?"

"Naught. Please believe me." He tucked a stray hair behind her ear. "You are more tempting than any woman I've ever met, but if I take this where I'd like to, your sire would hang my head on a post in front of our gates."

She watched him as his free hand subconsciously went to his neck. Her sire. Fear of her father had once again interfered with her life. If it were up to her father, she'd probably remain untouched forever.

"But…"

He lifted her chin and kissed her gently. "We cannot get carried away. I'm glad you came, but I think it's best I leave before we are caught. I will see you on the morrow."

She stared after him, unable to move as she watched him leave, doing her best to understand what was happening between them—because she knew it was far more powerful than any of the other kisses she'd experienced.

Cailean MacAdam would not leave her mind anytime soon.

℃

Cailean stood in the great hall the next morn, seated across from the laird and his second. "Have you heard aught?"

"Nay," Torrian said. "Uncle Logan said he would return as soon as he could. I doubt my parents will be back for a sennight or so. Brenna will stay to make sure Uncle Alex heals." Torrian fiddled with a few knives on the table, the only clue to his anxiety.

Cailean dropped his voice to a mere whisper. "Do you think the Grants are in trouble with Alex gone?"

Torrian glanced up at him, considering the question carefully before he replied. He was not one to jump to conclusions. "I do not think Simon de La Porte has the manpower to mount an attack. From what Uncle Logan said, they lost many warriors in the battle, probably two-thirds of their men. They'll need to rebuild..."

Kyle interrupted, "If de La Porte is interested. I doubt he will get Duncrub, so he needs to find a place to train, though coin won't be a problem for him. He's reputed to be verra good at wheedling coin out of others."

"I think de La Porte will return to London to stir up trouble. He may go back and boast about taking down the laird of the Grants. Mayhap he will even claim 'twas his sword. Whatever he chooses to do, there is one thing I am sure will take place," Torrian said.

"What's that?" Cailean asked.

"Word will travel through the land as fast as lightning bolts in a Highland thunderstorm that the great Alex Grant is close to death." Torrian rubbed his chin.

"That worries me," Cailean agreed. Hadn't the same thought occurred to him?

"His castle is renowned as one of the largest and most extravagant. I worry more about other Highland lairds attacking than de La Porte. He has no allies here. You know there are groups that could band together. The area is isolated, and they'll expect the castle to be in turmoil."

"But the king would never sanction such a thing. How would they get away with it?"

Torrian replied, "King Alexander is in turmoil. 'Twas enough of a shock to lose his wife several years ago, but he's since lost a daughter and a son. His mind is elsewhere. If they do it correctly, claiming they wish to build a larger alliance for Scotland or to protect Grant land from a larger force, they could get away with it. I hope I'm wrong, but 'tis possible."

"They'd be fools to try it," Cailean said.

"Exactly. My fear is that a group of fools will band together."

Kyle chuckled. "They do not know the laird's sons or Loki if they think to try it. Loki is almost as good a swordsman as Alex."

Cailean took a deep breath and brought up the subject he'd been afraid to discuss. "What about us? Will word travel that Logan and your sire are gone? Do you think the attacks on Sorcha are related? And—"

"Whoa," Torrian held his hand up. "Allow me a moment to respond. I do not think word will get around about Uncle Logan. He'll be back before it happens. My sire? Mayhap. But I doubt they will attack us unless they are passing through on their way to London. There's no way to know which route they will take. I'll be sending more patrols out over the next sennight," Torrian said. "We shall see what we hear."

"I volunteer to patrol your lands, my laird," Cailean said, bounding out of his chair.

Torrian gave him a strange look. "Nay, you'll stay on the duty I assigned you yesterday. Follow my cousin Sorcha. I do not trust her. In fact, she was talking with Baltair down near the archery field. You must stay with her until her sire returns."

Cailean groaned loud enough for Torrian to stare at him in question.

"My laird, I'll do as you ask, but she's not the easiest to follow."

Kyle said, "I thought you might enjoy this a wee bit, MacAdam." There was a sparkle of humor in his eyes.

Cailean cast him a sideways glance. "Not enjoy, but there's no denying she is a challenge. I know she wishes to leave the grounds."

"Aye, but she's to stay inside the gate." After delivering this order, Torrian motioned for him to move on, so he did, whistling as he made his way through the door, wondering what he would find at the archery field.

His whistling stopped as soon as he drew closer to the archery field. The sounds of a huntress laughing caught his attention, forcing him to slow his steps to be sure she was laughing and not yelling, but as soon as he caught the teasing lilt in her voice, he hurried to the area in the periphery of the bailey. Gwyneth had created this spot for practice inside the walls, and everyone in her family had spent hours training here.

When he rounded the corner, he caught sight of Baltair standing behind Sorcha, attempting to help her with her aim, although he could tell that being that close to a beautiful woman had reduced the man to a stammering fool. A few guards had stopped at the top of the wall to watch them practice.

Cailean yelled up to them. "Move on. Do you wish to be caught standing there when Logan Ramsay returns?" He didn't understand why, but he felt a sudden need to throttle each of them.

The idiots all left without complaint, fully aware of their transgression. Kyle Maule's booming voice could be heard from the courtyard as he moved toward the gates, bellowing his displeasure at seeing his men facing the wrong way on the wall. Had they noticed his approach, they wouldn't have allowed themselves to be caught gazing at Sorcha.

Sorcha fired her arrow and shouted with joy when she hit the target square on. She bounced from foot to foot, throwing lavish gratitude at Baltair. Cailean couldn't help but release a snort of laughter as he came up behind the sweet swaying hips.

Her hands settled on said hips as she twirled around to acknowledge his presence. "What was that sound supposed to mean? You do not think I've done well?" Her gaze narrowed as she stared at him.

He chuckled. "Nay, you did well, just as well as you've been doing for years. 'Tis a lovely act you've put on for Baltair." He knew his words reeked of jealousy, but for some reason he didn't care. He fought the frequent urge to yell, "Mine," whenever he was around her.

"Truly, Cailean. I know not of what you speak. Baltair, would you mind retrieving my arrows for me?" She cast him a wide smile, and the young lad scurried off toward the target, anxious to please Sorcha.

As soon as he was out of hearing distance, Sorcha turned on him. "Must you be here to ruin everything?"

He laughed, leaning against a nearby tree, his arms crossed in front of him. "Aye, I must. Instructions from my laird. But please, carry on. I'll not bother you again. I'll enjoy the entertainment."

"I'm just being nice to someone who volunteered to help me."

"Looks to me like you're trying to substitute for someone you met in private last eve. Mayhap you cannot get that *someone* out of your mind, so you've settled on the nearest lad." How he wished it were true. The truth was that *he* couldn't get a certain temptress out of his mind. She was causing him to test every promise he'd ever made to himself.

She sneered at him. "Do not flatter yourself. Baltair is a good person, and there is naught more to it than that."

He threw her an innocent look, doing his best to look like an injured soul. "You did not enjoy our jaunt in the kitchens, lass?"

He licked his lips. "I have fond memories of tasting someone in the dark. I cannot recall who 'twas because of the darkness, but she surely had the softest curves I've ever felt." He waggled his eyebrows at her.

She gasped and spun away from him, calling to Baltair.

He stepped up behind her as quietly as he could and whispered in her ear, "You're blushing, my sweet. And I remember every inch of you."

She twirled around and stepped back. "I thought you said you could not recall who you met."

He let the smile slip from his face. "Och, I remember you well." He winked at her. "We are perfect together."

"Did you not tell me you would never marry? If you feel that way, why kiss me?" She tilted her chin up as she awaited his answer.

He hated being put on the spot, and yet he could not deny the truth: she'd made him question every belief he'd ever had about his life, including his vow never to marry. "Mayhap I cannot stop myself." He stared off after Baltair before he glanced at the clouds above them. "Mayhap I can only think of you and how you feel in my arms." Then he directed his gaze back to her. "Listening to you with another man brings out the savage beast in me."

"Cailean, please cease your teasing. I do not wish to hurt Baltair's feelings. There is naught between us."

Baltair came barreling toward them, retrieved arrows in his hands. "Sorcha, you hit the last target dead center. 'Twas perfect. Well done."

She smiled and glanced over her shoulder at Cailean. "My thanks, Baltair."

The lad nodded to her, then shifted his gaze to Cailean. "Do you wish to take over her training?"

Cailean decided to let the poor man finish training her. He knew the lad devoted most of his time to helping his sire and did not often entertain lasses. This was probably a thrill for him. "Nay, go ahead. I'll stand back here. I'm assigned to her protection until her sire returns." He moved back to the tree, sitting underneath it to watch.

"My thanks, Cailean," Sorcha said. "Baltair has given me some useful pointers."

He contained his snort, not wishing to offend Baltair. The man was doing his best, no doubt, but Sorcha had been taught by the best archer in the land.

"My thanks for helping me. I have not practiced with Mama much since she hurt her ankle. It seems I've forgotten a few of the essential elements of archery."

This time a small snort escaped, but she ignored him. Unfortunately, he could not ignore her. She was just too enticing.

Baltair continued his instruction, and Cailean found it hard to shift his gaze from the lass in front of him. He couldn't help but wonder what it would be like to go to bed every night with a woman like her in his arms. He couldn't imagine waking up to her every morning only to return and make sweet love to her again at night.

It made marriage seem almost...appealing.

Sorcha continued on, not actually flirting as he'd suspected. She was just being nice to Baltair, and the lad clearly enjoyed being in her presence.

Who wouldn't? A lad would have to be nearly dead not to see her beauty.

The warning from the gates came from out of nowhere. "Attack! We're under attack!"

Cailean bolted up from his spot under the tree in time to see Torrian running down the path toward the gates. The laird halted upon seeing them. "Cailean, I need you. Sorcha, you will stay inside the gates. Understand?"

Sorcha, her eyes wide, just nodded.

Cailean took one look at her and said, "Promise me you'll stay." He couldn't bear the thought of someone shooting at her again, trying to hurt or kill her. The very idea of it did something strange to his insides.

She nodded again, whispering, "I promise."

Cailean hauled off in the direction of the gates, running behind Torrian. They quickly scaled the wall when they reached it and looked down below. At least a score of men on horseback were stealing Ramsay horses and fighting the patrolling Ramsay guardsmen outside the gates.

They exchanged a look and hurried back down, Torrian yelling orders to the men running in from the lists. "Full attack. Horses, everyone on horseback."

The lads from the stables saddled up as the entire bailey erupted in chaos.

Cailean ran for a horse, leaping atop a stallion directly behind Torrian and heading out the gates to do battle with the intruders.

Who the hell were they?

CHAPTER SEVEN

ᐃ

SORCHA'S HEART WAS IN HER throat as she watched the men of her clan draw together to fight the invaders. Who dared to attack the Ramsays? How she wished her sire and Uncle Quade were here now. Chasing up the stairs to the curtain wall, she leaned out over the valley below, wondering if she would recognize the plaids of the attackers.

They were too far away.

Baltair had followed her and popped up next to her, leaning over the wall the same way. "Who are they?" he breathed out, a panicked expression on his face.

"I don't know. I cannot see a plaid, can you?"

Baltair shook his head. Two of the Ramsay guards went down, arrows protruding from their bodies.

"They have archers. Where are they?" Sorcha asked. "Can you see them in the trees or are they on horseback?"

Both of them scanned the countryside for the archers, but none were clearly visible. Baltair shook his head. "I don't see any archers on horseback. They must be hidden in the trees." Another man went down because his horse had taken an arrow to its flank.

"Over there." She pointed to the spot she'd seen the arrow come from. "Someone needs to go in that direction. The arrows are coming from over there, and no one has noticed."

The Ramsay guards were overpowering the invaders on horse-back, but the arrows continued to shower down on them. Sorcha tried to yell warning to their warriors, but nothing could be heard in the melee. Unspeakable. She was watching her people come to harm when she knew how to help them.

"I cannot stand here and watch this. 'Tis horrid watching our men and horses drop. I'm going out there, Baltair. Are you coming with me?" Sorcha pivoted and headed back down the staircase. "I'm going to the stables for a horse." She grabbed her bow and arrows and ran.

It could not be Horsie, of course, for her mare had likely been injured by the very people who were attacking them now. The thought only made her madder.

Baltair's voice rang out behind her. "What are you going to do?"

"I'm going after the archer in those trees. I'll shoot him down myself."

"But you promised our laird and Cailean you would stay here," Baltair said uneasily.

She stopped short and he ran into her. "Would you really have me do naught while our clansmen are shot down, one after another, by the same archer? At present, you and I could be the best archers on Ramsay land. It looks like there's only one, but if I'm wrong, you can take one out and I'll get the other. I'll not stand idly by any longer."

She took off to the stables and grabbed a horse the stable lad had already saddled. "Are you coming?" she hollered to Baltair.

"I guess I am." His voice was heavy with resignation.

Good. Baltair mounted a nearby horse and followed her out into the chaos.

She drove her horse as fast as she could toward the patch of trees she'd noticed from the curtain wall. Baltair caught up with her quickly and stuck by her side until she reached her mark. Motioning to him, she rode off to the side, away from most of the action, hoping to see more arrows fly from the trees.

But there was silence—no arrows, nothing. She searched the field, noticing that the Ramsays were gaining control, fewer strangers were doing battle with them. Most of the attackers had been defeated and now lay scattered across the grounds. She was about to go back when she heard the sound of an arrow sluicing through the air. She turned toward it and everything else happened at once.

Baltair took the arrow to his side and fell off his horse.

She screamed.

Her horse bolted.

Two horsemen followed her.

Sorcha did all she could to get her horse under control, pulling on the reins to slow him down, making soothing noises, but he broke through the trees, forcing her to duck branches and lean in close to keep from being knocked out of the saddle. They raced over uneven ground until she thought her bottom would split in two, but a quick glance over her shoulder revealed the two horses were still in pursuit, one in front of the other.

She did her best to veer off to the side to get a better look at the riders chasing her, but she could not. The horse jumped over a burn, and she only managed to stay atop him by clinging to his back with all her might. Her heart beat so fast she swore it would stop and never beat again. Out of the corner of her eye, she saw the wild face of the horse directly behind her. The rider was not wearing a Ramsay plaid.

She spurred her horse onward—faster, faster—praying he would not turn lame from the uneven ground they traversed. A loud grunt came from behind her, followed by another. The rider from the horse closest to her went toppling to the ground, but she knew not why. She did not slow to find out. There was a small clearing up ahead where the ground was a bit more level, so she pushed her horse forward.

The sound of more horses reached her ears.

What if it was the attackers? What if they captured her, carried her off to their camp, and raped her until she lost consciousness? Every fear she'd ever thought reared up in her mind, making her more and more frantic, her horse sensing her fear and tensing even more. Hoofbeats came closer to her and the next thing she knew she was flying through the air, a warrior's large hand grabbing her by the waist and tossing her across his horse with an oomph.

She pushed herself up and struggled with her attacker, flailing her arms wildly and connecting with flesh. "Nay, nay, nay! Leave off, you brute!"

Swinging her fist, she caught him in the jaw, knocking them both off-balance. They fell to the ground in a heap, but she heard a shout as they tumbled down together. "Sorcha, stop. It's me."

She opened her eyes, only then realizing she'd squeezed them shut in fright. It was *Cailean* on top of her, grappling for her hands and holding them over her head as she struggled. When she finally saw his face, she was so relieved that she threw her arms around his neck and sobbed.

He sat up and tugged her onto his lap. They did not notice they were no longer alone in the clearing until a frightening voice filled the clearing and a sword appeared out of nowhere.

"Take your hands from my daughter."

Her sire.

☾

Cailean held onto Sorcha a wee bit too tight, but he couldn't stop himself. He was so relieved to have gotten her off that wild horse safely—and away from her pursuer—he wished to hold her for the rest of the day. "You are not hurt, Sorcha? Say something, please?" He kissed the top of her head and tucked it under his chin, clinging to her.

That was when the sound he'd dreaded most rang out in the trees around them.

"Take your hands from my daughter."

Logan Ramsay had a sword aimed straight at his neck. He threw his arms up in the air as a sign of concession, not wishing to anger the man further. "Aye, I'll not touch her again, my lord, but you must remove her from my lap." He did not wish to have his throat cut with one quick slash.

"Sorcha, get up." Logan had been joined by two other guards, Torrian, and Cailean's brother.

Sorcha lifted her head long enough to say, "Nay, Papa. Cailean saved me. There was another chasing me, and my horse…" Her breath hitched and she rested her head back on Cailean's chest, her arms wrapped around his waist.

Alan spoke up in Cailean's defense. "My lord, she was being chased by one of the reivers. I was a ways behind the man, but I saw he was after your daughter. My brother took him out and scooped her from her wild horse." He pointed off to the clearing, where the poor horse had run in a circle until he found the burn again. Now he was drinking heavily and foaming at the mouth.

"Sorcha, is that true?"

"Aye, Papa." She turned her head to her sire, and this gesture finally moved her father to drop the tip of the sword from Cailean's neck and hold his hand out to her. She threw herself into her sire's arms. "Papa, I was so frightened. What if Cailean had not followed me? What if that horrible man had stolen me away, what if…"

Torrian said, "I assigned Cailean the job of protecting Sorcha because I was worried she would not stay inside the gates in your absence, Uncle Logan." Turning toward her, he said, "Did you not promise to stay inside when I ordered Cailean to horseback?"

Sorcha sobbed, unable to stop. Cailean wished to hold her until she calmed, but he would not risk angering Logan more than he already had.

Sorcha babbled at everyone. "I saw where the archer was hidden. I thought I could stop him. Baltair. Where is Baltair?" Her hands flew up to her face in near panic. She stepped away from her father, moving closer to Cailean. "Baltair, he was hit with an arrow. I saw him go down." She took another step toward him.

"Why the hell was Baltair out here? He's not a trained warrior." Logan began pacing the clearing, radiating annoyance and anger.

"Sorcha, he's being tended," Torrian said. "From what I could see, 'twas a flesh wound."

"I feel so bad. I forgot he was injured." Her crying turned into a wail. "'Tis…my…fault."

Cailean could see her hands trembling and thought she was near to collapsing, though he couldn't understand why. Her father and cousin were here, and the Ramsays had successfully repelled the attack. He couldn't stand to see her shake any longer. He took a step forward and hauled her up against his side, wrapping his arm around her and letting her lean against him.

Logan stopped in his tracks and turned to him. "You dare touch her in front of me?" he growled out.

Sorcha cried louder.

"Aye, my lord, with due respect." He wished to shout at the man, but he controlled his impulse. "She's shaking, and 'tis the only way I can be sure to catch her if her legs buckle."

Logan Ramsay's eyes narrowed, and Cailean thought his own legs would buckle under the man's scrutiny, but he managed to stay strong. Still, the sweat on his brow nearly dripped into his eyes, his heart threatened to burst out of his chest, and he was ready to move fast should the massive man jump toward him.

It did not happen.

Instead, Sorcha's arms curled around his, making everything he'd risked feel worthwhile. Her crying slowed, so he asked, "May I request to return the lass to the keep, my lord?"

"She'll return with me," Logan said, giving him a weighing look.

Sorcha stepped over to her sire's horse, casting a last glance at Cailean over her shoulder, but her sire tossed her up onto his horse as if she were little more than a feather. Then he mounted behind her and sent his horse into a gallop.

The rest of the group followed, but Alan stayed behind for a moment. Once everyone was out of earshot, Alan asked, "You all right?"

Cailean nodded, letting out a breath between his pursed lips, puffing his cheeks out.

"You're not like our sire."

Cailean turned his head toward his brother, wondering what had made Alan think of such a thing.

"If you were like our sire," Alan continued, "you would have lost control and screamed at Logan for accusing you falsely, but you did not. Da would have."

He thought about it for a moment before nodding.

"Did you yell at Sorcha for leaving the keep?" Alan asked.

"Nay, I couldn't. I was too relieved she'd survived."

"Da would have."

Mayhap he was correct. "My thanks, Alan."

Alan laughed. "Now all you have to do is protect your bollocks from Logan Ramsay."

His brother had never spoken truer words.

CHAPTER EIGHT

ॐ

S ORCHA PACED IN THE SOLAR, awaiting her sire's return. He'd agreed to speak with her here after he delivered instructions to Torrian and Kyle. Her mother had returned home as well, but she'd gone directly to see Brigid.

How Sorcha wished Cailean was there to support her. She couldn't believe he'd been brave enough to wrap his arms around her so close to her sire. Lads never dared to touch her in front of the renowned Logan Ramsay.

But she no longer thought of Cailean as just any lad. Settling into the chair, she straightened her tunic, doing her best to remove the dirt and leaves. When it became clear her attentions were not helping, she gave up with resignation. What did it matter? Somewhere along the way, she'd changed. While she loved being with her father more than anyone, she was no longer the wee lass who craved being the center of his attention. Now she craved Cailean MacAdam's attention.

Had she gone from being a lass to a lady? She snorted, answering her own question with a flourish. Lady, perhaps not; woman, aye. She'd grown in ways she hadn't expected.

Once she discovered how Uncle Alex fared, she would confess all her failures to her sire.

Everything. The burden of carrying it inside was too much, regardless of what Maggie had said. He might never know the truth if she didn't speak with him, but *she* would always know.

The door flew open and she jumped out of the chair, though her sire's abrupt entrance shouldn't have surprised her. It was the only way he ever entered a room—with a bang. He strode over and sat behind his brother's desk, giving her a puzzled look. "What is it?"

She didn't know how to answer that question, so she ignored it for a more important topic. "Uncle Alex? How is he?"

"He'll be fine. You know how strong your uncle is—he's an enigma to every Scotsman. He won't go down yet."

"The truth, Papa?" She knew her sire's tendency to bend the truth if he thought it was in a person's best interest. Her hands twisted in her tunic as a bothersome thought occurred to her, but she pushed it aside, needing to hear about her dear uncle.

He sighed and leaned his chair back on the two rear legs. "Och, my daughter is old enough to know my tactics. Fair enough. Aunt Brenna and Aunt Jennie were verra pleased with the surgery. He opened his eyes for long enough to tell Maddie he wasn't going anywhere. Aunt Brenna stayed because he's not stable yet. She wished to wait a few days, so your mother and I returned early to help Torrian. We all agreed this was likely to be a time of upheaval across the Highlands. Aunt Brenna does not often ask for special requests, so when she does, I honor them."

"Aye, and because she saved Lily and Torrian. Grandmama used to say you'd do aught for Aunt Brenna, that you fell to one knee at her wedding and vowed to protect her forever."

He nodded, though Sorcha guessed it was difficult for him to admit he was indebted to anyone. She was secretly pleased it was a woman. Her father held women in higher regard than most men, something that pleased her immensely.

Her father sat forward in his chair, his lips twisting—a common expression when he was deep in thought. "It will be a long time before Uncle Alex holds a sword again. 'Tis the only truth I can give you. He is down for a bit, and there is always the chance of fever, but as you know, he has the verra best caring for him. I believe he'll be hale in a moon, though mayhap not quite as braw as he once was."

She stared at her hands still twisting her tunic in her lap. Uncle Quade was limited in movement due to a bad knee; Uncle Alex had been downed by a sword injury. Her father could be next. He was the eldest of the group after Uncle Quade and Uncle Alex. She said a swift prayer to keep him hale and healthy.

Tears welled in Sorcha's eyes, begging to be set free, but she fought the urge and won. Her life was filled with such sweet memories of the clans coming together for the yearly Ramsay festival. The elders always loved to gather together and talk of what was to come. What *was* to come? Would there be more battles, more pain? Did they have anything left to look forward to?

"Daughter?"

"Papa, I must tell you something."

"Go ahead. I'm listening."

This time she lost her control over the tears. "I…I…'twas all my fault."

His brow lifted the way it often did when he waited for her to continue. He tipped his head toward her—an indication that he was growing impatient.

She swiped at her tears and forced herself to tell her tale and be done with it. "Brigid. When Brigid and Jennet were kidnapped, 'twas my fault. Mama will hate me forever." More tears tumbled down her cheeks. "I know how tortured Mama was while Brigid was missing, and…and poor Brigie was upset for days after she returned. I'm so sorrryyyyy." She couldn't stop the wailing sounds coming from her own mouth, though she tried her best to see through the flood of tears. She deserved to see her father's reaction.

"How was it your fault?"

"Because…" There was no rage in his face—yet.

"Sorcha, control yourself enough to answer my question, please. Because why?"

His exasperation was beginning to show in the tic in his jaw, so she forged ahead. "Because, because I was supposed to sleep with Jennet and Brigid that night." She had to stop to catch her breath, but then she plowed on. "I begged Bethia to switch with me so I could sleep with Maggie. We were talking about lads and I wasn't ready to go to sleep yet. Bethia *was* ready, so she switched with me."

"And, if you had been in the chamber instead of Bethia, you think you could have stopped Bearchun and Shaw from stealing the wee lassies? One lass against two Ramsay warriors?"

"I could have tried. Bethia just panicked. You know how shy she is. She didn't dare to do aught against the attackers."

"Are you sure you would not have panicked when you found two men in your chamber in the middle of the night? Lass, they would not have stood there and waited for you to awaken and clear the sleep from your eyes. How fast do you usually arise in the morning?"

"I...I..." She frowned, considering his point. Her sire was correct about that. She hated getting up in the morn.

"Frankly, I'm glad you switched."

Her eyes widened. "What?" Had she heard her sire correctly?

"Had you been in that chamber, you would have fought them. You could have gotten yourself killed." Her father's voice softened. "And I would be lost without my wee lassie."

"But you just said I probably would not have even stirred..."

"You're *my* daughter, and those men came to steal two wee lassies you love. You would have fought and kicked with your entire being. They still would have kidnapped your sister and your cousin, but you would not have walked away uninjured."

Her father got out of his chair and circled around to the front of the desk, leaning against it and crossing his arms. "Sorcha, how long have you been carrying this guilt around on your shoulders?"

"I...I..." Blast it all, why could she not think?

He tugged her to her feet and lifted her chin until she met his gaze. "Bearchun and Shaw are the only ones guilty of what happened that night. And did you think your mother and I did not know you'd switched with Bethia?"

She swiped the tears away from her face in bafflement. "What? You knew?"

He nodded, a smug grin on his face. "Your mother and I know everything you do."

"Everything?" Her eyes widened.

"*Most* everything. Answer me one more question. Is that what you were thinking about when you twisted your hands so much that you put a hole in your tunic?" He tipped his head toward her middle, where a touch of her skin showed.

She gasped, covering it with her hand and staring at him, appalled at what she'd done. "Papa..."

"The truth. Were you thinking about Brigid?"

She shook her head, not daring to lie to him when he was this close. Instead, she threw herself at him and wrapped her arms around him. "Nay, I was thinking about you and hoping you would not be the next one to get hurt after Uncle Quade and

Uncle Alex." Down came the tears again.

"Hmmm. Seems we have a similar problem."

She tucked her head under her father's chin, taking in his usual scent of pine and the outdoors. He always made her feel as if she were standing in the middle of a summer forest, the sunshine breaking through the needles of the pines and releasing the aromas of the grass, leaves, and earth. "What problem do you have?"

In a quiet voice, something so unlike him, he said, "The problem of seeing my daughter prefer another man's comfort to her father's for the first time."

She pulled back to stare at him. "What?"

"Do you think 'twas easy for me see you move toward Cailean MacAdam and away from me, especially since you are my first-born?"

"But I was frightened. He saved me. Papa, 'twas not meant to hurt you."

He brushed her hair back from her face and planted a huge kiss on her forehead. "I know what it meant, lass."

"Papa, I'm not your first daughter. Molly is."

"Nay, she is not. We had you before we adopted Molly and Maggie. I love you all, but you will always be my firstborn wee lassie. I did not have the privilege of holding Molly and Maggie when they were newly born like I did you. And neither of them look back at me with my own eyes. Brigid looks at me with her mother's eyes."

"Oh, Papa. I love you, too." She kissed his cheek, surprised to see her small gesture in the woods had hurt his feelings.

"Now, I'd like to hear more about Cailean. According to Torrian and Kyle, I missed quite a bit while I was gone."

She stepped back and sat down, covering the hole in her tunic with her arms. "There's not much to tell."

Her father's brows rose and she sighed. "All right. Cailean was the one who saved me from the arrows on our hunting jaunt."

"Your mother mentioned as much to me. Now tell me why you were hunting. You're not a hunter. You hate taking animals down."

"I know. I just wanted to make you proud…to do something for the clan while you were gone."

"And how is Horsie?"

"She's better, Papa, but I was so upset she got hurt. I did not intend for her to get hurt, just as I did not expect Brigid to get hurt when I switched places with Bethia."

"Who was the archer aiming for?"

"Everyone seems to think he was shooting at me. 'Tis why Torrian asked Cailean to protect me."

"And what do you think?"

She thought back to that day, how close each arrow had come to her. In a small voice, she said, "I think he was aiming for me."

"Did you get a look at him?"

"Nay. I was too frightened when Horsie was hurt."

"And what did Cailean do?"

"He pulled me off my horse to protect me, just like he did today."

A knock sounded at the door. "Just a moment," her father bellowed.

She peered up at her father, feeling much better now that she'd confessed her guilt. Now all she had to do was come up with a different way to make him proud.

"That will be Torrian, Kyle, and Cailean." He grinned, showing all his teeth. "I'll see if Cailean is man enough for my daughter."

"Papa, nay. Please do not treat him like that."

"Are you interested in him?"

"I'm not sure. Besides, he says he'll never marry."

He chortled. "I used to say the same. Then I met your mother and here I am with five bairns."

"You thought you'd never marry?"

"Most men do not. 'Tis a woman's plan we get ensnared in. I've never been happier. Back to Cailean, aye or nay?"

She fidgeted in her chair, still playing with the hole she'd made in her tunic. She didn't know how to inform her father she was most definitely interested in Cailean. Perhaps it was better if she said nothing, because if she admitted it to him, he would keep pressing for more information. She wasn't ready to admit how *much* she was interested in the man.

She unquestionably did not want her sire to know that Cailean occupied her every thought of late.

Her sire tipped his chin toward her tunic. "You'll make the hole larger if you don't stop."

She stopped her fumbling, resting her palms flat on her lap.

Why would a man say he never wished to marry? She'd always assumed they all wished to marry, but if her sire was right, mayhap there was a chance. Hadn't Cailean admitted that he had started to reconsider his convictions?

"What is it? I can see the thoughts whirling through your mind."

She forged ahead, hoping he would be honest with her. "Papa, why didn't you wish to marry? I don't understand."

He pursed his lips for a moment, then said, "I never wanted the responsibility of children. I watched my brother's struggles with Torrian and Lily, and it scared the hell out of me. And see? I have you, and look what you're putting me through with your questions about lads. Now, until Cailean or some other lad thoroughly impresses me, your brother and I will be the only males in your life. Do you hear me, daughter?" He tugged her to her feet and bounced her up and down until she promised to love only him. It was a silly game he'd often played with them when they were wee bairns.

She couldn't help but laugh at his antics. He'd teased her and her sisters often about never having suitors. He'd always said he'd hurt any man who touched them without his permission. Being naïve, she'd assumed that day would never come.

That day was here.

He drew her in for a quick hug, then stood and moved toward the door. "You need to go upstairs and bathe. You're a mess, and you'll want to look beautiful at the festivities this eve."

She hurried to his side and her sire grinned. "I thought you'd like that."

"What festivities?"

"I've ordered a celebration in honor of Uncle Alex. All the guards who are not on duty will be invited to attend," he said, waggling his brows.

She leaned in to kiss his cheek. "My thanks, Papa. I cannot wait."

"Enter," he shouted, throwing the door open.

Torrian, Kyle, and Cailean came through it. Sorcha smiled at each of them before she disappeared.

She couldn't help but notice that Cailean's skin color was a faint shade of green.

CHAPTER NINE

᚛

CAILEAN ENTERED THE SOLAR BEHIND Torrian and Kyle, hoping to slip in unnoticed by Logan. That was not to be.

"Must I force a wedding, MacAdam?" Logan's voice bounced off the walls.

"What? Wedding, my lord? I don't understand," he stammered. He wasn't prepared to marry Sorcha. Mayhap Alan was right about their father...but he needed more time to consider it. He could never enter into a marriage without being certain he would not follow in his sire's footsteps.

"You had your hands all over my daughter. I understand you saved her from a possible attack, and for that I give my thanks, but are you man enough to deserve my daughter? You need to speak up or stay away. Make your choice."

"I...I considered saving her as part of my assignment. Torrian had assigned her to my protection..."

"True, Uncle. She has a tendency to run free, as you know, so I was concerned about her leaving the protections of the keep."

Logan motioned for the three of them to sit while he paced behind Quade's desk. Torrian took his position at the desk opposite him. Since he and his father shared the lairdship, they also shared the solar.

"So she does," Logan said. "Her nature is not unlike my own." The stare he drilled into Cailean felt like the point of a sword. "If you have no interest in my daughter, MacAdam, you're to stay away. I'm here to protect her now. Otherwise, I'll meet you at the end of my sword at dawn."

Cailean quelled his need to charge out of his chair and argue with the man. His self-control reminded him of what Alan had said. Mayhap he could… Nay, it was too soon to decide. And Logan Ramsay was not the kind of man who would accept a half-hearted answer. "No need, my lord. I was doing my job, not pursuing her. She has been under a great deal of stress from both incidents."

"We'll drop that topic for now. I wish to discuss the reivers today. How many?" He took a seat behind his desk, shifting his attention to Torrian.

"Five dead, probably another score on the run, many of them injured. Our warriors did a fine job of gathering quickly and taking care of this threat."

Kyle added, "We had our men patrolling our land. I don't know how they missed them. Did you recognize any of them? I did not."

"Aye. I'm afraid I did." Logan nodded. "The one after Sorcha was one of Duncrub's men. They must have resorted to stealing to make up for the coin they were promised by the baron. Dead men don't pay."

"Do you think there will be more attacks?" Kyle asked.

"Unfortunately, there could be. I made sure to spread the word that Gwynie and I are back, but tidings of Alex's injury have traveled far and wide. I'm more worried about the Grants."

"What do you propose?" Torrian asked.

"Nothing yet." He stroked his chin as he stared into space. "Now, we all know an archer came after Sorcha the other day. I'd like to know if any of you think today's archer was aiming for my daughter."

"A few others were hit with arrows before she came outside the gates."

Kyle added, "I have three with injuries from the arrows, including Baltair. All three will survive. A fourth fell from his horse because an arrow pierced the beast's side. His worst injury was a broken arm."

"Baltair was near Sorcha?"

"Aye, he was just a bit behind her when he was hit. I saw him go down," Torrian replied. "I can't say for sure that Sorcha was the target."

"But it's possible?" Logan asked.

Torrian nodded first and then turned to Kyle and Cailean to see if they agreed.

Cailean hated to admit it, but it was entirely possible that the archer had been waiting in the trees in the hopes Sorcha would be lured out.

Hellfire. He would still be in protection mode, and her sire would be watching.

He'd have to be careful.

(c

A few hours later, Sorcha spun in a circle, seeing how her new skirt would flare out when she danced. She giggled with glee and clasped her hands together.

Brigid flew into her chamber. "Sorcha, will you fix my hair? I don't like the way Mama did it. Please?"

Her mother stood in the doorway behind her, an exasperated look on her face. "She's growing up too fast, Sorcha. Spin your magic. I'll see you both downstairs."

Maggie entered the chamber just as their mother left. "You look beautiful, Sorcha. That gown is stunning."

She smiled and twirled again because she *felt* beautiful. The dress was a dark lavender, one of her favorite colors, with pink ribbons across the bodice and down the back of the gown. "Maggie, you always look lovely in blue."

"Do you think so?" Her sister peered down at her dress and fussed with her blue and green ribbons.

"I like that one best of all your gowns," Brigid said to her.

Sorcha set Brigid on the bed in front of her, then began to work her magic with her sister's thick, brown locks, giving her several small braids and one large one. "Maggie, where's Bethia?"

"She's not going."

"Why not? Is she ill?" She tied off one braid and started another. "Brigid, stop wiggling or I'll have to start over." Her wee sister giggled.

"Nay. She just doesn't wish to put a nice gown on. Says she doesn't have any." She shrugged her shoulders and flopped onto the bed.

"Tell her to come here. I'll find her something to wear. She cannot stay up here alone. Aunt Brenna is gone, Jennet is missing her mother and clinging to Lily. She *has* to go. It's a celebration for Uncle Alex."

Maggie nodded, climbed off the bed, and disappeared. She was back in a few moments, saying. "She won't come in here either."

Sorcha finished up with Brigid's hair, then said, "Brigid, go down to the hall with Maggie. I'll get Bethia."

"She's not verra happy," Maggie whispered. She ushered Brigid ahead of her down the passageway while Sorcha hurried toward Bethia's chamber.

Knocking on the door, she chewed on her lip, trying to think of a way to convince her cousin to join the festivities. Bethia had always been shy, much like Uncle Quade, though he was forced to talk to people because he was laird.

She heard a muffled sound in the chamber, so she opened the door, only to find Bethia prostate on the bed sobbing her eyes out. She stepped into the room, closing the door behind her, and sat on the edge of the bed. "Bethia, what is it?"

After several minutes and much coaxing, Bethia finally raised her head and then pushed herself to a sitting position, wiping the tears off her red cheeks. "Mama's not here."

"I know. We all miss her. But time will go faster if you enjoy yourself."

"You don't understand."

"What is it?"

Bethia pointed to her chest against the wall. "Nothing fits."

Sorcha frowned. "You're correct, I don't understand. You have many beautiful gowns. Just pick one."

"Promise you'll not tell anyone?" Bethia whispered.

"I promise. What is it?"

"I'm always growing bigger around the waist. Mama fixes the gowns for me right before I have to wear them. I tried them all on. I'm even bigger than the last time."

"Bethia—" Sorcha climbed off the bed, "—you have the biggest heart of anyone I know. The reason your gowns don't fit is because your heart has grown even larger, not because of your waist. Here. Allow me to help you. I'll find something."

She guided her cousin over to the chest and selected several gowns for her to try on, but to her surprise, Bethia was right. Nothing fit. "Wait here. I have an idea." She hurried back to her chamber and pulled out the gown she'd been making for herself. It was a glorious gold, a shade she'd never seen before, and she'd been so excited to find the fabric for it. She'd finished most of it except for the final seams for the last fitting. The bodice was fitted, but her bust was larger than Bethia's, so that shouldn't be a problem. The skirt, which flared out beneath the bodice, was still much too big for her. Would it fit Bethia? She held it up and a small moan escaped her lips as she thought of giving it up, but she made up her mind and took it into her cousin's chamber.

Bethia gasped when she laid it out on the bed. "Sorcha, that is the most beautiful gown I've ever seen. Whose is it?"

"I was making it for myself, but I haven't done the final fitting yet. Try it on. See if it fits. It has a different fit that I think will be flattering for you."

Bethia stood up and gazed down at the gown, fingering the material as though it were actually made of gold. "Are you sure, Sorcha? This gown is so beautiful."

"I didn't really like it when I tried it on. The color wasn't good for my skin, but it will be lovely against your brown hair. You must try it on for me. If I don't wear it, Mama will be furious with me. 'Twas expensive fabric."

"Will you help me?" Her cousin stared up at her with so much hope in her eyes. She couldn't possibly deny her.

"I'll do your hair, too. You'll see."

Nearly an hour later, the red in Bethia's eyes was gone, washed away by the huge smile on her face. Sorcha spun her around in a circle and declared, "'Tis more beautiful on you than on me. I wish your papa were here to see you."

Bethia beamed the biggest smile she'd ever seen. Drawing Sorcha into a hug, she whispered, "Many thanks to you."

Sorcha tugged her down the passageway, and when they stopped at the top of the stairs, a hush fell over the gathering beneath them. She turned to Bethia and whispered, "You see? 'Tis for you. You shall go down first."

She was so proud of her cousin. She *did* look beautiful, and all eyes were on her as they descended the staircase. Well, except for two pairs that settled on her and stayed—her sire's and Cailean MacAdam's.

Her father came over and fussed over Bethia just as she'd hoped he would do. Then he leaned in to kiss her cheek. "I know what you did, daughter."

His voice was full of pride. Tears pricked Sorcha's eyes, but she choked them back and gave him a huge smile. After talking with her family, she moved away from them and made her way toward Cailean. There was only one problem.

Cailean had disappeared.

What had she done wrong? Had her sire said something to him earlier?

She snuck out the door just in time to see him heading down the pathway toward the gates. "Cailean?" She lifted her skirts and chased after him.

He walked along as if oblivious to everyone around him. When she finally caught up to him, she touched his shoulder and he spun around as if she'd set a flame to his back. The terrible expression on his face startled her. "Cailean, what's wrong? Did I do something wrong?"

Cailean shook his head, his shoulders hunched over as he glanced around, looking for who? Her sire? "What? Nay, you've done naught wrong. I'm going home to visit my uncle."

"But I thought you'd dance with me tonight. 'Tis not often we have these festivities. Please come back." She couldn't make out the expression in his face, but this was not the Cailean she was familiar with—the one who teased her, made her laugh, and took care of her.

He ran his gaze up and down Sorcha. "Sorcha, I cannot…I wish to…"

She could see how he struggled with his words. Her sire *must* have said something to him. He'd never acted like this with her before. He placed his hand on her lower back and ushered her off to the herb garden, hiding underneath a huge oak tree.

"What is it?" She set her hand on his forearm, but he pulled away.

"I've told you I don't wish to marry. I *like* you, more than I've ever liked any lass, but 'twould not be fair to start something with you when I have no intention of marrying. I'm not assigned to protect you anymore, so let's end this as friends."

There was no laughter, no teasing, no gleam in his eye. She could see how unhappy he was, could see how he fought his urges. There was only one reason this man could be acting completely different than the last two times they were together.

Her sire had said something to frighten him away. He'd probably threatened to kill him. Her hands fisted at her sides. "My father. What did he tell you today? Did he threaten you?" She'd find out if he had.

"Nay. He said naught except to thank me for saving you. There was no problem between us."

His gaze stared off into the distance over her shoulder. He was lying.

A fury built inside her that she wasn't sure how to control. She'd find her father and tell him he needed to leave her be, leave Cailean be. How dare he interfere in her life? She stomped off toward the keep but then stopped abruptly. If she went inside, Cailean would leave, and her father would win. She whirled around to face him.

Her sire was not going to win this time. She raced back to Cailean and threw her arms around him and kissed him, parting her lips to invite him in. Her hands fisted in his hair because he tasted so unbelievably good, and she wasn't about to end this quickly.

Cailean pulled back and gazed into her eyes, "I lose all control when I'm with you, do you know that?" He kissed her again, a strong, possessive kiss that caused her to moan into his lips.

He lifted her into the air, his hands under her bottom, and set her down on top of the stone fence that surrounded the garden. It was a dark, hidden corner—a haven where they could be together away from everyone else's prying eyes.

"I want you, Sorcha, more than I've ever wanted anyone." He ravaged her lips and ran his hands over to cup her breasts, teasing her nipples through the cloth.

She arched against him, wanting more of his touch, his caresses, everywhere. His sweet torture was too much, more than she could handle. To her surprise, his hands reached around to her back and fumbled with the ribbons until he'd loosened the bodice enough to slide her sleeves off her shoulders, freeing her breasts from their confinement.

He cupped her breasts in his hands and stared at them, his thumbs flicking against the taut peaks until she wished to scream. "Sorcha, you are perfect. So beautiful…"

His head lowered to her breast and she gasped when his tongue teased her nipple, laving it. Then he took her breast full in his mouth, suckling her until she cried out. "Cailean, do not stop." Her hands gripped his head, holding him close.

She whimpered as his head bent to the other breast, repeating his delicious torture, tasting her, suckling her until she wished to scream.

A voice interrupted them. "Cailean."

It was Alan, calling to him from the beginning of the path. Cailean tugged her bodice back up, covering her breasts and then her shoulders. "What is it, Alan?" he shouted back.

"Ramsay is coming. He's looking for Sorcha."

"Delay him," Cailean said, his hands now fumbling to tie her ribbons in the back.

Alan took off and Cailean pulled her off the stone wall and stood behind her, fixing the ribbons. "Sorcha, forgive me. This was wrong…I should not have…" He grabbed the plaid she'd had around her shoulders and covered her.

She cupped his cheek with her hand. "Stop, Cailean. I am not sorry. We need to talk. Why do you keep saying this is wrong? It is so *right*. You cannot mean what you say."

"Sorcha?" A booming voice called out in the distance.

"I'll explain later. I'll return you to your sire." He did his best to straighten the hairs that had fallen astray.

"Nay, I'll just go alone." She headed back up the path.

He chased after her. "Nay, I'll never disrespect you. I will escort you back. No matter what your sire does, I must accept responsibility for my actions."

She nodded and he tucked her against him as they moved out onto the path in the courtyard.

Just in time. Her father came around the corner and asked, "Where have you been?"

His gaze moved from Sorcha to Cailean.

Cailean started to speak, but she interrupted him. "Cailean took me for a walk. He explained to me how he'll never marry. I'd like to go back to the festivities. Cailean is going home." She nodded to him and brushed past her sire.

☾

Logan Ramsay stared at him, his hands on his hips. Cailean said, "Have a good eve, my lord."

"MacAdam, did you not tell me you were not interested in marrying my daughter?"

"Aye, 'tis what I said."

"Stay away from her or you'll break her heart."

Then he nodded and went home, half expecting a sword to cleave him in two. It never happened.

Too bad. He deserved it.

CHAPTER TEN

ᠵ

MORE THAN A SENNIGHT HAD passed, and naught more had happened. In fact, Sorcha hoped she'd be allowed outside the gates soon. She hated being cooped up like a prisoner. The only activity she enjoyed was watching Horsie get better. Each time she visited her horse, she hoped Cailean would be there, but so far she'd been disappointed.

The night of the festivities had not been as enjoyable as she'd hoped. She'd had little interest in the event after Cailean's departure, though she'd stayed to honor her uncle.

To her chagrin, she hadn't seen Cailean since then. He had taken to avoiding her, and she knew just who to blame, though she hadn't confronted her sire yet about his apparent threats to her suitor. She'd hoped her father would calm down after a few days. Mayhap today would be the day to speak with him. Staying away from Cailean was not working; she only wanted him more.

She took her time before going down to the hall to break her fast, though she was well past the normal time. When she sat down, Maggie joined her from the hearth. "Bethia is still talking about the celebration. She had the time of her life."

"I had hoped she'd dance a bit more than she did." Sorcha had danced most of the night to take her mind off Cailean, which was why her feet had plagued her the next morn.

"She's shy, Sorcha. She may never marry."

Sorcha stirred the porridge that the serving lass had brought her. "And what about you?"

Maggie shrugged her shoulder. "I will if I ever want to."

"Are you not missing Molly?" She took a couple of bites of her porridge, but the distraction did not prevent her from seeing the glimmer of pain on Maggie's face before she recovered.

"I am, but I'm also happy for her. She and Tormod are well suited."

The door opened and their sire barreled in, heading straight for them. "Good, you have your leggings and tunic on, Sorcha. And it's one without a hole, too. That helps." He grinned at her.

"Why, Papa? Are we going somewhere?"

"Aye, once you finish your porridge, come to the stables. I'm taking you hunting. You did such a nice thing for your cousin the other night that I've decided to teach you myself. There have been no more attacks, so I think we'll be safe. MacAdam is coming, too, though only to help guard you. I still do not trust that the trouble is completely over, but no one will dare bother you if you're with Maule and the MacAdam brothers and me."

She jumped up from her seat. "That sounds wonderful. I'll get a few things and be right down."

He spun on his heel and left, yelling back over his shoulder, "Maggie, of course you are free to join us."

"Nay, I'll stay here, Papa. I'm going to see how Brigie is. Mama wants me with her later."

He gave them a final wave and left.

Sorcha grabbed Maggie's hands. "I'm so excited. This will be fun. Come along."

"Nay, I'll pass. I don't want to be there to see the disappointment on Papa's face when he realizes your excitement comes from the fact that Cailean is there."

"What?" Sorcha was stunned to hear Maggie assess the situation so clearly. "Nay, I'm happy to be going with Papa, to be allowed outside the gates. I do not care about Cailean. I have not even seen him since the night of the celebration. Besides, he tells me he'll never marry."

"Keep telling yourself that. Mayhap you'll believe it, but I won't. I know where your heart is, and I think he's fooling himself, too. Now run along and enjoy your new friend."

Maggie winked at her and chuckled as she left the hall to find their mother.

Sorcha vowed not to let Maggie's comment bother her. It was true that she knew what she wanted: Cailean. But while he clearly wanted her, too, and had told her as much, he seemed to be standing fast by his refusal to marry. Why, then, would it be worth her time to pursue him?

Because she quite simply enjoyed being around him. He made her smile, made her feel special. What more could she ask for? Until he blatantly refused her, she'd continue to pursue him—fool that she was. Plus, she still clung to the idea that her father had said something to keep Cailean away. He'd probably threatened to kill him or something else foolish. All the lads feared her sire.

When she finished her porridge, she ran to her chamber for her bow, then headed out to the stables. Her sire was chatting with Torrian and Kyle, and Cailean was nowhere to be found. *Mo creach*, where was he? Would he not be joining them after all? She didn't dare ask about him, or her father's eyebrows would do that jumping up and down thing again.

Her cousin Lily came down the hill with the wee lassies strapped to her—one to her back and one to her chest. "Uncle Logan, wait, please."

When Lily reached them, Lise, strapped to her front, smiled a toothless grin at Kyle. He laughed and tickled her, then snuck around to Lily's back to play with his other daughter.

"What is it, Lily?"

"I was just thinking. I spoke with Kyle about this last eve. Uncle Alex has always been so fond of wee lassies that I thought it would be nice if the lassies and I took a trip to visit him. Mayhap the girls' smiles will help cheer him up. Is he still at Aunt Jennie's?"

Logan thought for a moment, pausing to plant a kiss on each wee one's cheek, prompting a giggle and a flurry of kicking feet from the bottom of their plaid contraption. Then he growled to tease them more, and this time both of the babes *and* Lily giggled. Sorcha's smile stretched across her face—she adored seeing her father this way. He was always so gentle with Lily, his favorite niece, and her daughters.

"Kyle, what say you about this?" Logan asked without looking at him.

Kyle cleared his throat and glanced at Lily before he spoke. "While I agree with Lily about cheering Uncle Alex up, I am of two minds about this."

Lily's hands parked on her hips. "And what are the two minds,

Kyle Maule? You didn't share those thoughts with me last eve."

"I'll share them with you now. I gave this a lot of thought after you fell asleep."

Logan grinned at Lily. "Do you think he's wishing to get rid of you, lass? Lily, the man followed you everywhere. Do you think you'd be rid of him so easily? Give the man a chance to talk. He's one against three in his house."

His teasing made Sorcha smile, but Lily scowled, first at Logan and then at her husband. Kyle wrapped his arm around her and said, "Sending you away is the verra last thing I would want to do. Will you not hear me out?"

Rubbing the pale strands of hair on Lise's head, Lily said, "Go ahead, Kyle. Uncle Logan, I'd rather not hear any more from you." She tipped her head away from him when he chuckled.

"I am against you traveling because I prefer you and the lassies to be here by my side, but 'tis a most selfish feeling. I am in favor because I do not like what has been happening with Sorcha," Kyle said. "We were also attacked not long ago and the thought of anyone getting inside our curtain wall makes me quite ill. Seeing them so close to our gate changed everything in my mind. I believe I would feel better if Lily and the lassies were in a safer place until the Highlands are settled again. I know naught more has happened in the last sennight, but our scouting guards have heard more rumblings about unrest and uncertainty. Cameron land is home to Lochluin Abbey, so 'tis as safe as any place can be. Reivers know to stay away. Your mother and father are there, too. I know I belong here at Torrian's side under the circumstances, but I would feel better if you went to stay with the Camerons."

Logan's face turned serious. He nodded and said, "Kyle, I cannot disagree with you, but we may arrive only to discover Alex has already returned to Grant land."

"What is he talking about, Papa? Under what circumstances?" Sorcha asked. All of a sudden, she did not like the tone of the conversation.

"We're in the middle of uncertain times, lass. With the laird of the Grants down, unrest may follow. We could have problems here or on Grant land. Lochluin Abbey may be the safest place in the Highlands. Verra few will go against the church. Lily is one person protecting two wee ones. Her husband is second to the Ramsay laird and cannot be by their side all the time. I'll escort her myself on the morrow. Torrian, you decide who will travel with me. Now, Sorcha, are you ready for your hunting lesson?"

She dismissed the other thoughts because they frightened her too much. "Aye. I'm ready, Papa. Are you sure 'tis safe?"

"I'll be with you, and we're taking Maule, both MacAdams, and several other guards. I'll be watching. Mount up."

Alan MacAdam joined them just as they set out of the gates. "Cailean will be right along." He nodded to Sorcha and pulled his horse up close to her.

"Good, MacAdam. Stay close to her until your brother arrives. Then I want the three of you guarding her."

"Aye, my lord." Alan moved closer to her, tipping his head in a greeting to Logan. "Cailean's on his way. Do not fear."

"I have no fear, Alan," she said with a grin. "Did you not know that? Look, I'm free again!" She tipped her head back to soak in the sun and spurred forward, Alan and Kyle on either side of her. She couldn't help but be happy with the wind in her hair on such a beautiful day. Even though so little time had passed since the incident with the arrow, she'd felt trapped in the castle.

"On we go. Maule, you and MacAdam stay with her."

A deer burst out of the brush ahead of them, and Sorcha's father shouted to her, "Shoot it! Perfect target!"

Shocked by how fast it had happened, she fumbled with her bow, but her father rode up next to her. "Calm down, lassie. You need a steady aim. Slow your horse. That deer is close." He gave her a few more pointers before she was able to settle down.

She calmed her breathing as she aimed, remembering something Molly had told her, then let the arrow go. She watched it heading straight for the deer, but the animal was on the run now, and at the last second it darted off to the right, out of the line of her arrow.

"Papa, I missed." It had been so close.

"We've only just started," he said. "I think I hear boar in the distance. I'm going in to rustle the trees, see if I can send one your way. They're a bigger target for you. That doe was too sleek to hit from behind."

Her gaze followed her sire into the woods, but then confusion clouded her mind—followed by searing pain.

An arrow sailed by her face.

Cailean had experienced more sleepless nights than ever before, and it had nothing to do with the painful memories of his parents' last days.

Instead, he was haunted by dreams of a honey-haired beauty with green eyes and a smile that made him think of things he'd never considered before—like marriage. He'd frozen when Logan Ramsay had stared him down, demanding that he either ask for Sorcha's hand or leave her be, but how could he not have reacted thusly? The beast of the Scottish Crown had threatened to meet him at dawn with his sword in hand. He would have been cut down in a matter of moments.

On the other hand, he'd heard that Logan Ramsay preferred to taunt his enemies, playing with their minds, just as he'd done with MacNiven. His words had led the villain straight into the path of his daughter Molly's arrow.

Perhaps Logan was playing with Cailean's mind—the better to destroy him.

What could be more frightening?

He'd buckled under the pressure, promising to stay away from Sorcha.

But then he'd failed himself. The lass had been stunning in that purple gown. Accustomed to seeing her in her tunic and leggings whenever she was going for a long ride outside the keep, his jaw had dropped at the sight of her on the stairs. Everyone else had been looking at Bethia in her golden gown.

Not him. He'd been so smitten he'd forced himself out the door so as not to be tempted by her beauty. His self-control had its limits, and when she followed him down the path, calling to him, entreating him to spend time with her, he had first told her that he planned never to marry and then proceeded to ravage her in the corner of the courtyard.

What a sight they'd been. He had no excuse other than that he'd lost his ability to reason the moment he touched her perfect breasts. True, he was enchanted by every part of the lass, but those breasts had truly cast a spell on him. And every moan, every whimper, every sweet word that had come from Sorcha had gone straight to his groin. Then his brother's voice had awakened him from the sensual spell.

He was still appalled by his behavior, shocked by how he'd lost control in the courtyard. An honorable man would have been on his knees asking for her hand in marriage, but he hadn't acted honorably. They'd hidden their activity from her sire, and he'd gone running home.

Now he would do as he promised. He would join them for the hunting expedition, which was mayhap another of Logan's manipulations. But he was weak around her, so the best thing he could do was wait to join the group until the last moment. He couldn't risk being around Sorcha too much, not when he had so little self-control around her.

He found an urn and threw water on his face, cleaned his teeth as if doing so could wash the thoughts from his mind. He failed. Sorcha haunted him, just as she'd haunted him all night. He wanted her, and it was more than pure lust. He wanted her around him, laughing with him, challenging him, teasing him. Sorcha Ramsay had brought him happiness he'd never experienced before.

True, she was good company, but there was more to it. When she had sought his comfort rather than her sire's after the archer's last attack, he'd thought his chest would burst. Was it happiness, pride, or what?

The other eve, he'd tasted the saltiness of her skin, heard her passion, seen the evidence of her desire.

He'd sworn he'd do anything to hear her laughter, but now he knew not what he preferred, her laughter or her testaments of desire. All he knew was that she caused his chest to do strange things, and that he didn't want to be away from her.

"You cannot let her go, can you, lad?" His uncle joined him.

Cailean decided not to hide his feelings any longer. Mayhap his uncle would have some advice for him. "Nay, I cannot. I try to remind myself of all the reasons I should let her go, but naught drives the woman out of my mind."

"And what are those reasons?" Uncle Isaac sat at the table.

He joined his uncle, flopping down with resignation. "I probably should not marry due to my temper, and Logan Ramsay has warned me away from her."

"You have a new word in your reasoning that I like. *Probably.* You *probably* should not marry. It gives me hope that you're starting to see the truth. There is no good reason for you not to marry. You do not have your sire's temper, and in fact, your sire's temper was not as bad as you seem to recall."

"Suppose I am beginning to believe you. We still have the second problem to settle. Logan Ramsay has warned me to stay away from his daughter."

"I've known Logan Ramsay all my life. He is not an unreasonable man. Now, he may not stand off to the side and allow some young lad to play with his daughter without promising marriage, but I think it would please him to see her matched with a strong Ramsay warrior. I know not why he would disapprove of you. You are a hard-working lad. What has happened that you're not telling me?"

Cailean pushed away from the table, gathered his sword and moved over to the door. He paused before he left. "You have the right of it, Uncle. I told him I'd never marry, so he's told me to stay away. But 'tis one of the most difficult things I've ever done. I don't wish to be away from her." He gave his uncle a short wave and left, thinking of his dilemma.

Logan Ramsay was back, and he would be watching every move he made. Hellfire, he was doomed. He could postpone his duty no longer. It was time to defend the woman who had found a way into his heart, loath though he was to admit it.

He swallowed hard as he mounted his horse, flicking the reins to head toward the gates of the Ramsay castle. The group had not made it far, and he had no trouble finding them in a clearing not far from the curtain wall.

He started off at a full gallop, trying to catch up with them, but something enticed him to slow his horse. The scene before him urged him to stop and watch.

In the middle of a sea of warriors sat a golden lass bouncing on a black horse, appearing to be in her glory. Her father rode up behind her, pointing to a deer in the distance. She slowed her horse, controlling her mount with her knees as she readied her bow, took aim, and fired. Sorcha Ramsay was gorgeous, that much he understood. What he didn't understand was the way he felt in her presence. In the past, he would spend all day wandering in the woods and the castle, searching for something unknown, something elusive. Searching for a piece of himself that was missing.

Not anymore. The urge had died as soon as he started spending more time with Sorcha.

His insides calmed at the sight of her. It was as if he'd finally found that missing something.

What did that mean? *You know what it means, fool.* He'd have to speak to Logan Ramsay and tell him he'd changed his mind. He could not leave her be. For Sorcha, he could take the risk of marrying. For her, he would be a better man than his sire.

Spurring his horse, he charged up to the group in front of him before moving down the middle of the line toward Sorcha. Something caught his eye.

There was an archer hidden in the trees. He bellowed the Ramsay war whoop and headed straight for Sorcha just as chaos erupted. Her sire was far into the woods and would be unable to help her, but Sorcha herself knew something was off. He could see her panic. Then he saw something worse.

There was an arrow flying directly at Sorcha, and there was no way he could reach her in time.

CHAPTER ELEVEN

෪

CAILEAN THOUGHT THE ARROW HIT her, but he wasn't sure. A second arrow lodged in his brother's thigh. As he raced toward the hunting group more arrows flew at them. Clearly, there was more than one archer—and they all had a single purpose. He reached Sorcha just as she was about to topple off her horse. She'd been hit. Fear knifed through him, but his determination to save her was stronger.

Logan Ramsay was heading straight for them at a dead gallop, but Cailean reached her first, lifting her off her horse and onto his mount, slamming her against his chest.

"Alan, can you make it?" he yelled to his brother, who was wincing from the direct hit.

"Aye, get her away from here. I'll follow you."

He peeked at her and almost flinched at the shock in her pale face. This time there was no fight in her. She grabbed his arms in a death grip as he swung his horse around. Then he galloped to the farthest point away from the archers, giving them his back to protect her. "I've got you, love."

"Cailean?"

"What?" He glanced down and she lifted her left arm to him as if she'd just noticed the blood dripping from a wound in her forearm.

"I...I don't feel well."

"Hush, hang on." She tipped in one direction, but he grabbed her, righting her in front of him. He quickly examined her arm to see if there was an arrow protruding, but he neither saw nor felt one.

Gwyneth Ramsay's voice rang out across the meadow. "Where?"

Glancing over his shoulder toward the castle, he saw another slew of warriors riding out to assist them, Torrian and Gwyneth leading the group. As they got closer, he watched Sorcha's mother stand in the stirrups and shoot in the direction of the assassins. She fired one arrow after another into the trees with deadly accuracy.

Alan came up beside him and said, "Is she all right?"

"Aye." He glanced at her pale face before shifting his gaze back to her wounded arm. The blood had slowed, thankfully. "Surface wound. You?"

"Aye. The arrow's out. I'm going back to fight."

"Be careful." He found a small group of trees off to the side and led his horse into the small clearing in the middle of them.

Alan followed him long enough to ensure he could find them again, then turned back toward the melee.

"Tell her sire she's all right," Cailean yelled after him.

Alan nodded, running his hand down his sore leg as he rode.

Cailean positioned his horse so that he could see anyone coming near them. Then he reached down to lift her chin to his. "How bad is it?"

"Cailean. I don't feel right." She held her arm up to him.

"Here, let me see." He turned her so that she partially faced him, giving him better access to her injury. Cradling her arm with his, he ripped a piece of her tunic off so he could see the wound clearly. He tore a piece of his plaid and used it to wipe the blood away as gingerly as he could, hoping not to cause her any more pain, then tied it around the wound to staunch the bleeding.

She was right. She didn't look well to him. "Look, Sorcha. 'Tis a surface wound. The arrow nicked you. 'Tis not deep at all. You'll be hale in no time."

She glanced at her wound, then leaned against his chest, burying her face into his neck. "Why does he not leave me alone?"

"He's not alone this time, sweeting."

"There were two of them?" She stared off into the distance, her voice devoid of the lilt he loved so.

He could feel her weakening, though he didn't understand why. She hadn't lost much blood. Mayhap she was just tired. She shivered uncontrollably. He wrapped her in his embrace, giving her what heat he could, though the day was warm for the Highlands.

"Alan was hit within a few seconds of you. The arrows had to come from different archers. The angles varied, too."

She peered up at him and said, "Alan was next to me, where you usually are. Why have you not gotten hit before?"

"They mustn't be verra good archers. I'm big enough." He laughed and she joined him, though it was an effort for her.

A few moments later, she glanced up at him. "Cailean?"

"Hmmm?" He rubbed his hand across her thigh, nothing suggestive, just a comforting touch. He tipped his head over hers so he was close enough to take in her scent.

"I like you big."

He almost choked on air.

She lifted her gaze to his and gave him a smirk, waggling her eyebrows.

"I guess you're improving," he said.

She sighed and snuggled against him again. "I am, but please do not let go."

He noticed everything had quieted, so he led his horse out of the trees. Gwyneth and Logan were headed straight for them. "Sorcha?" Gwyneth shouted, her tone urgent. "Is she all right?"

Cailean met them halfway and said, "She's pale, but I don't see anything other than a flesh wound in her forearm. Looks like she was nicked by an arrow." He held her arm out to show her parents that the bleeding had stopped from the bandage he'd made. He looked at her sire. "Did you get them?"

Gwyneth had tears in her eyes, but she swiped them away. "We got two."

"*Gwynie* got two," Logan added. "I swear there was another, but he disappeared."

"Logan, I should have come with you. I told you so…" Gwyneth was beside herself over the attack. It was written all over her face.

He shook his head, glancing from Sorcha back to his wife. "Nay, you wouldn't have wanted to be here. It only matters that you got them."

"But I could have…"

"Wife. Had you been here, you would have seen the arrow strike your daughter. You would have watched her lose color and topple off her horse. 'Twas not easy to watch."

Gwynie swung her head to her daughter. "You fell off?"

"Nay," Logan said. "I died another ten deaths, knowing I was too far away to help, as I watched her start to go over. Her closest guard had been hit, too, but just then this big brute came out of nowhere and lifted her to safety. Nicely done, MacAdam."

"You'd have done the same if you were closer."

"I owe you my thanks, Cailean." Gwyneth nodded to him.

Sorcha lifted her head, kissed his cheek, and whispered, "He always saves me, Mama."

☾

Sorcha took a long tub bath, then allowed Jennet to bandage her wound. Her cousin loved being the healer in her mother's absence, even though she was only eight years old. She fussed over Sorcha and gave her strict instructions to come see her once a day, acting as though she were eight and twenty.

Her father had sent for her, asking that she join him in the solar after Jennet bandaged her wound. As she headed down to the solar, Sorcha's heart lurched at the thought of seeing Cailean again in front of so many witnesses. If they were alone, she'd launch herself at the man and kiss him senseless. He'd saved her again, but this time she hadn't fought with him, they hadn't tumbled to the ground, and she'd allowed his tender ministrations to her wound.

It felt as if something had changed between them, and she could only hope it was true.

In the meantime, they needed to learn who the bastards had been, the men who'd been shooting at her. At the Ramsays. Who had dared to come to Ramsay land on three separate occasions and survived to tell the tale? Well, survived two attacks, anyway. She assumed they had lost their lives from Gwyneth's arrow. Her mother never missed.

She knocked on the door to the solar, and a few moments later, a small group filed out. Torrian and Kyle were followed by Cailean and Alan.

"Alan, your leg?"

"I'm going to see wee Jennet. She's insisted on bandaging it, but it doesn't hurt. And your wound?"

"Aye, 'twill heal with no problem."

As if understanding their unspoken wish for a moment together,

Alan moved along. Sorcha could feel her heartbeat speed up just from being close to Cailean. He stood behind his brother, a concerned expression on his face. The man grew more handsome every day. She glanced at Cailean and whispered, "Take care of him. I feel horrible that someone was hurt again."

"Alan will be fine. How are you?"

She held her arm up for his inspection. "Jennet."

"She loves healing, doesn't she?" he asked with a smirk.

"That she does."

"Sorcha! Your turn," her sire barked.

She smiled and headed into the solar. Her father and mother were the only two inside. "Mama, Papa, what did you discover?" She found a chair and sat.

"'Tis as I suspected. They are warriors who fought with Baron Duncrub. Men who have no leader or allegiance. What I do *not* know is why they would be targeting you. We found evidence of three men in the trees. Your mother killed two of them. One escaped. What do you think?"

"Papa, I have no idea why they wish to kill me—and they *must* wish to kill me. If they wished to take me captive, they would sneak in as they did to steal Jennet and Brigie. This makes no sense."

Her sire's eyes bored into her, the way they often did when his thoughts were moving too quickly for him to share. She'd learned long ago to allow him to work through information on his own.

"Mayhap it really has naught to do with you. It could be that they're just picking one person out of the group to target. In every instance, you've been the only female."

Her mother asked, "But why?"

"Mayhap they are merely doing what reivers love to do. They love to unsettle things, stir things up, and it's done to hide their true mission." Her sire got out of his chair to pace, running a hand through his hair as he walked. He stopped at the mantel above the hearth, staring at the weapons hanging on the wall above him.

"Which would be what?"

"Gwynie, I don't know the answer to that yet, but I'll continue to think on it. Can you come up with any reason, Sorcha?"

Sorcha played with the bandage on her arm, too upset to let them know how she felt. "I don't know. Does this mean I'll have to stay inside the gates again? Never mind. After this fiasco, I'll stay inside on my own. Seeing my own blood frightened me. They hit me and they hit Alan, too." What she really wished to say was that she wished to stay with Cailean.

"So what do we do?" Her mother looked to her sire.

"I believe we have no choice. I've already promised to escort Lily to Cameron land, so the solution is for our daughter to go with me." He turned around and swung one leg over the edge of the desk, sitting in front of her. "Sorcha, I'm taking you to the Grants."

"What? Why?" Nothing could have surprised her more.

"The archer is aiming for you," he said, his brow furrowed. "'Twould be best for you to leave."

"Who is going with us? Maggie? Brigid?" *Cailean.*

"Nay. Gwynie will stay here with Maggie, Brigie, and Gavin. You will come with me. I have wished to see how the Grants are doing without their laird, so 'tis a good time for a journey. But we'll already have Lily and the twins with us, and I cannot risk bringing any other females when the danger is so great. Pack your things. We leave at dawn on the morrow."

"How many guards are we taking? What if he follows us?"

"Sorcha, this time they were taken by surprise. Your mother killed two of their men. They cannot have too many. They will regroup before they do aught else. They'll have to. This is the best time for us to take our leave. We'll travel with a score of guards, or mayhap thirty, but I have to leave a good number here. There's still a score of them with Uncle Quade."

All of a sudden, she found it difficult to swallow. "Who, Papa? Which guards go with us?"

He lifted himself off the desk and stood in front of her with his hands on his hips. "Not the one you want."

CHAPTER TWELVE

ᖇ

LATER THAT NIGHT, CAILEAN WAS in the warriors' camp, brooding about Sorcha, when Maule arrived to deliver news.

The warriors gathered around him, waiting for him to speak. "I have an important mission," Kyle said. "In fact, naught could be more important than this mission in my eyes. The men who were killed earlier previously fought for Baron Crichton. In other words, they are men without a leader who have gone without pay and are probably angry. Logan has decided to take his daughter Sorcha to the Grants. I have chosen to send my wife and daughters to Cameron land for safety. We will take thirty guards. I'll be going with them as far as I deem necessary. Then I will return to my position as my laird's second. Those of you who go on the mission will be answering to Logan Ramsay.

"This is the list of guards who have been chosen to travel with us at dawn on the morrow. If your name is on this list, you are excused from camp this eve to ready yourself and your families for your journey. While a few of you may remain with the Camerons, most of you travel on to the Grants and will be gone at least a fortnight, mayhap longer. Prepare yourselves and be ready to travel at the break of dawn. This may not be an easy journey."

He waited for their attention before he continued. "The warriors who will be making the journey are as follows."

Cailean expected to hear his name at the beginning, but he wasn't first on the list. No matter. He'd have to speak with Alan, as his brother would be unable to travel with his recent injury. Maule finished the list, and many of the men left immediately. There was only one problem. He hadn't heard his name.

"Maule, I must have missed my name."

Kyle peered at him, his lips in a tight seal as he shook his head. "Your name is not on the list. 'Twas created by your laird, Logan, and myself. You're staying back, MacAdam."

Cailean couldn't speak, unable to process what he'd just heard. "What? There must be a mistake. You know I've been the one to save Sorcha on three occasions. I should be going as her protector."

"We do not anticipate the archers will follow us, so you may not be needed. If you have a problem with the decision we've made, seek out Logan."

With that, the laird's second left, no doubt to prepare his own family for the voyage.

Cailean knew why Kyle had said that. No one with their wits about them would dare go near Logan Ramsay. Alan appeared at his side, limping.

"Leave it be, Cailean," he said in an undertone, looking around to ensure their conversation was not overheard. "Mayhap 'tis best you do not go." He reached up to massage his neck, clearly bothered by their situation.

"I need to go." A tightness in his chest told him he *was* going, a sensation that would not be ignored.

"Have you considered that mayhap you are too emotional when it comes to Sorcha? You're falling hard for her. I can see it. I imagine her sire and our laird see it as well. He only wants to bring men who are able to fight with calm control. Do you have that at present?"

They both knew the answer to that. Cailean tapped his foot at a frantic pace he knew Alan would notice. He grabbed a fistful of his hair, then let it go. "I am the one who has been there every time she needed someone. Mayhap I am the best protector for her because I have her needs at the top of my list, unlike others. Had you considered it from that point of view?" He wanted to do something, throw something, beat his fists against a wall. He'd not be left behind.

"I see that you're upset. Go walk the anger off, or you may find yourself in more trouble than you expected. Once you've mastered your self-control and have the words you wish to speak prepared in your mind, talk to Logan Ramsay. I wouldn't advise you to talk to him in the state you're in."

"I'll walk it off." He spun on his heel and headed out of the warriors' camp.

"Where are you going? Mayhap I'll follow," Alan yelled after him.

Cailean paused long enough to yell back, "Nay, I go alone."

"Where?"

"After Logan Ramsay." He strode down the path, trying to come up with any words he could to convince Logan to allow him on this journey. He didn't have to go far. Once he reached the inner bailey, he found Sorcha's sire leaning against a tree, his gaze fixed on him.

"MacAdam."

"Why are you here, my lord?" Cailean asked, confused by his relaxed demeanor.

"Waiting for you." He grinned the grin they all hated to see.

"I respectfully request to be added to the list of warriors escorting your daughter to the Grants." He stood prepared for a fight. One did not go against Logan Ramsay without a backup plan in place. This time, running was not one of his choices. He needed to do this for Sorcha.

"Request denied." Ramsay pushed away from the tree, then crossed his arms and stood in his battle stance. Other than his arms, every inch of the beast screamed attack mode.

Sweat broke out across his forehead, and he tried to wipe it away, but it only returned even heavier. "My lord, you know I'm the only one who has saved her each of the three times she has been in danger. Whether you approve or not, I'll be following along. I am best equipped to protect your daughter."

Ramsay moved like a bolt of lightning out of the sky, and Cailean found himself slammed against a tree with a dagger pressed to his throat, the man's massive arms pinning him. Of the two, Logan was the smaller man, but he was a beast. The tales of the man's prowess had not been exaggerated, nor had the wildness in the eyes that now stared Cailean down from a nose length away from his face. "Allow me to tell you what's been on my mind, MacAdam. Who is the only warrior who has been near my daughter each time her life has been threatened? You. Mayhap it has not occurred to any-one else, but it *has* occurred to me. 'Tis possible you are the threat instead of the savior. I don't know what has been going on with her, but you'll stay back or I'll cut off your bollocks and feed them to the vultures. Then you'll have no desire to follow my daughter."

Had Cailean not just relieved himself a short time ago, he would have pished himself for sure. Unable to move, he waited to see what Ramsay's next move would be. The fire in his eyes hadn't calmed at all.

"Do we understand each other, MacAdam?" he ground out.

He moved the tip of the knife enough for Cailean to manage one word. "Aye."

"Good." He dropped his hand from his neck. "Stay away from her. I want her to live."

Logan Ramsay disappeared into the night as fast as the lightning bugs that popped on and off in the dark. Cailean rubbed his neck and coughed, making sure everything was still functioning. Since he was alone, he didn't bother trying to stop his next impulse, reaching down to make sure his balls were still firmly in place beneath his plaid.

He had to speak to Sorcha.

❦

Sorcha stood in the kitchens, hoping and praying that Cailean would show up. She hadn't spoken to her father again and didn't know what she should do. What she wished to do more than anything was to refuse him, just refuse to go. She knew that was useless, however—he'd just pick her up and tie her to a horse.

Her mother rarely went against her father's wishes. She understood why—her sire was usually right.

Not this time.

She was sick over the thought of leaving Cailean. She wanted the chance to explore her feelings for him, and that wouldn't happen if she were on Grant land. For all she knew, they could be there for a month or more.

A door closed off the back, so she hid, tugging her plaid around her. She wouldn't be caught in just a night rail this time. Peeking around the corner of the post, she saw it was Cailean. As soon as he set his small candle down on a nearby shelf, she launched herself in his direction, jumping into his arms.

"Lass! Make sure I see you coming next time. I almost didn't catch you."

She cupped his face in her hands and said, "You always catch me, Cailean."

He smiled. "Aye, 'tis true."

Sorcha kissed him, then said, "Cailean, I do not want to go alone. Come with us, please? Can you not talk with my sire or Torrian?"

He sighed and closed his eyes. "I tried. I insisted I on going with them."

"Good. Then you'll be leaving with us on the morrow?"

He stared at the ground. "Nay. Your father threatened to do serious damage to me if I follow you."

She chuckled. "What? Did he threaten to cut your bollocks off? I've heard that before."

He rolled his eyes and nodded. "Something like that."

"He did?"

"Aye. He says I'm to stay away from you."

"But why?" She gripped his tunic in her hands. "I don't understand. He was there when you saved me from falling off my horse. He saw it with his own eyes."

"I could not argue with his reasoning. I don't agree with him, but I have no evidence to support my claim." He had to swallow twice before he could speak.

"What could he possibly have said?"

He caressed her cheek, running his finger across her skin. "He said that I am the only one who has been with you each time, and that the attacks may have something to do with *me*." He took her hands in his. "Tell me you don't believe it."

"What?" She pulled back to stare at him. Her sire had surely lost his mind. "That makes no sense. There were others along with us each time."

"But he's correct." His gaze searched hers and she could see how difficult this was for him. "I could not refute his logic. I was the only one by your side each time."

"Alan was there every time, too," Her sire was wrong, he was just wrong. She'd make him see the truth.

"Nay, not when Baltair was hurt."

"What about Kyle?" Her mind was fraught with panic over the implications of what he was saying. There had to be someone else who had been with them each time. She wracked her brain, trying to come up with a solution, but she failed. Her father was right.

She moaned when the realization settled on her shoulders. "Nay, Cailean. Nay. It cannot be. Aye, you were there every time, but what would have happened if you had not been nearby? He cannot believe what he says."

"I know." He reached up and rubbed his thumb across her lower lip. "Tell me you don't believe I would ever do aught to hurt you. Please tell me that you believe in us."

"I *do* believe in us. I have also been thinking about these attacks, but I have come to a different conclusion." She gripped his forearms, wanting to remember everything about him in case this was their last time together for a moon or more.

"Tell me. Give me aught to convince your sire he's mistaken. I knew naught about the attacks."

"What if the archer is not targeting me, but the men around me? An arrow almost hit you in the first attack, Baltair was wounded in the second one, and Alan was hit in this last one."

"I don't follow. Why would the archer go for Alan?"

"Because I was speaking with Alan just before we moved out to hunt."

He stared at her, still confused.

"Can you not see it? It's as if the archer is jealous. Whenever I speak to a man within his eyeshot or earshot, he shoots at him. He wants me."

"But this time an arrow hit you."

"Aye, but 'twas aimed for Alan, who was beside me. The first arrow passed in front of my face and caught me in the arm. The second arrow hit him. I believe both arrows were meant for him."

"But we suspected two different archers."

"But if we're wrong? What if 'twas the same archer and he was aiming for the person closest to me?" She squeezed his hands, hoping he would understand her reasoning, see her logic. If so, they could convince her sire to allow him along on the journey.

A smile spread slowly across Cailean's face as he stared into her eyes. There was that special glitter in his gaze again. "You could be correct. I could imagine a love-sick lad wanting to kill anyone who was interested in you." He hugged her tight. "I could convince your sire of this. Have you said aught to him?"

"Nay. He is still upset with me, so I have not mentioned it."

He fingered the fine strands of her hair, then massaged her scalp.

"Why is he upset with you? I thought you had a long talk with him."

"I still think he's upset with me. 'Tis difficult to explain, but he's…different." She didn't know how to tell him that her sire was back to acting the way he had before all the attacks. He'd look at her and grumble as though the mere sight of her was enough to upset him. She tried to please him, to make him proud, but to no avail. He still marched around her like he wished to kill someone.

"I'll try to speak with him on the morrow. Listen, I know I said I would never marry, but 'twas foolish of me. I have been giving it much thought. The time we've spent together has changed my mind. I don't want to be here without you, and I would never, ever, hurt you."

His words bloomed inside her. He wanted to marry her. He wouldn't leave her. "Oh, Cailean, I know you would never hurt me. Your hands are always there to protect me, to support me when I need it most. You give me a strength I did not know I had." She leaned her head against his chest, just wishing to listen to his strong heartbeat, feel his warmth. "I'll talk to my sire." When had her father become so unreasonable? She'd always been able to speak to him before, because he had always been willing to listen, but now he'd become daft.

He ran his hands down her back, rubbing lightly. "I promise I'll be there at dawn in case he changes his mind."

"I don't want to leave you. This cannot be happening." She peeked up at him. "Cailean, I do not wish to go. Can we not run away?"

He closed his eyes, then leaned his forehead against hers. He kissed her, the most tender kiss she'd ever had, and she wished it would go on forever.

When he ended the kiss, she whispered, "Cailean? Take me away, please. My sire is unreasonable."

"I cannot. Sorcha, there's naught I'd rather do than run away together, but the Highlands are treacherous. There is someone trying to kill you or the people around you. If we go anywhere alone, I would be making us an open target. I can't do that. I care about you too much."

Tears slid down her cheeks. "But I know not when I'll be back. 'Twill feel like forever."

"Your sire is only doing what is best for you. I cannot disagree with his decision to take you away. I've watched arrows nearly kill you three times. 'Tis too dangerous for you to stay. I'll not argue that with him, nor would I argue if he chose to take ten score guards to protect you. Two hundred would not be enough for me."

He kissed the tears wetting her cheeks. "But I will continue to argue with him about leaving me behind. I'm your best guard. I *will* protect you. I promise you I'll be there at dawn."

She'd talk to her sire. He had to listen to her. He just had to.

She was falling in love with Cailean MacAdam.

CHAPTER THIRTEEN

GLENN OF BUCHAN PACED THE dais in his great hall, a hall full of his best warriors and many new ones he'd drawn into his lair, all awaiting his announcement. His dream of controlling the Highlands was about to come to fruition. He'd had no idea the chance would come again so soon.

The Grant had been taken out, but they had no idea whether or not he still lived. He wished he'd struck the bastard down himself.

He stopped his pacing, waiting for the animals in front of him to end their trite talk and give him their full attention. When all was quiet, he continued.

"The Grant is down."

The hall erupted into cheers and applause, boots stomping on the stone floor as the men hooted their pleasure. He let them continue, secretly pleased with their response. They wanted this as much as he did.

He raised his arms to silence them.

"I wish to congratulate all of you on our first successful attack on the Ramsays. Aye, 'twas a small attack, and many men fell, but it did what I wished it to do. It has them in chaos as they scramble to ready their defenses. I want them confused. Attacks at the Grants followed by an attack at the Ramsays will make them uncertain as to where to go next, where to concentrate their forces. I'm pleased with what we were able to accomplish with such a small assault.

"In our travels since the Grant went down, I've encountered several men who have volunteered to join our ranks, anxious to twist the balance of power in the Highlands at long last." He nodded to a guard by the door, who held it open while several men marched into the hall, moving to the front of the cavernous space to stand before him.

As soon as word had reached him about the Grant's injuries, he'd made it a point to travel the Highlands searching for lost fighters.

And he'd found them. He'd encountered many who had just come from the battle, and others who'd tired of all the Grants and Ramsays. He couldn't be more pleased.

Hellfire, but he'd waited a long time for this to happen. Wresting power away from the two united clans was a dream he'd shared with his own two sons, Dugald and Cormag, and the neighboring laird, Ranulf MacNiven. One day, they'd pledged, they would reign over the other clans in the Highlands. All three men were now dead, killed by the Ramsays and the Grants. Only his dear daughter, Davina, had been left to him. But his dream had not died. He had carefully built up his army of warriors in anticipation of another battle. One he would finally win.

That day was here. With the Grant down, the best place to do battle was at Grant castle since he guessed they were in a turmoil. His sources told him the Grant had gone to Cameron land, and perhaps he was being put to rest near Lochluin Abbey. Some had tried to talk him into attacking the Camerons, but that was a line he would not cross.

Lochluin Abbey was off limits. He would not go against the heavens. Others did not respect the power of the church, but he did.

Once all of the new men had been ushered in, Glenn waited for the crowd to quiet. "The men you see in front of you are verra familiar with the Ramsays and the Grants. Some of them are former guards—men who know the strategies of the clans' leaders. At present, the Ramsays' guards are controlled by Torrian Ramsay and his second, Kyle Maule. Quade is still alive, but he is unable to do battle.

"The Grant laird is down. Expect his brothers, Brodie and Robbie, to take his place, with his two eldest sons, Jake and Jamie, also capable and mighty with the sword. Their neighbor is Loki Grant, a strong swordsman in his own right.

"I must remind you that the mightiest of all, and the ones we should all fear the most, are Logan Ramsay and his wife Gwyneth. Aye, 'tis true. We've all witnessed her talents, and many of you saw her skills on our recent attack. Never doubt her because she's a woman. While there is talk that her aim is not as strong of late because her sight has weakened a touch, she is still capable of taking you out in the trees or on horseback. You have all heard the famous tale of Gwyneth splitting a man's bollocks in two with an arrow. I care not to be the one to test the truth of that tale. Stay out of her sight. Trust me when I say that her husband will hold you down with a grin on his face while she does as she pleases to you. Do not make light of the fact that she is a woman. Their daughter Molly is the one who took both MacNiven and Warwick out. Rumor is she did it alone, but I know she acted with the assistance of her sire and her husband.

"Our strategy will be to break them up. Together they are invincible, apart they're not. Anyone who takes out Logan, Gwyneth, or Molly Ramsay will be promoted in my ranks."

He let that information settle as he motioned the men he'd just introduced to find seats in the hall. He had one more surprise for them.

"I am pleased to introduce my new acting second. This man helped take down the Grant. He knows the area and knows their fighters. He *will* lead us to victory." He nodded to the man at the door, who opened it. A man strode in and posed, his legs planted apart and his hands on his hips, larger than life.

"This is Simon de La Porte."

La Porte spat on the floor and said, "Get your lazy arses outside in the lists. We'll see who the real men are."

CHAPTER FOURTEEN

ᴄ

C AILEAN RACED TOWARD THE GATES, planning to make one more effort to convince Logan Ramsay he should join the travelers. Once there, he breathed in a sigh of relief. He'd made sure he was here before dawn so he wouldn't miss them.

He glanced around the area. There was no one outside the gates. No one.

Something was wrong. He raced to the gates and shouted, "Open up. I need to be inside."

The guard yelled down to him. "Cannot open it until daylight. You know the rules when we've been under attack, MacAdam."

"Frang, open the gates. Please. I need to speak to Logan Ramsay."

Frang snorted. "You're a wee bit late for that."

Alan came up behind him. They'd left the camp at the same time, but his limp had slowed him down.

"What the hell does that mean?" Cailean shouted.

"It means the contingency headed for Cameron land has already left."

"Left? They said they were leaving at the break of dawn." He started to pace, his worst fears bouncing inside his head.

"Logan Ramsay decided they'd leave before dawn. Lily was here with the twins, Kyle, Logan, Sorcha, and several guards. Even Lily's tamed wolves went with them. They didn't waste any time. Logan ushered them out as if the brush behind them were on fire."

Cailean whispered, his hands trembling as they fisted in his hair, "Shite. 'Tis too late." He picked up a rock and threw it as far as he could, then he did the same with another and another, a loud bellow erupting from his chest with each throw. "Bastard outsmarted me besides. I hate that man. I hate him. Sneaky bastard."

Alan looked at his brother and said, "Come back to the cottage. I'll make porridge. Naught to do until the sun rises, Cailean."

His shoulders slumped and he followed his brother home, filled with uncertainty and unease.

When they reached the cottage, Cailean was surprised to see his uncle was already awake, making the breakfast porridge. He spoke without turning around. "Alan, I've decided to visit the carpenter today. Mayhap you are both correct. 'Twould be good for me to get involved with our clan again." Uncle Isaac turned around to face him, surprise on his face when he saw Cailean was with Alan. "Cailean, you didn't go along?"

He'd shared his plan with his uncle and his brother the previous evening.

Cailean fell into a chair, and Alan took a seat beside him. "Nay, they were already gone. The bastard snuck out early."

"You didn't chase after them?"

"Nay. Lily's wolves are with them. Ramsay wouldn't hesitate to send them after me."

Uncle Isaac set bowls of porridge down in front of both of them. "Mayhap this is a good time for a discussion. I've been thinking about how to tell you the truth…"

Cailean stared at his bowl forlornly. "About what? I don't need a discussion, I just need Sorcha."

"Why do you not ask her sire for her hand in marriage? Logan Ramsay is not the type to stand by and watch some foolish lad play with his dear daughter. He'll only allow a lad who's serious enough to consider marriage to court her."

He glanced at his uncle, desperation so heavy on his shoulders, he could not think clearly. He had to go after her. He had to. "You know I didn't intend to marry, Uncle Isaac. I…I would never subject Sorcha to someone with a temper like Da. But I *do* want to marry her. I've never wanted anything more."

His uncle heaved a sigh. "Mayhap I've kept the truth from you lads for too long. Your parents never wanted you to know, but 'tis time."

Cailean had no idea what the man referred to, but he could tell it had something to do with marriage and his worries about Sorcha. He looked at Alan, who appeared equally as puzzled. "Go on."

"Your memories of your parent's unhappiness are mostly from their last year together, true?"

Cailean nodded. Alan said, "'Tis all I remember, tears and yelling."

"Your parents were verra happy together until that last year. My brother was a good man and a good husband, despite his occasional outbursts. Your mother carried their third child, a wee lassie, almost to the end of her time, but she was devastated when the babe was born dead. Your sire sent you away when they called for Lady Brenna to tend her. Even your sire knew her belly wasn't large enough to be carrying a full-size bairn. 'Twas too early. They had not even told you lads there would be a new bairn coming."

Alan asked, "We had a sister?"

"Aye. She was a wee lassie. Your sire said she was a delicate beauty, but she never drew a breath. She passed while still in the womb. There was naught Lady Brenna could have done."

Cailean said, "I don't understand. Why did they wish to hide this from us?"

"They felt you were too young to understand death, so they never told either of you. The reason I tell you now is because of what their loss did to their marriage. You have memories of your mother crying and your sire yelling at her, and it did happen, but you probably never knew why. You think 'twas because your sire had no control over his temper, that his temper caused your mother to sob so often. 'Tis wrong, Cailean. Your mother cried so because she had lost her wee lassie. Your father used to beg her to stop crying because he couldn't bear it. In fact, he wished to have another bairn in the house to ease your mother's pain. She refused. She'd taken measures to be sure she'd never carry again."

"But why? That seems the perfect solution to me," Alan said. "Mama would have loved another bairn."

"She said it would be too painful if they lost another babe. But this is the reason for your parents' arguments. They kept their feelings hidden from everyone."

Cailean whispered, "Mama died from a broken heart, did she not?"

"Something like that. She died in her sleep, and Lady Brenna said her heart had given out. The anguish and exhaustion were too much for her. You lads suffered because of it, but she couldn't see it. Your sire nearly lost his mind after she passed."

Cailean said naught as his mind spun through his last memories of his parents, reinterpreting them. His mother crying, his sire yelling at her to stop…that memory had played over and over in his mind. He'd thought she was upset because of his sire's cruelty.

His mother's tears had naught to do with his sire.

They sat in silence while they finished their porridge. He suspected Alan was struggling to make sense of this new information, too.

"My thanks, Uncle Isaac, for breaking your promise. This means everything to me. All those years, I believed Papa had an uncontrollable temper that he would turn on Mama to make her cry. Now I see it differently."

"I'm sorry you don't have other memories of them," his uncle said. "They were in love, and they adored you both. Alan, you were too young to remember much beyond their last year together."

Alan turned to his brother, "Cailean, you need to go after Sorcha. You cannot let Logan Ramsay or the memory of Papa's temper hold you back. You must offer for her."

"I'll leave in an hour," Cailean said, nodding. It was unthinkable to sit here and wait for an entire moon to pass. "I should be able to catch them in no time at all. I'll just have to pray that Lily will call her wolves away from me."

"Mayhap, but I wouldn't if I were you," Alan said, limping over to the counter with his bowl.

"And what would you do?" At the moment he was stumped, so stymied by the fact that he'd been outsmarted and robbed of the chance to say goodbye to Sorcha that he couldn't even think straight. Did she think he'd given up on her? That he hadn't fought for her?

"I'd wait at least three days and then head out."

"Three days? That could be too long." What the hell was his brother thinking? He couldn't just sit here for three days while Sorcha could be under attack. He had to know she was safe.

"Slow down and think. If you chase them now, and stop them, who will you have to battle besides Logan Ramsay?"

Cailean groaned.

"You've understood my meaning, I see. If you leave now, you'll have to deal with Kyle Maule *and* Logan Ramsay, not to mention that you'll be holding them up while Lily and the twins are riding with them. Maule will kill you with his bare hands. They'll be stopping on Cameron land for at least one night, mayhap more.

"If you wait," Alan continued, "my leg will be much improved, and I can go with you. You know the two of us will travel faster than that group with Lily and the twins. The wolves will remain on Cameron land so we'll not have to worry about them. Besides, the trip through the Highlands is slow for twenty or more. We can catch them easily. You pick the time and place to let them know we're behind them."

Uncle Isaac said, "Alan's right. He's a smart lad with no emotion invested in this. Listen to him."

Cailean clasped his brother's shoulder. "Brilliant, Alan. Now that's a plan. It gives me time to decide how we'll do this."

☾

Sorcha was heartsick. Her sire had stopped trying to talk to her, something for which she was grateful. Whenever they stopped, she assisted Lily with the twins, and changing their raggies with their wild kicking legs kept her so busy that she had little chance to talk to him anyway.

She needed time to think.

Her father had been her favorite person for a long time, but now he confused her. How could he not see that Cailean had helped her? That he wished to help her even more?

Later that day, they had just changed the babies again and strapped them onto Lily's chest and back when her cousin said to her, "Your sire does not wish to lose you."

Sorcha jerked her head to face her cousin. "What do you mean?"

"You're his first daughter. Aye, he loves Maggie and Molly, but he did not raise them from wee babes the way he did you and Brigid."

"What difference does that make?" Even as she said it, she remembered her sire saying much the same thing after the attack on the castle.

"I'm not sure, but I know it does make a difference. I have not shared this with anyone, but my sire made me sit on his lap before he sent me away to Edinburgh with your mother and father."

She gave Lily a puzzled look, unsure how to interpret what she was telling her.

"He wanted me to marry Kyle, so he asked him to take me to wife without telling me. I was a bit upset, especially since Kyle turned him down. Even though he already had a bad knee, my father made me sit on his lap and lean my head on his shoulder the same way I did when I was little. He wouldn't accept aught else. He acted like he was doing it to placate me, but I believe 'twas because he feared losing his first daughter. I think 'tis why he chose Kyle. He wanted to be sure I'd stay on Ramsay land."

"What are you saying?"

"That you are still your papa's wee lassie. He has trouble seeing you any other way. He's not ready to give you up to another, even if a part of him realizes 'tis time."

"You might be right, but how do I change his mind? At least your sire wished for you to marry. My sire hates Cailean."

"Why?"

"He thinks Cailean may be involved in the attacks against me."

"From what I've heard, 'tis a ludicrous suggestion, but it tells me your sire is grasping for any vine drifting from the trees from above."

"What?" Her dear cousin had a unique way of putting things.

"He's searching for any excuse within his reach not to accept the fact that Cailean has captured your heart."

"He does not know that."

Lily smirked and rolled her eyes at Sorcha. "Everyone else knows it, and your sire is far from foolish, so he's denying what everyone else is telling him, even his own eyes."

Sorcha couldn't believe what her cousin had just said. "*Everyone* knows it?"

Lily giggled then peeked at Liliana tied to her front, two fingers presently in her mouth. "You knew it, did you not, Liliana?"

The wee lassie squealed and kicked her feet, ending in a giggle.

Lily glanced over her shoulder at her other daughter, bound to her back, and asked, "Lise, what about you? Did you not know it?"

Lise repeated the movements of her sister, right down to the giggle. Lily shrugged her shoulders. "Aye, 'tis obvious to all how smitten Cailean is, and we can see it in you, too. You may think no one knew you were in the kitchens together, but…"

Sorcha gasped and waved at her cousin, indicating her wish for her silence. "Hush. Do not allow Papa to hear you."

"'Tis not of import now. What matters is that your sire is having a hard time thinking about you marrying, and you must convince him."

"How do I do that?"

"Your sire wants to be sure you won't replace him with Cailean in your heart. He has to know there's enough room for both of them. If he can see that, he'll see the rest. He's fighting the idea of a man grabbing your heart, it does not matter which one. Cailean is no different than any other, except…"

"Except what?" Sorcha had no idea where her cousin was going with this, but that was not unusual.

"Outside of your cousins and Kyle, Cailean is probably the strongest of any of the guards. Kyle has told me so. That could make him more of a threat to your sire."

Their conversation was cut short when Kyle came back to check on Lily and the girls. Sorcha nodded to her cousin and mouthed the words, "My thanks."

❦

By the time they arrived on Cameron land, Sorcha realized Lily had been correct about everything. She'd been looking at the situation completely wrong, and she knew exactly what she needed to say to her sire.

Now, would she get the chance before they were too far north?

Another worry quickened Sorcha's heart as they entered the gates. What if Uncle Alex had not healed yet? What if he was still abed and sickly? She could not imagine her uncle in such a state.

Kyle dismounted from his horse before moving back to help Lily down. The girls were still bound to her chest and back. She chattered uncontrollably, the same way she always did when she was upset about something. "Come, lassies, you must greet your uncle Alex. Grandmama and Grandpapa are here, too." She took off toward the keep.

Kyle barked, "Lily!"

"What is it, Kyle? I can hardly wait to greet Uncle Alex."

He beckoned her back. "Lily, I must return to assist Torrian." He leaned down and kissed both girls until they giggled and waved their tiny fists at him. "I shall return for you when I know it's safe."

She threw her arms around Kyle's neck, hugging him around their wee one, and said, "We'll miss you, Kyle. Please be careful."

He kissed her thoroughly, then pivoted and took off toward his horse. Lily watched him go and then turned back toward the keep. Reciting a quick prayer that they would find Uncle Alex well on the way to healing, Sorcha followed her in. She couldn't help but notice that her sire continued to keep his distance from her. Logan was ignoring her, pouring all his attention into helping the stable lads settle the horses, who were rebelling against the nearness of the wolves. But that was a problem for later—now, she needed to spend time with her uncle.

Sorcha almost bumped into Lily when they entered the hall, but she soon realized what had stopped her cousin. Uncle Quade was tucked into a chair not far from the hearth, and he was sound asleep. When had she ever seen her uncle asleep, especially in daytime?

As soon as the girls began their giggles, he woke up, turning his head toward the visitors. He waved to them but didn't rise because of his knee. Aunt Brenna came out of the kitchens carrying a bowl of broth, headed for the hearth. As soon as she caught sight of them, she set the bowl down and threw her hands into the air. "Oh, Lily, you've brought the twins for Aunt Jennie and Uncle Aedan. They'll be delighted. I cannot wait to hold my dear lassies again." Aunt Brenna kissed all three of them—Lily and each wee babe—then turned toward Sorcha and greeted her the same way. "Sorcha, you grow more beautiful every time I see you."

Aunt Jennie came out of the kitchens and squealed, rushing over to them. She hugged and kissed all of them, her two daughters not far behind her. She led them over to the hearth, grasping Lily's hand. "I'm so glad you've come to visit. I've been longing to see the twins."

Lily's curiosity got the best of her, and Sorcha was glad for it. Horrible possibilities had popped into her mind about Uncle Alex. "Mama? Where is Uncle Alex?" Lily asked. "I love Aunt Jennie and Uncle Aedan, but please tell me Uncle Alex is hale."

Aunt Jennie said, "He left for Grant land a few days ago. He's doing much better. With all that has transpired, he wished to go home. Your mama and I did our best to convince him to stay a few more days, but he refused. We all agreed with Maddie that he would not rest until he was home, though I'm sure it was a slow journey for them."

Uncle Aedan came in through the front door. "He'll not be swinging his sword anytime soon, but he's doing much better. He was willing to go back in the cart, which surprised us all. I think he's worried about repercussions from the battle."

Aunt Brenna nodded. "I promised your aunt we'd stay on for a few more days. She has a new poultice she wished to try on your sire's knee."

"Aye, we rarely get time together," Aunt Jennie said. "I love having my sister here so I can fuss over her. Lily, please introduce me to those two wee lassies tied to you."

Lily laughed and stood facing him. "This is Liliana, Aunt Jennie."

Liliana giggled and chewed on her fist. Then Lily pivoted so she was facing away from Jennie. "And this is Lise. Lise, greet your grand auntie."

Lise giggled and shook her arms up and down, then kicked her legs through the openings in Lily's contraption.

"Here, allow me to help you," Aunt Jennie said. "Your back must be sore from the ride, Lily." She took Lise out from the back and cuddled her close, kissing the top of her head while Aunt Brenna helped her with Liliana. "Oh, Lily. She's darling. They both are."

Uncle Quade glanced at his wife, his lips pressed in a straight line. "Brenna?" He held one arm up, his elbow bent.

"Of course, Quade." She settled Liliana in his lap, and he wrapped an arm around her. "Now he's happy. He just adores the twins." She helped free Lily from her trappings. "Uncle Alex is doing much better, lassies, but he was worried about how his bairns fared. He does not like to be off Grant land for long. 'Tis too quiet here for him."

Lily said, "I had so hoped to visit with him, but I'm pleased he was well enough to go home."

The door banged open and they all turned to see Logan enter. He strode over and stood in front of Uncle Quade. "I hear the Grants have gone home. There must be a good reason you've stayed on if Alex is gone." He clasped his shoulder fondly.

"Aye. Whenever Brenna is around Jennie, they cannot seem to part." He rubbed his knee. "Besides, I believe Jennie has found something that eases my pain. I'll stay a few more days if it will ease my knee enough for me to have an easier time of walking. All is well at home?"

Sorcha glanced at her sire to see if he would tell his brother everything that had transpired on Ramsay land. As soon as he pulled a chair over to the fire, she knew they wouldn't be leaving until the next day.

Mayhap more. She was beginning to believe she'd never see Cailean MacAdam again.

CHAPTER FIFTEEN

SORCHA TWISTED HER SKIRTS IN front of her. In the middle of the night, she'd bolted up in bed after a dream. She needed to speak with her sire—about *everything*. There could be no more delays. In the dream, someone had stood on the other side of a dark cloud and said, "Your suspicions are correct. Go to your sire. Do not hide your thoughts any longer."

Her sire came down the stairs and waved her over to Aedan's solar off the hall. He'd ignored her ever since they'd arrived, but she'd sent word through Aunt Jennie that she needed to speak with him.

Once her sire closed the door, he sat at the desk and motioned to the chair in front of it. She refused, too full of excitement to do aught but stand. Her sire arched an eyebrow at her, but she did not back down. She had to convince him of Cailean's innocence.

"Papa, I would like to speak to you about Cailean."

Her father shot out of his chair and headed toward the door, not saying a word.

"Papa, I know why you do not like him."

He turned a slow half-circle until he faced her, his eyes narrowed. "And why is that?" His voice came out in a tone she didn't recognize.

"Because you don't wish to lose me."

A smug look crossed his face. He returned to the desk and sat down. "Daughter, I know someday you will find a man who wishes to marry you, but he will have to meet your mother's and my expectations. We will not marry you to just anyone. He must meet certain standards. But that is not why I refused to bring him on this trip."

"Then why, Papa? I like Cailean. I feel safe around him. He saved me when you weren't there, and even when you *were* there."

Cailean had told her what her sire believed, but she wished to hear it from his own lips.

"I must be objective about the attacks, and the truth is that there is one possibility that no one else has considered. Cailean Mac-Adam was there for all three of the attacks. I want to know why, but I wasn't at home for long enough to question him or talk to anyone else about it. Did you ever consider that he may have *known* the archers were going to attack? That he was the one who ordered them to do it? Mayhap he thought to earn my gratitude by saving my daughter, that his actions would allow him to advance through the ranks of the Ramsay warriors."

"Papa, nay! You have this all wrong." She so desperately wanted him to listen to her, to consider there was another possibility. "Please, I beg you to give me the chance to explain."

He crossed his arms and tipped his head toward the chair behind her. "Then sit down and I'll listen."

"My thanks." She sat down and settled her hands in her lap, hoping she could keep from kneading a hole in her gown. "Papa, I've thought about this with care, and I believe we've all misinterpreted the situation."

"Go ahead. Tell me your thoughts." He leaned back in his chair, his hands clasped behind his head.

"The archers weren't aiming for me. Before each attack, I was chatting and laughing with one lad in particular, ignoring the others. The lad who held my attention most was the target."

Her father dropped his arms and sat forward. "So the first time you were attacked, who was he after?"

"He was after Cailean, who was riding next to me. I don't think his aim is true. He missed several times and then hit Horsie."

"Let's say I'd like to believe you. Who was the next target?"

"Baltair. He was showing me how to shoot inside the gates. In fact, I'll admit that I was flirting with him a bit to make Cailean jealous. Then the attack started, Cailean had to leave, and I wanted to go out and help. Baltair insisted on following me. I was nowhere near him when he was hit. That archer was not aiming for me at all, but for Baltair."

"And the last time?"

"Alan was protecting me. We were laughing and chatting before we moved out. Cailean was not even there. The archer shot Alan because he'd been talking to me."

The gleam returned to her sire's eyes. "Brilliant." He stared at her again, lost in his own thoughts.

"Your pardon, Papa?"

He stood up and placed his hands on the desk. "I believe you could be correct. They weren't after you, but whomever you were closest to at the time. It makes perfect sense."

"What does that mean?"

He chuckled and moved to her side, giving her a quick hug. "He's jealous. And you're the only one who figured that out. This archer, whoever 'tis, has been eliminating his competition. He wants you for himself."

"But I'm not sure about the other archers that day. Mama took two of them down. Mayhap he's dead and will never bother us again."

"It's entirely possible that this archer had a different purpose from the others. They might not have even known he was out there. Your mother hit the two closest shooters. She missed the one the farthest away. He was alone and could be the one after you." He thought for a moment and said, "Well done, Sorcha."

"Does that mean Cailean can come now?" She could send a messenger to summon him.

"Nay." He left the room. "Don't be ridiculous. He still hasn't proven his worth to me."

She'd gained nothing.

☾

Cailean was more determined than ever. The depth of his feelings for Sorcha had become even clearer to him after spending three days without her.

Alan trailed behind him by a short distance. His brother had tried to talk him into slowing down, but he was too afraid he'd miss his opportunity to talk to Logan Ramsay. They'd already passed Cameron land—the tracks had informed them that Logan's party had already left. They were close now, and might encounter Logan and Sorcha anywhere along the trail.

Cailean had gone through at least one hundred different ways to approach Logan, but each idea brought him back to the same approach. It was definitely a risky move, but he doubted anything less would register with the man.

They hadn't gone far when he found fresh tracks. He pointed to them as they passed to let Alan know he was not about to slow down.

The day was more than half gone when they finally caught up with the Ramsay guards at the back of the group, though the gray clouds hung so heavy and low it was hard to tell. The guards brought them to the front of the group, to Logan.

He looked neither surprised nor pleased. "MacAdam, I told you to stay on Ramsay land."

"I'd like a private word with you, my lord. I'll be as brief as possible."

"Nay, go back. Turn your horse around and head home." He did not even shift his attention from the road ahead.

Cailean glanced at Sorcha, whose grin was as wide as her beautiful face. She indicated that she wished to speak, but he hushed her. If he didn't settle this with Logan, the man would never respect him.

"Nay," Cailean shouted to the stubborn man ahead of him, "I'm not going back. I am here to protect Sorcha as I've been doing for the last fortnight. Her life could still be in danger. My brother and I can be of assistance should aught happen."

Logan stopped his horse, holding his arm up to the guards to indicate they were to stop, too. "Did you just refuse a direct order?"

"Aye, I did." Glad he was still on his horse, he did his best to stop the slight trembling of his body. He was less successful in banishing the vision of his bollocks hanging from a nearby tree.

"MacAdam, I'll not slay you in front of my daughter because she has feelings for you. If I have to steal your horse and leave you in the woods tied to a tree until we return, I will."

Cailean thought twice before he took his next step, but in his heart he knew this was the only plan that would work. He dismounted and drew his sword. "My lord, I love your daughter, and I'm going along with you."

He couldn't see Sorcha's face because his attention was pinned on Logan, but he heard her gasp. Hopefully, it was good news. He would have preferred to tell her in private first.

"Are you challenging me, lad?"

"Aye, if that's what it takes, then I'll gladly spar with you. I will prove to you that I am worthy of protecting your daughter. I have worked hard, and I believe I am one of the top Ramsay warriors. Allow me the chance to prove it."

Logan laughed and dismounted, pointing to a clearing in the distance. He gave curt instructions to his guards to parole the area. Cailean followed him into the clearing.

Logan asked, "You're sure you want to do this? There's no going back once it starts." He pulled his sword out of its sheath. "I'll not allow you to quit just because you are losing. You'll stay until I knock the sword from your hands."

Cailean unsheathed his sword, swinging it with both hands over his head to loosen up his muscles. He'd trained for years. While he'd never gone against Logan before, he had trained with both Kyle and Torrian, and his skills were good. He planted his feet and lowered his sword. "I'm sure."

"Whenever you're ready. You may have the first swing."

Cailean took a deep breath, said a quick prayer, and glanced over at Alan and Sorcha, who stood just outside the clearing. He only hoped he'd prove his mettle. He took a wide swing and moved toward Logan Ramsay with a grunt, but Logan took him by surprise with a quick move that tossed him flat on his back. The older man put his boot on Cailean's chest and said, "That did no' take long. Now you'll take your leave and forget about my daughter."

He heard Sorcha's voice whisper, "Papa!" There was something in her voice—hope, an entreaty for him?—that gave Cailean the motivation to continue. With one hand, he gripped Logan's boot, which the man was balancing on with all his weight, and flipped him to the ground. "I'll not forget your daughter. I love her, and I don't give up that easily." He stood back and allowed Logan to stand and get his bearings again, giving him the first swing when he was ready.

Cailean easily deflected his blows, fueled by the necessity to prove himself for Sorcha, blocking one after the other. They parried evenly for a short time.

Then Cailean noticed Logan's sword arm tiring.

That couldn't be possible. He was the mighty Logan Ramsay.

He lightened up his swing, not wanting to do any damage. This was not a fight to the death, but only a test of strength and ability.

And that was a big mistake. Logan out played him, surging forward with strength he'd yet to show. He swung hard and Cailean had to pull from his gut to stay on his feet. Ramsay had turned the fight so that he was now on the offense and Cailean was fighting defensively.

"Never underestimate your opponent, lad." He swung and swung, knocking Cailean to his knees twice, but he came back each time. "You're done now. Foolish strategy. Do not take it easy on an old man. Say goodbye to your friend, Sorcha. He's done."

The grin on his face fired Cailean like nothing else could. The grin and a sweet voice that squealed, "Cailean!"

He came back with a growl. "Nay, I'm not done, old man." He swung from the side, but his shot was blocked. So he came at him from the other side. "'Tis time to put an end to this."

He made his swings as fast as he could until the tone of the battle changed. Now Cailean was on the offense, and Ramsay on the defense, taking many steps backward. Recognizing this as his opportunity to speak, Cailean panted out, "I'm following you to Grant land, and I'm asking you for your daughter's hand in marriage. I respectfully request that you accept it. I love her and I'll protect her." He swung three more times, each blow blocked by a panting Logan Ramsay.

Then Sorcha's sire surprised everyone and tossed his sword to the ground. Cailean stopped his swing mid-air.

Ramsay, heaving from exertion, said, "My daughter's worth fighting for. You had to show me that. Well fought." After a few more breaths, he said, "You may travel with us. I expect you to guard my daughter with your life."

Cailean nodded, sheathing his sword with a small smile. "May I have her hand in marriage?"

"Nay." Logan snorted. "Now you're being foolish."

He walked off into the woods toward a nearby stream, and Sorcha threw herself into Cailean's arms.

"I love you, too," she whispered.

He closed his eyes with relief. One step at a time.

CHAPTER SIXTEEN

T HE FARTHER THEY TRAVELED, THE more the weather declined. Lily had stayed behind at her parents' insistence since Kyle had already returned home. The rain had started about an hour before, and Sorcha was chilled through her plaids and leggings. Rumblings of thunder could be heard in the distance, and uneasiness crept up the back of her neck.

Her sire shouted out to them, "I'd like to get through this next pass, though it's a difficult path. 'Tis a bit steep to travel in the rain, but if we can get to the other side, there's a deep cave where we can spend the night. We're almost to Grant land, so we just need to push ahead."

Cailean said, "I hope we can get through before that storm hits. If it rains any harder, we could be in trouble." He rode his horse on one side of Sorcha to protect her from the blowing wind.

She'd love nothing more than to be riding in the shelter of his warm embrace, but her father had forbidden it, with good reason. It would be too difficult for a horse to get through the next pass with two riders, especially if one of them was the size of Cailean.

"We're almost there," her father shouted back.

Sorcha did not like this one bit. The path was narrow, barely allowing for two horses to climb abreast, and it was steep besides. She could feel the jitters in her horse as he plowed ahead. A small part of her was relieved that dear Horsie was still healing. She would not have managed this journey well. What in heavens name did the Grants do in the winter? She'd made this journey before, but never in unstable weather.

She pulled the plaid scarf down over her face in an attempt to keep the wind from stealing her breath away. Her hair, plaited down her back, stayed mostly in place, but a few flyaway strands danced around her eyes. The bulk of her hair remained dry, fortunately. Otherwise, she'd be shivering for certain. She peeked ahead at the path in front of them, gritting her teeth as she urged her horse forward.

"Almost through," Logan bellowed.

The skies opened up and the steady rain shifted to a downpour.

"Hurry! I fear the path will wash out." Her father waved them forward. "Sorcha, get ahead of Cailean. The path narrows up ahead."

She maneuvered her mount forward. Cailean said, "Are you all right? I'll build a fire to warm you when we get to the cave."

She smiled, but that was all she could do before her horse's hooves slipped in the mud, trying to find a grip but failing. Her horse dropped out from beneath her, the rain propelling them in a mudslide off to the side of the path. She screamed and glanced back at Cailean, who jumped off his horse in an attempt to grab her as she rolled off her horse's back. Her horse got caught by a tree sticking sideways out of the ground just over the cliff, but she and Cailean hurtled past the tree at a speed that frightened her.

Cailean wrapped his arms around her and pulled her on top of him as they plummeted down the ravine, tossing, turning, banging on rocks and bushes and mounds of mud. They finally came to a stop with an oomph, Cailean's large body caught by a line of bushes on an outcropping. She gripped his forearms and glanced over his shoulder and squealed. There was *nothing* beneath them. They would have fallen and fallen for minutes, it seemed.

He glanced down there with her and said, "Don't look. I've got you. We're not going over. We're on a solid ledge, caught on a strong bush, and we're protected from the worst of the rain." But even as he said the comforting words, he gasped for air. She knew he was equally shocked, equally frightened, and their fear gave them pause to just huddle together, grateful they were still in one piece.

"What will we do?" She looked back up the path they'd just traveled and said, "Oh, how will we ever get back up that hill? 'Tis treacherous."

"Do not think of that. Are you hurt?" He turned her face, doing his best to straighten her scarf to protect her. His hand traveled down her arm, searching for any wounds or broken bones.

She wiggled both feet a wee bit and didn't feel any sharp pain. "Nay, I do not think so." Glancing at his side, she gasped. "You're bleeding. Where is it coming from?"

A bellow came from above. Her sire yelled, "Sorcha? Where are you? Sorcha?" She could hear the panic in his voice.

"Here, Papa. We're here," she shouted, desperate to comfort him.

"What? Are you all right? Louder."

She opened her mouth, but Cailean hushed her. "Nay, my voice carries better." He covered her ears and yelled. "We're fine. I have her and we landed on a ledge that's mostly dry."

"Do not move or you'll cause another mudslide. I'll get the rope and we'll pull you out. There are enough of us, plus the horses."

She gazed into Cailean's green eyes and whispered, "You fought for me and look what happened. You would have been better off if you'd stayed on Ramsay land."

"Nay, I would have been daft from worry." He did his best to wipe the mud from her face. "I'm exactly where I need to be. Where would *you* be if I had not come along? Your sire was too far away from you."

"Cailean, I'm frightened. 'Twas a horrendous fall and the rain is not stopping. Will he be able to get us out? Look at it, 'tis so steep. We fell a long distance."

He chuckled and said, "I'd rather go up than down."

She shivered and huddled against him. What else could she do?

He kissed her forehead and held her face against him, protecting her from the brutal weather. "I have complete faith in your father. He will find a way to get you up the cliff."

"What about you?"

"*That* I'm not so sure about. He may decide 'tis an easy way to be rid of me." Her horror must have shown in her expression because he chuckled. "I'm teasing you. Your father is not a cruel man. I'll get myself out if I must. I'm more worried about you climbing such a rough terrain." He glanced up the cliff. "There is little to grab onto because it's all wet. You're going to need strong arms, but I believe in you."

"Are you not sore? And you're still bleeding, though it has slowed." She felt along his upper arm, then down his side. "I think 'tis your arm. Does it not bother you? I hurt from the first time I hit the ground. I'm sure my hip will be bruised."

He gave her a sly grin, his one brow waggling at her. "Do not worry about me. I'll make sure and kiss any bruises you have. I'll make it my priority to check your skin for wounds." He squeezed her hand and kissed her knuckles.

She shivered against him, wondering what would have happened to her if he hadn't jumped with her. He'd borne the brunt of the rocky journey, tucking her inside his embrace so she wouldn't hit.

"MacAdam," her sire's voice carried down the small canyon. "I'm throwing the rope down."

"Lass, I have to move you a bit. Don't make any jarring movements." He lifted his upper body, scooting her into his arms.

"I think the rain is slowing." She glanced up at the gray skies, turning dark now that night was nearly upon them.

"We have to move quickly. We need to take advantage of it before it starts pounding down again." He shifted her to one of his hips to free up an arm and then reached for the rope. "I've almost got it," he yelled, "but it'll take a moment to get it tied around her." He sat up, glancing around for a solid spot for them to stand. "Look. See that spot there? You can hang on to the tree trunk sticking out. It's a small one, but it will hold your weight. I'm going to help you to stand and I want you to lean in that direction so you have something to steady you."

"MacAdam, you're coming with her," Sorcha heard her father bellow. "Place her in front of you. She'll not make it on her own."

She glanced at him, hoping he agreed with her sire. Climbing together sounded much better than trying to do it on her own. And she wouldn't have to worry about his safety. As if he read her mind, Cailean said, "He's right. I'll be right behind you."

They sat up together, his arm still around her, the rope almost within their reach. He assisted her to a kneeling position and she maneuvered her way over to the tree trunk, wrapping one arm around it. She turned to him and said, "I've got it."

"Does it feel as strong as it looks?"

She tugged on it. "Aye. It'll hold me."

"Good. Now stand up so I can get behind you."

She did as he asked, but then her eyes, as if controlled by someone else, veered down to the long drop beneath them.

"Don't look down! Look up. I want you to look for your sire so we can see what direction we're headed."

Lord in heaven, she could not look down again or she'd lose the insides of her belly for sure. She gladly gripped the tree and stared up, looking for any signs of movement above them. "I think I see him. Papa?"

All she could see through the branches was a hand, but it was definitely part of a person. "We're almost ready. Not quite."

Cailean pushed himself to a standing position and reached for a tree above her, grasping the thick trunk to steady himself. The rope was finally within reach.

"Are you ready?" came the shout from above.

"Nay. A few more moments. I'll let you know." Cailean shifted himself so he was directly behind Sorcha. He whispered in her ear. "Here's what we're going to do. I'm going to turn you around and you're going to wrap your legs around my waist rather than wrap the rope around you."

"Oh, Cailean."

"It'll be all right." He helped her pivot until she faced him, his left arm around her and the other hanging on to the tree. "I'm going to let go of the tree and grab for the rope. Do not move when I do that. As soon as I wrap the rope around my arm, I'm going to tell your sire to start pulling. One of your arms should stay around my neck at all times, but you should use the other hand to grab onto trees or branches, anything that will help steady us and guide our path as we move up. My left arm will move back and forth between protecting you and grabbing the rope in case I need a two-handed hold. Whenever I move my hand, you have to hang on tighter, understood?"

She peered up at him. "Aye. Cailean. I love you, just in case…"

"We'll be up in a matter of moments. Your father is like a bull. He'll have the guards pulling us so fast, it will make your insides spin."

He kissed her on the lips, a kiss that lingered just long enough to tell her exactly how he felt. "I love you, too. We'll make it because I have to get your father to agree."

"Agree to what?"

"Och, I almost forgot. Sorcha, will you marry me?" He glanced down at her with a smile that melted her heart.

How could she ever refuse this man? "Aye, Cailean. I'll marry you, but please get me up the ravine first. I would just as soon make it to our wedding."

He gave her a quick kiss, grinned, and yelled, "Ready. Start slow until we're steady."

A moment later, they were in midair, swinging back and forth, branches hitting them as they passed. She squealed but hung on to Cailean with all her might.

"Ramsay, slow down or you'll behead us!"

She felt his grip loosen a touch. "Cailean?"

"I've got you. Now, both hands on my neck for a moment." He let go of her to maneuver them around a boulder sticking out of the dirt. "Almost there." Then he wrapped his arm around her again, pinning her to his chest.

She glanced up to the top, surprised to see the guards coming in to view, her father at the front of the group, Cailean's brother, Alan, behind him, their hands gripping the rope as they tugged and pulled, grappling to keep their feet steady in the mud. She could see they'd braced a log between a few trees to wedge their feet—a safeguard against slipping in the mud.

They passed the tree where her horse had been, but he was gone. She tried her best not to think about him. They hit another outcropping and swung wildly beneath it. She squealed, feeling Cailean's grip on her weakening.

"Do not panic. If I lose my grip, you have your legs wrapped around me. You're going nowhere. I need you to stay calm."

"But it's so far down. What if…"

"Nay. Do not think…"

A sudden jolt stopped them and she peered up to see the rope was almost shredded in two from the sharp edge of the outcropping. "Cailean…the rope…" Tears misted her eyes. It hurt worse for this to happen when they were so close.

"Stop pulling," he shouted.

Her sire's voice was so close. "What's wrong?"

"The rope is tearing…do not move a muscle."

Turning back to her, Cailean said, "I'm going to turn you a bit. I want you to grab onto that tree trunk. Can you reach it or at least grab ahold of the closest branch? We need something to hang on to in case the rope breaks."

He pushed her sideways and she managed to grab the closest tree, dragging herself over until she could put two hands on it, her legs still around his waist. Cailean grabbed a branch above her a moment before the rope snapped in two, the part they'd been hanging on to plummeting to the ground beneath them.

It was a long time before they heard it hit.

"Sorcha!"

"I'm here, Papa. We're hanging on to a tree. We can't reach the other end of the rope."

Cailean grappled for a better grip and pulled himself up far enough to get a foothold on a rock. He switched his grip to a slightly higher tree and then reached for her. "I'm sending her up, Ramsay," he shouted. "You have to come down a bit to get her. There's no other way."

Sorcha could hear her sire barking orders to the men, but she ignored it. She glanced at Cailean and said, "But how? I cannot pull myself up any higher. There's naught to grab onto."

"I'm going to lift you up to this tree. It's stronger than the one you're holding. You'll pull yourself up into it. I think your sire will be able to reach that far. We're almost there."

"My arms are so weak."

"You're much stronger than you think." He gripped her hips and pushed her up. "Do not look down, Sorcha. Look up. Grab the branch first, then look for your sire."

Managing to scramble upward with Cailean's help, she finally shifted her weight to the stronger tree.

"Now, push yourself higher. Get your knee on that trunk sticking out sideways so you can reach for your sire. I think it'll bring you close enough."

She did as he said, pulling and pushing with all her might. "Papa?"

"I'm right here, Sorcha. And don't be looking for your horse. We already have him up here."

She glanced up and almost cried when she saw her sire's hand extended to her, perfectly within reach. He, Alan, and two other guards had created their own rope with their arms. Once her sire had a tight grip on her arm, he bellowed, "Pull us up."

She flew up the rest of the way and landed at the feet of her sire, who promptly scooped her up and wrapped his arms around her. She thought she actually saw a little moisture in his eyes.

She pushed away from him. "Cailean? Papa, we must help him." She leaned toward the tree to peek over the edge just as Alan tugged on something. Cailean's arm. His head appeared, and then he crawled up the side of the embankment, landing on his back with a gasp. Panting, he said, "Thanks, Alan."

"Och, I knew you could get yourself up the rest of the way," Sorcha's sire said. "Oh, by the way, I've had some time to think. You may have my daughter's hand in marriage."

Relief and excitement washed through Sorcha in equal measure. He approved. They could be together.

Cailean sat up and stared at her sire in shock. "What? Why did you change your mind?"

Her father held his hand out to Cailean to help him to his feet. "I changed my mind when I saw you jump over a cliff after her. I decided you must have her best interests at heart after all."

Sorcha threw herself into her sire's arms and said, "Thank you, Papa."

He hugged her and let her go before saying, "Two years. You have to wait two years before you can marry." He moved over to his horse in the front of the line. "Mount up. You two will have to ride together. Your horse is a bit lame, Sorcha, but he'll make it."

Cailean grabbed her and hugged her tight. "Two years. 'Twill kill me, but I can wait two years." He placed her up on the back of his horse before climbing up behind her.

She whispered in his ear. "I cannot." She giggled. "We'll wear him down."

Her sire could not possibly have heard her, but he chose that exact moment to shout back, "Touch her before then, MacAdam, and I'll kill you."

CHAPTER SEVENTEEN

IT WAS LATE BY THE time they stepped inside the Grant hall, but excited voices shouted out greetings all around them. Logan had pushed them into finishing their journey that night instead of resting in the cave. He said he was worried about something, but he wouldn't tell them what.

Cailean stood to the side, still clutching Sorcha's hand. He'd heard stories about the Grant castle all his life—the grand curtain wall, the parapets, the mountains around it. He wished he'd noticed more of it upon their arrival, but somehow he hadn't... Had he been sleeping? How was that possible? Sweat broke out across his forehead, but there was no reasonable explanation for it. It wasn't overly warm inside the hall. He glanced into the sea of faces, many of them staring at him, but he had no idea who they were.

He glanced down his arms to his feet. No wonder they were staring; he was caked in mud. This part of the Highlands must have red mud. He'd never seen such a thing before. "Look, Sorcha. The mud is red here." He pointed to his legs, coated with the thick red substance.

"Papa?" Sorcha called her sire over. Her voice sounded... strained...and now that he thought about it, she'd been giving him worried looks for a while now.

Logan took one look at Cailean and then turned toward Robbie Grant, Alex's brother. "Robbie, fetch Caralyn. Someone needs tending." He tipped his head toward Cailean.

Cailean found himself staring at the tapestries on the walls. They were of the castle in the different seasons. He squeezed Sorcha's hand, and he felt her hand on his face, but he couldn't tear his gaze from the tapestries. Oblivious to everything else around him, he had only one wish at the moment.

Sleep. He needed to close his eyes so he could forget the fire that someone had set inside his body in the last hour. Alan came over to him, staring at him strangely. Logan said something to Alan in a voice too low for Cailean to hear, but he didn't care. He was here with Sorcha, and Logan hadn't killed him yet.

He glanced at Sorcha again and noticed her face was wet. Reaching over to wipe it, he asked, "What's wrong, love?"

Alan stood on his other side and said, "Cailean, Sorcha is going to lead us to the Grants' healing chamber. Lean on me if you've the need. You took a nasty battering in your fall."

"What? I do not..." His left knee buckled when he took a step behind Alan, but he managed to hold himself upright. They walked a ways in silence.

"Come, Cailean," Sorcha said in that same strained voice. "You can rest in here. You look verra tired. This has been a difficult journey." She led him over to the one large chair in the healing chamber, bypassing the pallets.

Alan peeled off his plaid, tossing it over to a basket, probably because it was covered in that special Grant mud. That left him in his tunic and his boots.

Sorcha leaned over and kissed his cheek. "Caralyn will fix you up. You need to rest."

He couldn't see her anymore. "Sorcha? Where are you going?"

"I'll find you something to drink, Cailean. Alan and Caralyn will take care of you. You need a bath, so I must go." She kissed his forehead and patted his hand. "You know my sire would be upset if I stayed during your bath.

That was funny. He laughed at the thought. "I'll have an ale, if you please."

He heard her speak to Alan. "Please watch over him. I'll come back to sit with him after Caralyn cleans him up."

Sorcha's sire came flying in the room. "Nay, you will not. I'll sit with him if he needs anyone, but he needs sleep most of all."

Logan ushered her out of the room and then stood sentinel in the doorway while Alan helped to peel Cailean's tunic off. "Hellfire, MacAdam. Why did you not tell me? Alan, I knew he was in bad shape, but I had no idea. Did he tell you?"

Alan shook his head. "He's not thinking clearly. You've seen the way some men are after battle? Appears to be the same."

"Aye." Logan's voice came out in a whisper. "The ones who are badly injured." He didn't move, just stared down at him with a peculiar look in his eyes. "I should have suspected. I was too busy getting us out of that death trap."

Cailean had no idea what he meant, so he just stared at him. A woman came in through the door, and Logan introduced her as the Grant healer, Caralyn. Two lads followed her into the room, and Cailean distantly recognized them as Jake and Jamie Grant.

The healer took one look at him and said, "Oh my." Moving back over to the door, she yelled for some lads to bring in the tub and plenty hot water. Then she returned and started fussing with her supplies.

"We came as soon as we heard," Jake said. "Who beat him so badly?"

"The side of a cliff," Logan answered. "Sorcha's horse lost its footing coming through the craggy section from a mudslide. They took a tumble down the cliff."

"He was on the horse with her?"

"Nay," he said with a smirk. "He jumped after her, and according to my daughter, he cocooned her and took the brunt of the hits. It appears they did more bouncing than sliding."

"We know that spot well," Jamie said. "'Tis a dangerous passage during a rainstorm. I hope you thanked him. That could have killed Sorcha."

"I did. I gave him permission to marry her."

Jamie and Jake exchanged grins, and Jake clasped Logan's shoulder. "I never thought we'd see the day when you'd give up Sorcha."

Logan snorted. "Has not happened yet."

Cailean hadn't said anything up until then, too tired to speak. But this he couldn't let pass. "It will happen, Ramsay."

Logan replied, "We'll see. Rest up, MacAdam. You've earned it. My wee lassie has nary a scratch thanks to you."

Cailean stood to glance down at all the bruises, cuts, and scrapes on his body. He fell back into the chair, finally understanding why his body screamed in pain.

Sorcha sat with Kyla in the great hall, waiting for everyone to leave Cailean's side so she could go see how he was doing.

"How is he?" Kyla asked.

She shook her head. "I don't know. The embankment was covered with rocks and protruding branches, and Cailean's skin is torn to shreds in some spots. He has abrasions and cuts all down his body. 'Twill be a miracle if he has no broken bones." She swiped at the tears forming on her lashes.

"I'm so sorry, but Caralyn will help him. He seems to be a strong warrior. You survived, and you don't have many cuts at all. Just a couple wee ones on your face."

"Because he did it for me. He jumped after me as soon as the horse stumbled. He always keeps me from getting hurt. But you should see him. He's bleeding from everywhere. His body must pain him terribly, and he's talking nonsense. Do you suppose he hit his head?"

"That could be from the aftermath of battle. I've seen it in many before. We had several warriors talking nonsense after the battle with Duncrub. They were back to themselves the next day. The turmoil plays with their minds, Caralyn says. Didn't hurt his face much. Sorcha, he's one handsome man. You should marry him."

Her face lit up at this reminder of the best part of their journey. "He asked me to marry him and my sire approved."

"And you said?"

"Aye, of course. I love him. But it wasn't easy getting my sire to agree. He only allowed it because Cailean saved me going down the hill." She peered down at her tunic and leggings. "I feel so dirty."

"Come, we'll go to my mama's bathing room and find you something else to wear."

"I would appreciate that, Kyla. My satchel barely survived. It's drenched and covered in mud."

"And your dear Horsie?"

"Horsie was wounded, so I left her at home. The horse I was riding was injured, but he seems fine."

Her father emerged from the healing chamber and motioned for her to follow him into the solar. Struggling to get to her feet, she stood and beckoned for Kyla to follow.

"Papa, how is Cailean?" she asked as soon as she entered the solar.

"He's cleaned up and sound asleep. Do not expect him to awaken before the morrow. Caralyn gave him something to help him sleep."

He wrapped his arms around his daughter and kissed her forehead. "That big brute saved you. Every bruise on his body tells me he cares for you. Are you bruised?"

She replied, "Just one on my hip from when I first landed. Papa, that one hurts terribly. He must be in so much pain…"

"He's a Ramsay warrior and he's bigger than you. He can handle it, Sorcha. Do not treat him like a bairn." He moved over to the door and opened it as if he were expecting someone.

Kyla took her hand and squeezed it, as if she knew how much those words had stung.

"If he loves you, he'll heal just for you. I've seen it happen before." The sad look in Kyla's eyes that reminded Sorcha of why they'd made the journey to the Grants in the first place.

"How is your sire? I almost forgot. Forgive me."

"I understand. Papa is better. He sleeps quite a bit." Tears misted her lashes. "But I'm so pleased he's home. When he left with Jamie and my mother, I feared he'd never return. Mama says he'll heal— 'twill just take some time."

"I'm so happy to hear that. I must visit with him on the morrow."

Moments later, Jake and Jamie and Alan all filed into the solar. Once the door was closed, Logan gave his full attention to the Grant twins. "Have you had any attacks since your sire was hurt? I was pleased to hear Alex was hale enough to make the journey home."

Jamie smiled at the mention of his father. "He is much improved." He glanced at his brother. "Our sire is strong. We believe he'll heal, and Mama never leaves his side. Jake and I are acting lairds until he is able to return to his position. We've had more reivers than usual since the battle with Duncrub, but we cannot tell where they're coming from. Have you come with news? We were not expecting to see you so soon, Uncle Logan, though we are always grateful to see you."

Logan sat on the edge of the desk. "Sorcha has been attacked three times. Well, indirectly. There've been archers in the trees outside our gates on three occasions. They shot at her escorts, but we've yet to determine if they were attempting to kill her or her escorts. Sorcha thinks it could be the latter."

Jake nodded. "You interpret this as some kind of act of jealousy?"

"Exactly. We don't know for sure. I wanted to come this way to see how your clan fares. I worry that your father's illness may be enticing to groups hoping to overtake your castle."

Jamie snorted. "No one killed our five hundred guards. They would have to possess a major force to meet us in battle. Do you think that's likely?"

"Not likely, but possible. I'll need to send a messenger to Edinburgh, see what that area is like. One never knows what Glenn of Buchan is up to. I would not be surprised if he's busy stirring up a wee bit of trouble for us. He still lives for revenge, and MacNiven must have left a few men behind who could join forces with him, not to mention the men who survived your battle with Duncrub."

"We'll alert you to any problems," Jamie said.

"Take aught that happens verra seriously. I fear there could be a problem building in the Highlands. And Sorcha? Do not dare to step outside the curtain wall."

"Aye, Papa. I'll stay inside. I'll not leave Cailean's side until he's well again."

"Jake, if you see her outside, you'll let me know." He turned to point his finger at her. "You will not put yourself at risk. Understood?"

Why did she yearn to reach over and break his finger off?

☾

The next night, Sorcha sat in a chair in front of the hearth, staring at the flames. Kyla gave her a quick hug and then joined her.

"'Tis a cool eve, but the day was lovely. Crisp but lovely. Did you make it outside?" It was a gentle invitation to talk—if she was ready.

"Nay." Sorcha was so wrapped up in her own troubles, she hardly noticed the people who had entered the hall until the newcomers were almost upon them.

She jumped to her feet as Uncle Alex made his way over to a

cushioned chair by the hearth, assisted by Connor. "Uncle Alex! 'Tis so good to see you." She waited until he was seated before rushing over to kiss his cheek.

"Good eve to you, lass. Maddie sends her apologies as she's in her night rail. In truth, Connor is better at supporting me. From time to time, I still falter." He motioned for his youngest son to take a seat next to him.

"How do you feel?" Sorcha asked.

"Much better. I'll not be swinging my sword yet, but I'm improving every day."

She couldn't help but smile. His condition was so much better than the stories had inclined her to believe. His voice was as booming and authoritative as ever, and his body was clearly well on its way to recovery. "We have not stopped worrying since we heard the news. I feared the worst, Uncle Alex. I thought…Pay me no mind. Connor, you're almost as tall as your sire."

Uncle Alex chuckled. "He's trying to beat his brothers. Neither has surpassed my height, but Connor insists he will. He's convinced he has some growing time left. We shall see." Connor grinned and nodded his head in agreement. "I hear you had a difficult journey and there's a lad in the healing chamber who is in rough shape."

"Aye, a mudslide caught my horse, but Cailean went over the side with me."

Her uncle arched his brow at her.

"He was on a different horse, but his mount was right next to mine. He tried to stop me from going over the embankment— instead, we both toppled over it. He protected me." She wrung her hands, caught up in the entire event again. She'd never been so frightened in her life.

"Any good Ramsay warrior would do as he did. Your sire was not close enough?"

"Nay, he was in the front, leading us through the section."

"He was lucky Cailean was close by."

She leaned in closer and whispered, "Uncle Alex, would you mention that to him, please?"

Her uncle gave her a wide grin. "Your sire does not wish to admit you're a woman grown? 'Tis tough for us old fathers." He tipped his head toward Kyla. "I suppose I'll be forced to go through the same myself soon."

Kyla said, "Oh, Papa, you know I'll pick someone you'll like."

Connor chuckled, looking at his father. "But will he be good enough for you? I imagine you'll want to test his sword skills."

Sorcha rolled her eyes. "Papa already tested Cailean's skills."

"And did he pass?" Alex asked.

"Aye, or he wouldn't have been allowed to come along." She scowled, thinking again about the trials the poor man had been forced to endure just to travel along with the other Ramsay guards.

Just then, Sorcha's sire stepped out of the solar, closing the door behind him. A wide grin spread across his face as he moved to join them at the hearth. "Alex, you're looking much better." He stood by the big man's side, clapping a hand on Alex's shoulder.

"Aye, I'm improving. My thanks for getting my sister to my side so quickly, Ramsay."

"I doubt 'twill be long before you've got your hands on that sword again. Your son here can help you the first time. He's growing into a fine lad, I see."

"Do not worry. I'll be back." He shot a wry look at Kyla. "If for no other reason than to test the skills of my daughter's suitors, just as you did, Ramsay."

Her father smirked at her, but then turned back to Alex. "He passed. The poor lad took a rough tumble after that, but he's a Ramsay warrior. He'll survive. You're welcome to join us, laird. I need to confer with your sons and your brothers to see what's been transpiring in the Highlands."

Alex shook his head before nodding to Connor. "Nay, I'll leave all to the new lairds. Connor will help me back to my chamber. I'll sit with Maddie for a while."

With one last nod and grin, Sorcha's sire left for the solar. Kyla bolted out of her chair as soon as Alex started to lift himself up. "I'll help you, Papa."

"Nay, daughter. Stay and enjoy your cousin. Connor will come back to the solar in a few moments."

They watched the two cross the hall to Alex and Maddie's new chamber before they continued their conversation.

"So how is Cailean?" Kyla asked.

"I've tried to tend him, but he's barely alert. I worry about him. He opens his eyes, looks at me and smiles, then closes them again. I…I still worry he may have hit his head when he fell. Alan said he would sit with him for a while. I needed some time to think about all that's happened."

"Wait here for a moment," Kyla said. Sorcha just nodded miserably, staring at the flames.

Not long after, Kyla returned with Caralyn. The older woman took Sorcha's hand. "Do not worry about Cailean. I did not want him to wake up from the pain, and he did not, but he's struggling to stay awake. The amount of primrose root I give someone is always a guess on my part, and I may have given Cailean a wee bit too much last eve. He should be able to talk to you on the morrow."

"Are you sure he'll improve?" Sorcha was sick over the possibility that he may have suffered a permanent injury.

"I don't see any marks on his head or any swellings. 'Tis the effects of the potion, and he's still in pain. I think he'll be fine on the morrow. Still sore, but his mind will be back to usual. I know 'tis difficult for you, but let's allow him to rest. He deserves it after what he went through. In fact, you must be exhausted. Make sure you get enough rest." After giving Sorcha's shoulder another pat, she left them.

The hall had almost emptied after the evening meal. A few servants still circulated, cleaning and straightening. Sorcha's sire and the others were still in the solar, talking strategy or who knew what. She couldn't rouse any interest, not now.

She just wished for Cailean back.

"Tell me about Lily and the twins," Kyla said. "I would love to see them."

"Aye. The little ones already giggle like their mother does. Aunt Jennie picked one of the bairns up as soon as she could, but Uncle Quade prompted Aunt Brenna to put the other babe in his lap. He's so fond of his grandbairns." She reached over to pat Kyla's hand. Lily planned to visit your sire. She thought the wee ones would help cheer him up, but Kyle returned to Ramsay land before he found out your sire had already headed home. Papa did not dare travel through the Highlands with Lily and the babes without Kyle's permission. I wish they were here, but 'tis better they stayed behind with Aunt Jennie. The weather was too treacherous for her to be out with two bairns. Of course, Lily's Mama and Papa were still with the Camerons, so 'twas best for all. Uncle

Alex will get to meet the twins someday."

"I'm so glad you came. I miss all my dear cousins." Her eyes brimmed with tears again. "And I'm happy that you've found Cailean. Another one gone…and here I sit, still alone." She sighed and stared into the flames.

"What do you mean, another one gone?"

"I was happy for Loki when he married, then Jake and Jamie followed. I'm pleased to watch our *clann* grow. Then Ashlyn married and, of course, Gracie…"

"I felt the same way when Torrian and Lily married. But you have time, Kyla. You'll find the right lad for you. 'Tis funny how it happened so suddenly with Cailean and me. I've known him for years, but I'd never considered him before. He was young and small and kept to himself. Then he suddenly grew up. When his height shot up and his muscles started bulging and then he let his hair grow long…" She giggled and glanced at Kyla. They both laughed until they were both out of breath.

When she could finally speak again, Kyla asked, "So when will you marry? Right away once they catch the fools at your castle?"

"I hardly expect that. My sire said we could marry in two years."

"Two years?" She laughed out loud, a joyful sound. "Your sire is tougher than mine." She played with her dark hair, plaited but left down, twirling it around her finger.

"Mayhap. Do you truly feel your sire is hard on you?" They were both the firstborn daughters of strong-willed leaders. If anyone would understand her plight, it was Kyla.

"I used to, but no longer. He's softened a wee bit since my parents adopted Maeve. Why do you ask?"

"My sire seems like he's always annoyed with me of late. I know he dislikes Cailean, but 'tis more than that. He treats me differently than he used to."

Kyla tipped her head and arched her brow at her friend.

"What?" Sorcha asked.

"Your sire doesn't wish to lose you. Mama has been warning me about that for a long time. She likes to jest that I must fall in love verra slowly when the time comes."

Sorcha crossed her arms. Had she not heard something similar from someone else recently? "Lily," she whispered, tapping her finger to her lip.

"What about Lily?"

"Lily told me the same thing. But I don't understand…how can he lose me? He'll always be my papa and I'll always love him."

"Sorcha, mayhap your sire's afraid for you because of how much you favor him. You've always had his thirst for adventure. My sire always laughs about your sire, how he's always running in different directions. You're much the same."

"Nay, I'm not. I wish to stay on Ramsay land or Grant land, well, mayhap Cameron land, too, and I do love to visit Menzie land, and Uncle Micheil and Aunt Diana…"

"You see. You *are* like him. You love the outdoors. What do you do at home? Stay in the keep?"

She scoffed, "Inside? Never."

"You see, you *are* the same. Suppose you came here and fell in love with a Grant? Then where would you live? Probably on Grant land. Your sire would feel as though he lost you."

It was all beginning to make sense. Suddenly, she understood. "But why Cailean? He's a Ramsay."

"In a strange way, he may not want you to marry anyone. Mayhap he's having trouble accepting it."

"Hmmm…" She chewed the inside of her cheek. "He did mention that at home."

"What did he say?"

"He was upset because I sought out Cailean's comfort rather than his. Many thanks to you, Kyla."

Kyla nodded. "Fall in love slowly," she said with a smirk.

She snorted. "Too late for that."

"Tell me how he's been with Cailean. I'd love to hear about how he tested his sword skills."

"My sire would not allow Cailean to come along on our journey here. He had to follow us and take my father to task—show him he had sword skills."

"They actually battled? In front of you?" Kyla's eyes widened and she sat forward in the chair. "How romantic, Sorcha. He must really love you. I hope to find someone like him."

"Cailean is special. I just hope he really *is* better on the morrow." She sighed and slumped back, frustration getting the best of her.

Kyla clasped Sorcha's hand in hers. "Mayhap your sire will be kinder to him now that he was injured while saving you."

Sorcha sighed and leaned her head in her hand. "Probably not. 'Tis the fourth time Cailean has saved me. It has not softened him yet."

"But you said he gave you permission to marry."

"Aye, in two years!"

"Mayhap 'tis the only way he can handle it," Kyla whispered, causing the two of them to burst out laughing.

Once they calmed down, Sorcha said, "How are your sisters, Eliza and Maeve?"

"You mean Elizabeth? She does not like being called Eliza anymore, though Papa still calls her that sometimes. They are adjusting to Papa's illness. Maeve had him playing with her fabric puppies the other day."

"I'd like to see that," Sorcha said with a smile. "Come and get me if he does it again. I was so glad to see him."

"He's not moving around too much. I'm pleased to see him come out of his chamber, but I know he doesn't wish to lean on Mama. He waits until he can call on one of my brothers, I think. I'm surprised Mama managed to get him home, but he is stubborn. I'm sure he'll be about more often in a few days. He just does not want anyone to see him in such a weakened state. Some foolish idea about his reputation. Jake and Jamie put that idea in his head, so he's doing as they suggested."

The door opened and Finlay and Fergus, two of the Grant guards, stood there with a disheveled man wedged between them. Kyla jumped to her feet and hurried up to the door. "Art?"

"Greetings, Kyla," Finlay said. His tone changed to a sarcastic lilt. "Art has come to see Logan Ramsay. Says he has an important message. But who would believe someone like Art?" He gave the man a look of pure disgust. "Where is your sire, Sorcha?"

She pointed to the door to the solar, confusion and fear roiling inside her. This seemed important, though she wasn't sure how. The guards were treating Art with open disdain.

Kyla stood, moving toward Art. "They're in a meeting in the solar. Art, I thought you left the Grant clan?"

Art gave her a sheepish look. "I did. 'Twas not because I did not like it here. I appreciated the clan, but 'twas time for me to see more of England. I wished to explore Edinburgh, mayhap travel to Glasgow or London. I made a promise to Logan Ramsay, though, and I'm here to keep it." He leaned to the left to look around Kyla. "Greetings, Sorcha. I did not expect to see you here. What brings you to Grant land?"

Finlay barked, "Enough chatter. Sorcha, ignore him. He's no longer a Grant." Finlay strode over to the door and knocked. When it opened, he said, "Message for Logan Ramsay."

Sorcha's father appeared in the doorway. "What is it?"

Fergus gave Art a shove, pushing him to stand in front of Logan.

Sorcha watched as her sire lifted his brow and crossed his arms. "Art. What brings you back to Grant land? The last time I saw you, you deserted your clan to stay in Edinburgh."

Art squirmed, shifting from one foot to the other under Logan's sharp gaze. "I made a promise to you, if you recall, when I decided to stay in Edinburgh." He shifted his feet. "I left the clan because I wished to explore. You let me go, but you told me that if I ever learned aught in Edinburgh about a plot against the Grants and Ramsays, I had to come tell you or you'd kill me."

"Och, so you have a bit of wisdom in you. Go on…" Logan's gaze narrowed, not a good thing in Sorcha's experience.

"I headed to Ramsay land to tell you what I've learned, but a group of travelers told me you were headed to Grant land, so I came here instead." He scratched the back of his head.

"Never mind. Out with your information. What have you discovered?"

"When I was in Edinburgh, I was at an inn when two louts were in their cups and bragging about something. They said there was a group of them gathering with big plans. They talked about Laird Grant going down—they'd taken part in the battle and thought he was dead—and said they had a bunch of warriors who were going to take over the clan."

"And how does this relate to me? You should have come straight to Robbie Grant," he said, gesturing toward Uncle Alex's brother, who stood in the back of the solar.

"I would have, except there was something else they were laughing about…"

Sorcha crept closer, wishing to hear everything Art relayed. "Go on."

He coughed, then lowered his voice. "He said they'd just come from Ramsay land. They'd pulled off a small raid to confuse the

Grants and Ramsays. But there was one more thing."

Her sire leaned forward and grabbed the man by the tunic.

Art coughed again and said, "They'd hoped to steal your daughter for themselves."

Her sire's face turned the darkest shade of red she'd ever seen. His hand was still on Art's clothing.

"Their names?" Logan growled.

"I only caught one name. They helped with the attack on the Grants only to get closer to your daughter. They wish to pay the Ramsays back, not the Grants."

"Name!" her father bellowed. Uncle Robbie and Uncle Brodie rushed out of the solar, obviously concerned they would need to intervene.

"Bearchun. I heard the smaller one call him Bearchun. I don't know the other's name." He took two steps back, pulling his tunic free with trembling hands.

Her sire said, "I know it. Bearchun and Shaw." His hand flew to the hilt of his sword. "I'll kill the bastards.

Sorcha almost fell onto the floor. She'd never have guessed. The same men who had kidnapped Jennet and Brigid were after her.

She turned and ran up the stairs to Kyla's chamber.

CHAPTER EIGHTEEN

 ⏾

SORCHA COULDN'T SLEEP. KYLA WAS sound asleep next to her in the huge bed, but she didn't have the heart to awaken her to talk.

Nay, the person she needed was Cailean.

After listening to Art talk about Bearchun and Shaw, her gut had roiled with worry for the rest of the eve. While Shaw had always seemed harmless enough, Bearchun had often looked at her strangely, the way older men often did. The kind of looks that made her desperately uncomfortable. She'd never before considered the possibility that she might have been stolen alongside Jennet and Brigid had she been with them that horrid night. She clutched a Grant plaid around her shoulders and shivered.

Kyla, who'd lingered near the solar after the incident with Art, had told her that Logan seemed disturbed and out of sorts. He'd slipped back inside the solar; Jake and Jamie had escorted Art out the door.

Climbing out of bed as softly as possible, Sorcha slid the door open just enough for her to sneak through. The passageway was empty, so she padded over to the stairs and made her way down to the healing chamber.

Her heart was full of both hope and fear. Would he be well? Would he be himself?

Grabbing a candle from the great hall, she lit it from the embers in the hearth and made her way to the chamber, opening the door and hoping he would be the only one in there. He was. Not caring about the repercussions, she moved to the side of the bed. He lay on his side, sleeping, but his mouth was tipped into a small smile, as if he were enjoying sweet dreams. All she could think of was how much she loved him, how she could not wait until they were finally married.

They were alone, so she blew the candle out and set it on the table. She lifted the covers and snuck in next to him, letting out a soft moan when she felt his heat against her. She snuggled into the crook of his arm, wishing he'd wake up but not wanting to rouse him. Then she felt a pair of warm lips on her cheek, and something else dawned on her. He didn't have on a stitch of clothing underneath the covers. Had it not been the middle of the night, she would have seen all when she'd climbed in next to him. Suddenly, she felt quite naughty and smirked.

"Greetings, sweeting. Why are you here?" His warm breath tickled her ear.

"Cailean, are you better? Can you stay awake now?"

A light snore came from his lips. He'd already closed his eyes again.

"Oh, fine. I'll sleep here with you." And though sleep had eluded her all night, she closed her eyes and instantly fell asleep.

She had no idea how long she'd been asleep when she was awakened by a hand running down her side, over to her waist, and up her middle until it cupped her breast. He groaned into her ear and she giggled, grabbing his hand and moving it back to her hip. "Do not be too sneaky, Cailean MacAdam. I know you're awake."

He chuckled. "I know, but I've been dying to touch you, feel your beautiful breasts again, and you're right here, in the dark, all alone, no sire around…" His hand came up and cupped her cheek instead. "I do not think I've ever awakened to a more pleasant sight, Sorcha. You in my bed…beautiful." His eyes closed and he fell asleep again.

At least he'd recognized her and spoken a coherent thought. In those few short moments, he'd reassured her that he would be all right. She giggled and kissed his forehead while he resumed his snoring.

A few moments later, his breathing changed. She opened her eyes and found him staring at her. He kissed her and she parted her lips for him, allowing his tongue inside to tease her. When he deepened the kiss and moved over her, she gave him all he'd given her, dueling her tongue with his until they were both breathless.

He brought his lips down to her neck, kissing a path down to the bone above her chest, causing a sigh of pleasure to escape her lips as she tugged him closer, reveling in the hardness she felt against her belly.

She wanted him so much, wanted to feel every inch of his skin against hers, to explore him while he explored her. She was so anxious for them to be able to show their love for each other as married couples did. She'd heard so much from Lily and others.

She nibbled on his ear and whispered, "Make love to me, Cailean."

A light appeared inside, just bright enough for them to see something shiny. "You do and I'll skin you and leave the rest of you for the vultures."

Her sire.

She bolted out of bed and yelled, "Papa. What are you doing?"

"I think that question is better aimed at you and Cailean. Mayhap I'll get the priest and he'll marry you right now."

"Nay. Papa, put your dagger away."

Cailean struggled to stand, then fell back into the bed because he had no clothes on. He grabbed at the covers, glancing back and forth between Sorcha and her sire. "I didn't know, I do not remember how I got here. Sorcha, forgive me. Where am I?" He fumbled to cover himself, staring at her father all the while.

"Do not play the fool with me, MacAdam. You'll marry her right now. I'll scream and bellow until someone fetches a priest to marry you."

"Agreed. Naught would make me happier than for Sorcha to be my wife. I've asked you. I'll marry her this verra moment if 'tis what you want, Ramsay. 'Tis what I want, and I think 'tis what Sorcha wants."

Sorcha was furious. "Papa, I wish to speak with you alone."

Her father grabbed the nearby plaid and threw it at Cailean. "Get out, MacAdam. My daughter and I need to have a conversation."

Cailean glanced at her. "Sorcha, are you sure you do not want me here?"

"Go, please. This is between my sire and me. I've had enough of his accusations."

He grabbed the plaid and the blanket and made his way out the door, stumbling twice.

As soon as he was gone, her hands moved to her hips. "Papa, what is wrong with you? We're getting married. You said we could."

Her father covered his face with his hands, growling with frustration, and then dropped them to his sides. "You're getting married today so I do not have to deal with this anymore."

"Nay, I'm not, Papa. I'll not marry without Mama and my sisters here. I do not care how angry you are with me. I'll not do it without Mama."

"Angry with you? You are my wee lassie, and you'll always be my wee lassie. Have I not told you that before? Do you think 'tis easy for me to stand by and watch that big brute paw my wee lassie?"

"Papa, he's not pawing me, I'm pawing *him*."

A huge bellow erupted from her sire's mouth as he reached up to tug on his hair.

"I love you, Papa. Why are you so upset with me? Do you not want me to be happy?"

He stopped his bellowing instantly. "Upset with you? I'm not upset with you." But his actions belied his words. His hands fisted and he spun away from her, pacing in his usual fashion when he was upset.

"All you do of late is yell at me." She could feel the tears pricking her eyes as she stared at her father.

He stopped in front of her. "Lassie, where are you getting these foolish ideas?" His voice softened.

"Papa, you've done nothing but yell at me since Molly left. Why? He shook his head, unable to speak.

"Do you not recall the day you sent me away because you wished to speak to Molly alone? It seems I've upset you ever since that moment."

Her father sat down on the edge of the bed, his hands covering his eyes as he took a deep breath. He held his hand out to her. "Come here, please, Sorcha." He tugged her over until she sat down next to him.

Tears slid down her face. She'd said everything that had been in her heart for the last year, and she felt a bit relieved. Her father took her hand and cocooned in his own hands. "Sorcha, do you know why I sent you away that day?"

"Nay. All I know is that every time I'm near a lad, you get angry.

It upsets you to see me with Cailean. I thought you wished for me to marry someday." She swiped at the tears drenching her cheeks.

He turned to her and lifted her gaze to his. "Do you know why I sent you away that day?" he repeated.

She shook her head, her hitching breath preventing her from speaking. "Why?"

"Because Molly needed me more than you did. She had verra little love in her life for so long. I was trying to help her believe in herself. You've never had trouble with that. Aye, I've been selfish, but 'tis hard for me to see all my daughters leave me. You are my wee lassie. You are generous and caring, and I don't wish to share you...especially with a lad."

"What?"

"I'm being selfish." He groaned. "I knew this day would come. I knew I'd have to give you to another man someday, but he needed to be as special as you are. It would frustrate me if the man you chose didn't appreciate you."

"Papa, Cailean does. He loves me." She rested her hand on his shoulder and kissed his cheek. "He would never disrespect me, Papa."

"I'm beginning to see that. He does care for you verra much. But he had to prove to me that he would risk his life for you."

"And did he?" She gazed up at her sire, staring into the green eyes so much like her own.

"Aye, He did. Twice. The poor lout took a beating for you twice."

He wrapped his arm around her and she rested her head on his shoulder. "I'm scared, Papa. I heard what Art said about Bearchun and Shaw, and I couldn't sleep. I came down to check on Cailean because I needed to see him. It worried me when he wouldn't wake up before. 'Struth is when I first came in, he was still acting a wee bit daft from the potion and he fell right back asleep. So I climbed in next to him. It wasn't his fault. He hardly knows where he is."

"I suspected as much. I thought you wouldn't be able to sleep, so I came down here to see you. I expected you'd be sitting in front of the hearth. It does hurt my pride just a wee bit that you went to MacAdam instead of me, but you're growing up, lass. I need to accept that."

"I love him, Papa. He treats me well, and he makes me laugh, and he makes me feel safe."

"Uncle Brodie thinks you've picked a fine man, and I can't argue with his assessment. When I saw Cailean dive over the embankment for you, I was grateful. I do not care to think about what would have happened to you if you'd gone over alone."

"He saved me, Papa. I don't think I would have stopped on that ledge. His size kept us from plunging over it. 'Twas the worst experience of my life."

"I don't think I've ever been more afraid than when we pulled that rope up and it had broken off. MacAdam's a good man. I like the idea of two men protecting my wee lassie. Aye, I'm pleased with your choice."

"And we can wait until we get home to wed so Mama and my sisters can be there, and Gavin?"

"Aye, we'll wait."

"And you'll stop threatening Cailean's life?"

"I'll agree if you agree to stay out of his bed. I cannot handle seeing that."

"Agreed."

He pulled her in close and kissed her forehead. "I love you, Sorcha. Never forget that. And I'm right proud of you, too."

"I love you, too."

He helped her to her feet and they left the chamber together, his arm around her shoulders. Cailean bounded off the stool he sat on, almost tipping over.

Her sire strode over to him and said, "We'll wait until we return to Ramsay land for your marriage, MacAdam."

"Aye, my lord."

"If I haven't thanked you properly, I'll say it now. I'm grateful for what you did for my daughter on the trail. I gained a few more gray hairs from that episode."

Cailean nodded, his eyes trying to focus on them. He was clearly still woozy.

"Go back to bed, MacAdam. But you're going alone."

Sorcha giggled. "Sleep well, Cailean." She stood on her tiptoes and kissed his cheek.

Cailean moved away from them toward his chamber, but walked into the door first, banging his head.

"Cailean?" She watched him make a slow turn to them, but it

was obvious he was struggling to focus. "Papa, help him get back to bed."

Cailean held his hand up. "I'm fine. I'm almost there." He walked into the wall.

"Papa? You or me?"

Her father sighed and said, "You go to *your* bed. I'll make sure he gets to his."

She watched her father go after him. Just about to head up the stairs, she turned when the door opened, a cold wind catching her in the face. "Molly!" she screamed, running over to greet her sister. "Greetings, Tormod."

Her sire came out of the healer's room and caught sight of his eldest daughter. "Molly? What brings you two here in the middle of the night?"

Molly waited until she was closer to speak, but her furrowed brow indicated the news would not be welcome. "There is much going on in Edinburgh, Papa," she finally said. "Glenn of Buchan is stirring things up, and we've heard other names tossed about."

Sorcha's shoulders slumped. She didn't want to hear any more bad news. She wished to run off to a land where she could marry Cailean and they could all live forever.

CHAPTER NINETEEN

SIMON DE LA PORTE STALKED through the bailey toward the Buchan great hall, the laird running to catch up with him.

"What is your assessment? How battle ready are they?" Glenn asked.

"I need another fortnight with them. How many men are we going up against?" He wiped the sweat on his brow with his sleeve before spitting on the ground.

"My most recent report tallies the Grant at nearly five hundred."

De La Porte stopped in his tracks. "They did not lose many in the battle with Duncrub then, did they? We cannot take on more than one hundred at best. Do you have enough coin for me to bring in another two hundred of my mercenaries from England? The men thirst for the blood of battle, but they do require some payment."

"Aye, I have plenty of coin. Bring them in. With three hundred, we might have a chance."

"Believe me, two hundred of my men can handle four hundred Highlanders. We'll make a short battle of it with those odds."

Once inside the hall, Glenn of Buchan pointed at the few stragglers at the tables, signaling for them to leave. They immediately scooted around the two men.

"We have another problem," Simon stated.

"What is it?"

"A couple of the Ramsay guards we had have disappeared."

"Which ones?"

"Bearchun is the only name I recall. I think there were one or two others. Could they have been spies for the Ramsay?"

"Bearchun? Nay," Glenn scoffed. "He has revenge in his heart. He wants the lassies—two of them to be specific. Mayhap they've come to the same conclusion we have. With Alexander Grant down, the two clans are in turmoil. Mayhap he's made his own plans for taking what he wants."

La Porte spat again, his favored way of expressing his opinion, or so it would seem. "Forget them. We don't need them."

Two men opened the door to the hall, stopped when they noticed it empty except for two men.

"What is it, Earc?" Glenn yelled.

"We heard some news. Thought we would advise you of a recent development."

"What is it?"

"Bearchun and Shaw have headed to Grant land alone."

☾

Cailean awakened the next day with visions of Sorcha in his bed. Scratching his head, he glanced around the chamber, looking for any evidence that what he recalled had really happened, but he saw nothing.

Swinging his legs over the side of the bed, groaning from the pain, he rose to his feet. There was an urn of water on a chest, so he poured it into a bowl to clean up. Once he finished his ablutions, he decided he felt well enough to go into the great hall. His head was clear, which he hadn't experienced since the accident.

He had to find Sorcha to ask her if she had really been in his bed last night. Immediately after that thought, a vision of Logan Ramsay with a dagger in his hand filled his mind, but he prayed *that* hadn't happened.

He found his clean plaid and tunic, so he dressed—an arduous procedure, especially getting on his boots—and moved out to the hall. As soon as he stepped into the hall, the gentle timbre of conversation changed to silence, and all heads turned his way.

Sorcha hurried toward him. He noticed her sire also at the table, Logan's gaze inscrutable as he stared at him. Cailean kissed Sorcha, a chaste kiss for her sire's benefit—and since he wished to live—but took her hand to make his way over to join the small group eating. Kyla was there, along with the Grant's brother Brodie and a few others.

A bowl of porridge appeared in front of him, and he almost drooled. Had he eaten anything at all yesterday?

Brodie said, "Lad, you look as though you have not eaten in days and someone placed a slab of beef in front of you. 'Tis only a bowl of porridge, but eat up. Looks like you could use it. I think you better bring the man another trencher full," he said to the serving lass with a grin. "This one will be gone in two bites."

"You look better today, Cailean," Kyla said. "How is your head?"

He took a bite of the porridge and mumbled, "Much improved."

Logan had a wild smirk on his face when he asked, "Any memories of last night?"

"Papa. Leave him be." Sorcha reached for his hand under the table.

He glanced at her and whispered, "Should I? Mayhap...I'm not sure."

"Ignore my father." She waved her hand at her sire to hush him. Logan laughed, good-naturedly enough, and got up from the bench.

"Have I missed aught? Seems as though I've been asleep for days." He finished the one bowl and reached for the extra trencher the serving lass had brought out for him.

Sorcha replied, "Only that Art showed up on Grant land yesterday looking for my sire."

"Art? Who is Art?" He continued to shovel in the porridge in as fast as he could.

Logan strolled back toward their bench. "Art is a lad with no backbone. He deserted the Grant clan in Edinburgh. A group of warriors, Grants and a few members of my family, were on a mission to take down Ranulf MacNiven. I made Art promise to find me if he should hear of any threats against the Ramsays or the Grants." He cleared his throat and glanced around at the rest of the group before he spoke. "Art informed us that Bearchun is still thirsty for revenge."

Cailean bolted out of his seat, a fury in his countenance. "Bearchun? Was it Bearchun and Shaw who were trying to hurt Sorcha?" Bearchun was a twisted fool, one who had no honor. He'd had the nerve to kidnap two wee lassies and hand them over to one of the most wicked villains in the history of the Scots. Everyone in the clan knew that wee Brigid still occasionally suf-

fered nightmares. Underhanded and deceitful were the best words
he could think of to describe him. He'd kill the bastard with his
bare hands, twist his neck until his eyes popped out of his head.

Logan held his hand up. "Calm down, lad. Sit and eat. You'll
feel better with a full belly. Shaw has not been seen for sure yet.
Molly and Tormod also arrived last night. They came with news
about the unrest in the Highlands, and we'll be investigating further today."

The door flew open and two of the Grant guards stood in the
entranceway, blocking the door.

Brodie jumped to his feet, but Logan was twice as fast. He was
already approaching the two men. "What is it?" he asked.

"Two men have been caught on the periphery of Grant land.
They wear no plaid and have five guards with them. Some of them
carry bows. Our guards have detained them, but they claim they're
only scouts and there are another hundred guards to follow them.
Robbie's on his way now with a few men."

"Where are they holding them?" Brodie asked.

"Near the fork in the stream at the southwest corner."

Logan almost ran out the door, but he stopped himself with visible effort, "Any other information as to their identity?" he asked
the man.

"One's called Shaw."

"Is Bearchun with him?"

"Nay, we questioned them all—no Bearchun."

Cailean bolted off the bench so fast, it fell backward, knocking
the rest of them to the floor. He lifted Sorcha up and set her on
the table. "I have to go."

He kissed her and took off in a rush. She yelled after him,
"Cailean, you aren't well enough to fight yet," but her words didn't
stop him.

"The hell I'm not. I'll kill the bastard with my bare hands. If
Shaw is here, Bearchun can't be far. They're cousins. They were
never apart in their time with our clan." He followed Logan out
the door, reacting before the other lads could.

Logan looked back over his shoulder at Sorcha, waiting for the
other men. "That's my lad. We'll take care of him for you, Sorcha.
I have several ideas for the sneaky bastard Bearchun myself. I wondered how long it would be before he would resurface. I can be a

patient man when I need to be."

Cailean could tell he was not in his usual condition, but he had to be there when they questioned Shaw. He'd make the man pay for the anguish he'd put Sorcha through with the arrow attacks.

Of course, the former Ramsay guards had also stolen Jennet and Brigid. The Ramsays had waited a long time to encounter these men. Cailean was grateful he would be there. He'd twist Shaw's neck until he confessed all, and then he'd break it for sure. Then he'd find Bearchun and do the same to him. He was building toward a state of anger he hadn't experienced recently, but it did not matter. He passed Alan along the way and motioned for him to follow the group headed to the stables.

Alan called to him from behind. "Where are you all headed?"

"Bearchun and Shaw are trying to get to Sorcha."

Alan said, "Shite. I'm coming with you. I want to be there when you question them."

"You better hurry because I'll not slow, but stay in the background. You've already been hurt once. I want to kill that bastard slowly once he tells the truth of what he did."

Cailean paused only when he made it to the stables.

The horses were saddled and ready in no time, so he mounted his horse and flicked the reins. He slowed enough to allow Logan and Brodie and a few other Grants to get ahead of him, just then realizing he had no idea where the stream was other than southeast. In his present condition, his mind was still muddled enough that he wasn't sure he could find southeast.

Logan turned back to him from his horse. "If you feel weakened, you need to stand back. Do not allow your fury to slow us in this quest. I know you want your hands on the bastards, but you may not be capable of it yet. I'll handle them."

He nodded to his future father-in-law, though he knew he'd never stand back. It just wasn't his nature. When someone he loved was threatened, he would do aught he could to protect them.

A quarter of an hour passed and they still plunged ahead. Cailean swept his gaze across the sea of horses headed out to greet the two men and their scant guards. Suddenly, he had a bad feeling in his gut. There were so many guards traveling with them that he couldn't help but wonder who had stayed behind to protect Sorcha. Of course, she didn't need protecting if the two louts were being held, but was it possible Bearchun had gotten past the guards before his friends were caught? Could he have gotten inside the curtain wall in all the confusion?

What if he'd headed straight toward the keep? What if...? He turned around to glance behind him, surprised to see a slew of horses there. Aye, there were far too many of them. True, there would be guards left outside the gate, but had anyone gone inside to protect the lasses?

They'd left Sorcha and Kyla alone, or near to it.

"Alan, I'm going back. You go with the others—you know the questions to ask him."

"What's wrong? You hale?"

"Aye, but I have a bad feeling. I'm returning to make sure Sorcha is safe. Go in my place. I want you to tell me all. You know what happened when we were attacked. Do not accept their lies."

Alan nodded, so Cailean turned his horse around.

A feeling deep in his gut told him he had to get back to Sorcha.

CHAPTER TWENTY

T HE HALL FELT CAVERNOUSLY EMPTY after the men left. Sorcha rubbed her arms, covered in chill bumps.

"I'm going up to the parapets. Mama and Papa are already there. 'Tis Papa's favorite place and I'm like my da," Kyla said. "I love to watch the guards head out on their horses. Want to come along, Sorcha?"

"Nay, I'll stay by the hearth, await their return."

"May I come along, Kyla?" the serving girl asked. "I've never been up there before."

"Of course. Sorcha, we'll be back when they return. 'Tis a nice day to be up there." At the top of the stairs, she shouted down, "Join us if you change your mind."

Sorcha waved in acknowledgment as she watched them run up the staircase. Once they disappeared from sight, she turned to face the door so she would see anyone that entered. How she wished Cailean had stayed behind. Staring at the rafters, she realized how much she disliked the hall when she was alone—it was much too large and every sound echoed.

She shivered, staring at the door. It was so quiet, she heard the door to the parapets slam shut when Kyla and Fiona finally climbed up the stairs way at the end of the passageway. Though she would be loath to admit it, she didn't enjoy heights.

A while later, a sound came from behind her and she bolted out of her chair.

"Greetings, my love."

She stared, a sick feeling welling in the pit of her stomach. How she wished Cailean had stayed behind with her. What in the hell was this man doing here? She knew him, but…

"Are you not pleased to see me again?" He moved to her side and reached out to run his finger down her cheek, but she pulled back.

Apparently, that was the wrong thing to do. He grabbed her wrist, jerking her forward until she was close enough to see the coldness in his eyes, but they turned warm again in a second. Almost…hungry.

"Aw, do not fear me, dear Sorcha." He glanced around the hall again. "We're going to take a wee trip together." He tugged her over to the door, then peeked outside before nudging it shut again. He stood to the side of the door, grabbed a weapon from the wall, and held her in front of him with his hand over her mouth.

"Say a single word and I'll slice your neck."

The door burst open and Cailean flew in past them. "Sorcha?"

The lout reached out and clobbered Cailean over the head, knocking him out. He dropped the weapon and pulled her behind him toward the staircase.

"Cailean! Wake up. Please!" She ran backward, fighting the fool all the way.

"No one is here to save you, so you'll go with me through the tunnels beneath the castle. I have men and horses awaiting us. Now move along."

He shoved her up the staircase and she struggled against him, even biting him at one point. He took a swing at her, catching her on her cheek. "It doesn't have to be this way. Now move up the stairs."

"Nay. You'll not make me go." She kicked his shin and he swore again.

"Come along willingly, or I'll go back and stab your lover. I've seen enough of him. He was always with you in the forest. Always. Now, make your choice."

Kill Cailean? Nay, she couldn't risk it. She'd go along with the lout, hoping either Cailean or her sire would follow them and save her. "I'll be agreeable."

"Good, up to the laird's chamber and the tunnel entrance."

Just before they entered the chamber with the tunnel, Sorcha decided to make one last attempt to escape. She leaned over the railing and shouted, "Cailean. The tunnel!"

The man grabbed her and shoved her into the chamber so hard, she fell onto her knees. Yanking on her hair, he tugged her to her feet and shoved her toward the tunnel entrance. "Open it."

She did as she was told, deciding she had no choice. Cailean would wake up and realize she was missing. He and her sire would save her—surely they would.

"You lead the way. I'll stay in the back in case your foolish lover follows us. Just push everything out of the way. There's naught that can hurt you. Go down the steps carefully." She swung at the cobwebs slapping her in the face as they descended the stairs into the tunnel.

"The spiders are not going to drop on you as you walk," he said roughly. Once they reached the bottom, he shoved her to the side. "I've changed my mind. I'll lead you or we'll never get there."

He grabbed her hand and she did her best to follow along behind him.

"Why are you doing this?"

He stopped abruptly and turned to face her. "Why? Because I detest your sire. Can you believe that I found others who hate Logan Ramsay as much as I do?" He smirked and leaned closer to her. "We have this all planned out," he whispered in her ear. "Especially who gets you first. *Me.*" His eyes widened with glee. "I insisted. I cannot wait to take you in front of your sire. We'll truss him up, and then he'll get to watch all we do with you. He deserves it for treating me the way he did."

Horror washed through Sorcha, weakening her knees, but she forced herself to walk. If he carried her, it would be harder to escape.

He led the way through the dark tunnel, only bits of light coming through this rock or that. The candle he'd brought had almost extinguished. "I could understand your infatuation with that big brute MacAdam, but what the hell did you see in Baltair? The lad is just that—a lad, not a man. He's also an ugly clod, but as soon as he showed you how to shoot, you could not stop blathering around him. That was disgusting, I might add. I had to put a stop to him."

"You? 'Twas you who shot at me?"

"Aye. At first my only plan was only to track you, but after watching you with some of those fools on Ramsay land, I decided

I had to put an end to some of them." She had been right about the attacks. This man had been aiming his arrows not at her, but at the men around her. Somehow the thought brought her little satisfaction.

Sorcha closed her eyes and said a quick prayer. *Please, Lord. Wake him up. Cailean, hurry!*

The worst thing possible happened. They rounded a bend and up ahead, sunlight peered through various cracks in the wooden door. They were almost at the end of the tunnel.

If this man got her on his horse, they would never find her.

☾

Cailean woke up, uncertain of where he was. He pushed himself up, then grabbed his throbbing head with one hand and his sword with the other. The huge bump in the back was undoubtedly the cause of his pounding headache.

Sorcha.

He stood up, glancing wildly around the area. Kyla came down the staircase, the serving girl behind her.

"Where's Sorcha?" Kyla asked.

"I'm not sure." He rubbed his hand across his brow, hoping to slow the pounding.

"Cailean, you have a huge bump on the back of your head," Kyla cried out. "You're bleeding. What happened?"

Memories popped back into his mind. "I came into the hall and noticed 'twas empty. Then I was hit with something from behind and I collapsed. It must have been Bearchun."

"Bearchun? How?"

"I don't know, but he has Sorcha. Where?"

Kyla squealed. "Nay, oh my, nay! Sorcha, dear Sorcha. Where would he have taken her?"

A memory of Sorcha yelling something to him popped into his mind. He'd awakened enough to hear her voice. "The tunnel. Where is your escape tunnel, Kyla?"

"Up in my parents' old chamber," she said in a small voice.

Cailean followed Kyla up the staircase and into the chamber. The door leading to the tunnel was gaping open.

"Cailean, we have to go after her," Kyla said, looking at him with huge eyes.

"Nay, you and Fiona get help. Tell anyone you can find where
I've gone. I have my sword. I'll get him, but my head hurts. I'll take
any help I can get."

Cailean grabbed a tallow and hurried down the steps into the
dark. They'd definitely gone in ahead of him because the cobwebs
had already been cleared out. Whenever he came to a break in the
tunnel, he bent down to see which direction the footprints followed. Every time he stood up, his head roared with pain, but he
kept his mouth shut so as not to let on that he was there.

Eventually, he'd have to extinguish his light, loath that he was to
do it, but he could not risk letting Bearchun know he was behind
him. He crept along the narrow passageway, an occasional critter
brushing against his feet, but he never slowed.

Much as his head pounded, he would not stop until he had his
beloved Sorcha in his arms again. Surprised that he came upon
the end of the tunnel so quickly, he extinguished his candle and
slowly approached the door. It had been left open just a touch, so
he peeked out in the hopes he would see the villain who'd dared
to touch his lass.

Shocked at what he saw in front of him, he paused for a moment
before charging out the door after them. One man stood with
Sorcha in his line of sight.

It wasn't Bearchun after all...

CHAPTER TWENTY-ONE

ᛆ

CAILEAN BARRELED THROUGH THE OPENING, unsheathing his sword as fast as he could. "Art, let her go." He'd never seen the man before, but it could only be him. He had come to the castle to misdirect them—and he'd succeeded.

In one quick movement, Art spun Sorcha around and held her in front of him, his dagger at her throat. "Leave us be, MacAdam. I'm taking her away from here."

Apparently, his guess to the man's identity was correct. Cailean saw the fear in Sorcha's eyes and willed her to be strong. He caught her gaze, trying to tell her without words that he loved her and wouldn't let her go.

"Then why did you try to kill her?"

He'd keep him talking, hoping her sire or any of the Grants would follow them through the tunnel or circle around the bend. If Art managed to get her on that horse, Cailean had no way to follow him.

"I was having some fun by taking shots at her possible lovers. You were the only one I missed every time. My disagreement is with Logan Ramsay. He was a bastard to me in Edinburgh, and I swore I'd make him pay. She's just a wee extra piece of pleasure."

Two other lads appeared from around the corner—Bearchun and Shaw—each leading a horse.

Art grinned. "Imagine my surprise when I met these two and discovered they were equally as hungry for revenge. Set your weapon down, fool. You cannot take on three of us, but I'll leave you alive to pass a message on to Logan. Tell him to come and find his sweet daughter. He can watch the three of us enjoy her, then mayhap we'll set her free. What better way to take revenge on the man than to enjoy his beautiful daughter before we kill him?" He ran his hand down Sorcha's breast and she squealed. "He can bring all the Grant guards he wishes. We'll hide her and you'll not find her if you kill us all. Only when we make arrangements to meet with him alone will he have a chance to get her back…after we're done with her, of course. A few more of our men are awaiting our instructions."

Cailean was desperate to kill them all right then and there, slowly and with his bare hands. He gritted his teeth, watching the point of the dagger at her throat.

"Drop your weapon, or I'll cut her throat," Art said.

Cailean couldn't do it. If he lost his weapon, he'd be powerless to help her. He had no horse and only his sword.

Shaw climbed on his horse and said, "I'll ride ahead to make sure all is clear for our plan."

"Go ahead. We'll not need you here to help with this one. He's no fighter. He can hardly focus. Got a headache, my friend?" Art sneered.

Cailean swayed by accident, and Art's knife pricked Sorcha's tender skin in reaction to the movement, sending a slender trickle of blood down her neck.

As soon as he saw the blood on her neck, Cailean dropped his sword. "All right. You win, Art. Don't hurt her." He had to believe someone would be able to follow them on horseback and that the Grants would help him catch the fools. He had to have faith they would find her before these louts could hurt her.

In the meantime, as much as it pained him, he had no choice but to let them go. If this daft man cut her throat, all would be lost.

Once he dropped his sword, Art said, "Wise man. Bearchun, are you ready?"

Bearchun strolled up next to Art, leading his horse behind him. "Hand her over," he said to Art. "Time to take our leave."

In a matter of seconds, Bearchun reached for Sorcha and tossed her up onto his horse, then mounted behind her. Art mounted his own steed and they all took off, their laughter ringing out behind them.

"I love you, Sorcha," Cailean yelled, "I'll find you." He chased them as far as he could to see what direction they were headed.

Art smirked and dug his heels into his horse.

Cailean picked up his sword and ran back to the tunnel. He opened the door, shouting inside. "Anyone there?" Then he realized his efforts were fruitless because anyone in the tunnel would be equally helpless.

He needed a horse. The sound of a horse's hooves could be heard in the distance—in the opposite direction of the one Art had taken with Sorcha. Cailean raced through the trees into a clearing, pleased to see Logan Ramsay heading for him, followed by several more guards. He waved his arms, "Over here, over here!"

Logan drew his horse up and yelled, "Where is she?"

Cailean didn't hesitate. He ran over to the horse and yanked on Logan's leg hard enough to topple him off the horse. When Logan stood up to argue with him, Cailean said, "Sorry, my lord." He promptly punched him in the face, knocking him to the ground. He mounted and took off in the direction that Art had gone.

He heard Ramsay cursing at him from behind, and he called back, "Art's in league with Bearchun and Shaw, and they have Sorcha. And they want you, but we've no time to chat." He wanted Logan to know who the kidnappers were right away. It had been a surprise to him. Yet he did not want to give them what they wanted, and that was Logan Ramsay.

Cailean moved his horse as fast as he could, picking up Art and Bearchun's trail. True, he'd just made a big mistake and would pay for it later, but his need to get to Sorcha had outweighed every other consideration. Logan Ramsay could beat him to a pulp and he'd allow it—so long as Sorcha was safe.

He had to capture them first.

It didn't take long for him to catch up to them. Art had chosen a well-worn path that slowed him considerably. Cailean knew what he had to do. He'd seen Logan Ramsay hide an extra dagger in his satchel many times, the satchel that sat behind his saddle. He located the weapon, and as soon as he was close enough, he threw his dagger and caught the lout in his back, causing him to roll off the horse.

He'd kill Art first, then go after Bearchun.

By the time Cailean dismounted and ran to his side, Art had managed to stand up and unsheathe his sword.

Cailean didn't hesitate—he went at the man with all his power.

The lout was losing his strength, blood still pouring out of his wound.

"You'll never reach them in time," sneered Art.

Art made the mistake of running at him. Cailean easily knocked the weapon out of his hand, thrusting his sword into his belly in the same move. The lad fell to the ground, his eyes lifeless.

He mounted his horse and flew off in the direction of the horses' hoofprints. He had one dead and two to kill. He'd fought Bearchun and Shaw in the lists before. Shaw was no challenge, but Bearchun could be a beast. He had a mind that could spring off in strange directions, which made him hard to predict.

No matter, he'd do everything in his power to save his dear Sorcha, and he would not allow himself to think of the worst. He rode for a long while, finally accepting that he must have lost their trail. He had turned his horse around to go back when something caught him out of the corner of his eye.

Shaw was on horseback heading in the opposite direction. He was alone, Bearchun and Sorcha nowhere in sight. He made the quick decision to follow the man and choke him until he confessed where Bearchun had taken her.

Hadn't Art said they would hide her somewhere, only to reveal where when Logan came on his own?

He couldn't lose Shaw.

Cailean could tell the exact moment that Shaw had detected him—the fool spurred his horse before he even turned around to see who was behind him. But Cailean rode the mighty Logan Ramsay's mount, and his horse overtook Shaw's in no time. When he was almost upon him, he tossed his sword to the ground and jumped onto Shaw's back, taking them both off the horse and to the ground.

They landed perfectly, Shaw underneath him, though he had to roll him onto his back.

"Where is she?" Cailean bellowed, his hands around Shaw's neck.

"Go ahead and kill me. Then you'll never find her. Did you forget Art grew up on Grant land? He knows a spot hidden to all."

Cailean punched him square in the jaw. "Tell me."

Shaw spat on him. "Never."

Cailean moved off to the side and punched him twice in the belly. Shaw looked as if he was about to heave all over, so he changed tactics. "Where is she?"

"Kill me. I care not. I'll never tell you. Bearchun's the only family I have left. I'll not reveal his location or hers."

"Aye, you will."

Shaw's laugh started low, rumbled into a loud chuckle, and ended in a hoot and a guffaw that Cailean wished to beat out of him. A horrible fear took root in Cailean's mind. Would he ever hear Sorcha's laughter again?

"Where is she?" He punched Shaw in the face.

The man just shook his head and smirked.

Cailean hit him harder and knocked one of his teeth out.

Shaw smiled, spitting the tooth off to the side.

Cailean cuffed him on the side of his head—first one side, then the other—pummeling him until his eyes closed. A new fear gripped him. Had he let his anger get the better of him? "Nay, you'll not die yet, you bastard." He shook the man until his eyes opened.

Shaw's smile had slipped, and he started shaking his head.

Strands of light brown hair streaked with golden highlights filled Cailean's mind; the lilt of Sorcha's honeyed voice as she said, "I love you, Cailean." The feel of her curves in his hands, the warmth of her heart next to his, the scent of his woman—all sweetness, saltiness, and the aroma of the outdoors. The fear of losing her gripped him. "Where is she?" He pummeled and swung. "Where? Tell me or I'll kill you. Where is she?"

He sat back and pulled Shaw up by his tunic, but the man's head fell back. Cailean grabbed his hair, forcing him to look at him. "Where is she, Shaw? Or would you like to die this very moment?"

"The…"

He couldn't understand him. Shaking him again, he moved his ear toward his mouth. "Where is she?"

"The cave…"

"What cave?"

Shaw didn't respond, his eyes closing. Then he picked his head up. "He let me feel her breast before he took her away. Nice, verra nice."

Cailean hit him three more times before pulling him up. "Where is she?"

The man didn't answer, so he put his knee toward his groin, starting to press in.

Shaw's eyes flew open. "In the cave, near the burn."

He pressed again.

"Near the waterfall."

Cailean took his knee away. "Which way?"

Shaw's head lolled to the side, but he whispered, "North," before his eyes closed.

Cailean let his head drop to the ground.

He climbed onto his horse, looked at the sky and headed north.

CHAPTER TWENTY-TWO

S ORCHA HAD DONE HER BEST to keep the tears from falling, but after an hour or more, she couldn't stop them from
drenching her face.

Bearchun had left Shaw and told him to keep watch and guard
their location. Shaw had readily agreed, but as soon as they were
out of the man's hearing, Bearchun had chuckled to himself and
whispered, "Stupid fool. I'm glad to be free of you. My own cousin
thought he could tag along on my strengths and be as powerful
as I am."

Bearchun had brought her into this cave, hidden her behind a
rock, and tied her hands and feet together, barely speaking to her.
Just before he left, he halted and spun around, "Much as I'd like
to taste you myself, lass, I'm about to become one of the most
powerful men in all the land. More pressing matters await me than
revenge on your sire." He winked at her and rushed out faster than
he'd rushed in.

After struggling with her ties unsuccessfully, she'd forced herself
to scoot out from behind the rock, a slow, arduous process that had
scraped and cut her soft skin, only to find a strange hole in front
of her. She was far enough back in the cave to be in complete
darkness, so she didn't dare roll any farther. For all she knew, the
hole might be deep enough for the fall to kill her. Fortunately, the
slant of the stone had changed or she would never have noticed.

Cailean would come for her. She knew it; she just knew it.

A short time later, she heard some rustling outside, and did her
best to scream and yell through the linen gag the beast had stuffed
in her mouth. A shadow filled the opening of the cave and she

squealed because she recognized Cailean's shape.

"Sorcha?" He crept into the cave, his sword in his hand as though he expected someone to jump out at him at any moment.

When he came up to the hole, she squealed again, wishing she could tell him to stop moving. He couldn't afford any more injuries. He must have sensed something because he knelt down and ran his hand along the edge until he found it. Relief almost buckled her knees as she watched him make his way around the outside of the hole.

He tugged the gag out of her mouth and lifted her to him, crushing her against his chest. As fast as he did that, he set her back down and whispered, "Bearchun?"

She shook her head. "He's been gone for more than an hour, said he had more pressing matters ahead of him. I doubt he'll be back, he mentioned becoming the most powerful in all the land. Said he didn't care about my father." She sighed when she noticed the bump on his head, yet she was so glad to see him. "Cailean, you look terrible." She held her hands out to him and he untied her, first her hands and then her feet.

He clutched her to his chest again. "I was so frightened. Are you hurt?"

"Nay, he did not hurt me. Cailean, your hand. You're covered with blood. What happened?" She stood up and pulled him with her, deciding she wasn't sure she wished to know what had happened. He was here and Bearchun wasn't. That was what mattered. "Never mind. 'Tis of no import."

She took his hand and led him out to the waterfall, grateful it was early summer so the water would be cool but not like ice.

Outside in the sun, she peered at his hand. "Oh, Cailean." What had he done for her? He had a blank expression in his gaze, and his eyes never left hers. His plaid was covered in blood, so she removed it and tossed it aside. "Come, I'll wash you." He followed her into the small cave behind the waterfall. It was just a small one, so they could reach and wash without losing their balance.

She slid off his tunic, then stood on her tiptoes and drew him down for a kiss, teasing him with her tongue. "My thanks for saving me again."

He looked down at her, and she watched as his blank stare slid away, replaced by a look of fierce passion and deep feeling. "I love you, Sorcha," he whispered. "Never leave me?"

"Never." She pulled her gown off, tossing it onto a nearby rock, and then pulled off her chemise, too. She helped him remove his boots before she dashed beneath the brisk cool waterfall, tipping her head back to wet her hair. The need to wash Bearchun and Art off her forever was her foremost thought. Even Shaw had dared to touch her.

"Come with me, Cailean." She held her hand out to him and he joined her under the cool stream.

She held his hand gingerly under the water, the one plagued by cuts and bruises and raw knuckles, yet she still did not care to ask him why. She knew he'd done it for her and that was enough.

"Sorcha, I'm all right. Do not worry about me." He kissed her and ran his hands up and down her body, caressing her, fueling her need for him. "I cannot wait until we marry. I wish you were mine now." Once they finished washing, Cailean lifted her into his arms and carried her out to a soft spot hidden under a tree, moss-covered and private.

He gazed into her eyes and said, "I lost all sense of reason when I thought I'd lost you."

She tugged his mouth down close to hers and whispered, "Love me, Cailean. I want all of you."

Cailean set her feet down, growled and kissed her, a searing kiss of possession and love, of sudden urgency and need. He nibbled on her bottom lip, then thrust his tongue inside her mouth again, angling his lips over hers.

He ended the kiss and all she could say was, "Cailean." Her heavy breathing echoed his, and she realized she'd never before understood what want and need were. She writhed against his hardness, which stood strong against her belly, and managed to squirm until she could position that hardness exactly where she wanted it. He lifted her and settled her flat on the moss, resting on his side next to her so he could stare at her.

Her hands came up to his hair, tugging him toward her, then slid over the muscles of his back to his hips, finally settling on the strong arches of his bottom. Gripping him there, pulling him even closer, she said, "Make love to me. Make me yours, please, Cailean?"

He growled and nibbled her ear before trailing a path across her jaw and down her chest until he found the curve of her breast. He lifted the soft swell so he could take her nipple in his mouth and caress her while he raked the taut peaks with his tongue, and she responded by arching her back and thrusting herself closer to him. "More," she whimpered.

He chuckled and switched to her other soft mound, teasing the underside of her breast before taking her full in his mouth and suckling her until she cried out. His hand traveled down to the vee between her legs, teasing her, spreading her legs until he found her curls and her dampness.

His finger entered her passage and he said, "You do want me, do you not, Sorcha?"

"Aye, Cailean. No more teasing, no more leaving me aching with want and desire. Show me everything. I want you. I love you."

"You are the most beautiful creature that has ever walked this land, my sweet. You know this will hurt?"

"Aye, just finish it, please." Her hands came up to grip his biceps.

He settled himself above her, putting all his weight on his elbows. He teased her entrance, using her slickness to guide him in. She spread her legs to give him access, but also because she wanted him closer, wanted him inside her.

He gave one thrust and she felt the pinch deep inside.

"Forgive me, love. 'Twill get better. Tell me when the pain is gone."

"I care not about the pain. Please, show me."

He started slowly, a rhythmic pulsation that begged her to join him and she did, following his lead until the pressure against her woman's center drove her to seek more, pushing him faster, harder, until she crashed over the edge, screaming his name with pleasure. He didn't stop until he groaned, gripping her hips as he gave her his seed, whispering in her ear how much he loved her as he slowed, working to catch his breath.

"Now you're mine forever, and I am yours, lass."

℀

After washing Sorcha in the waterfall again, Cailean helped her dress, then looked at his plaid and tunic, both caked with blood. He could not stomach the thought of wearing either of them again.

Sorcha pointed to the horse. "My sire carries an extra plaid sometimes. 'Tis all you need. Check his satchel."

Pleased to find one, he pleated the plaid around his body, just now noticing all the bruises from his fall down the ravine and his battle with Art and Shaw. He helped her onto his horse and mounted behind her, a protective arm wrapped around her middle as he urged their horse to a trot back toward the Grant castle.

They didn't speak, both seeming to enjoy the quiet peace of the forest and their sweet uninterrupted intimacy. He caught sight of a group of horses coming in their direction. Despite what had happened earlier, Cailean actually hoped it was her sire. He had suddenly lost the strength to fight anymore.

As they moved closer, Sorcha whispered, "'Tis my sire, my cousins Loki and Jamie, and some guards."

"Good. I hope they caught Bearchun."

Once they met up with them, Logan slid from his horse and rushed over to Sorcha's side, staring up at her with concern. Cailean dismounted but left Sorcha seated. Jamie and the others rode up alongside the group.

"Sorcha, you are unhurt?" Logan bellowed.

"I am not hurt, Papa."

Logan glanced at Cailean, an unusual expression on his face, and said, "MacAdam, we found Shaw and Art, both dead, one by a sword wound, the other by direct blows. Do you know aught about it?"

Cailean nodded, and he glanced at Sorcha, reaching for her hand. "I might, my lord."

"What happened?" Logan asked.

Cailean shrugged his shoulder, his gaze on Sorcha. "They touched her. No one can touch her and get away with it. 'Tis not allowed."

Logan rubbed his chin. "Then they got what they deserved, lad. Where's Bearchun?"

Cailean turned his gaze back to the group of men. "I never found him. I was hoping you had."

Sorcha added, "He left me long ago, said he had pressing matters to attend."

"As I'm sure you've realized, Shaw was *not* at the gates," Jamie said. "Those men were paid coin to lie about their names and about the hundred warriors they claimed were behind them."

"You've not found Bearchun either?" Cailean asked, shifting his gaze to encompass the whole group.

"Nay."

Sorcha stared at her father, frowning. "Papa, what happened to you? Your eye is swollen."

He arched his brow and stared at Cailean. "You want to tell her, MacAdam, or shall I?"

Sweat came out of his pores as soon as he noticed the damage he'd done to her father. The man was bound to wake up with a black eye on the morrow. The group behind Logan could no longer keep quiet. They burst into laughter, and Jamie said, "Cailean was desperate to chase after you, so he pulled your sire off his horse, punched him, and rode off without a backward glance. Funniest thing I've ever seen."

Sorcha turned to him, her eyes wide. "Cailean, is that true?"

He nodded, a sick feeling washing over him. He may as well get it over. "Take your best shot, Ramsay. I deserve it, though I do not regret what I did." He moved Sorcha, still on the horse, off to the side and stood in front of Logan Ramsay, waiting for the fist, wherever he would land it.

Logan marched over to him, perused him from both the front and back, lifted Cailean's swollen and bloodied fighting hand and said, "I think you've taken enough abuse for my daughter. You're either completely in love or completely daft. Welcome to the family." He patted his shoulder, then headed back to his horse. "If you'd asked, I'd have given you the horse. I'm getting too old to chase after the bad ones. 'Tis about time you young ones took over."

❦

Two days later, they sat in the great hall making their plans to leave. Sorcha had enjoyed visiting with her cousins, but she was also anxious to return home. Bearchun had not been found, but it appeared he had only involved himself in the plot in order to be rid of his cousin so he could move on to something greater. They had yet to determine his destination.

"How long before you two marry?" Kyla asked.

Sorcha glanced at Cailean before she replied, "As soon as we can, depending on a few things."

"For instance?"

"What Mama says, when Molly can be on Ramsay land, when Uncle Quade and Aunt Brenna come home from Cameron land. I want everyone to be there."

Cailean leaned over and kissed the top of her head. "Whenever Sorcha's family says we can." He forced a smile at her sire. "Soon, I hope." He had his arm around her shoulder and she snuggled against him.

Caralyn entered the great hall and made her way over to them. "Cailean, I'd like to take a look at your wounds, make sure nothing has festered. I'm sure you'll be leaving soon, and I do not wish to see you travel with a fever. Would you mind coming into my healing chamber?"

Cailean shrugged his shoulders. "Sure." He dropped his hand from Sorcha's shoulder and kissed her cheek. "I'll be back shortly."

Logan growled at him.

"My lord, 'twas just a kiss on the cheek," Cailean said as he hurried off.

Kyla laughed. "I think you two should marry soon. Sorcha, will you come up to my room with me? I want to show you something."

"Sure," Sorcha replied.

She followed her cousin up the stairs. Overall, the trip had been a good one. At least the archer had been discovered, and she no longer had to worry about being hurt or stolen in the immediate future. She just wished to get married so she and Cailean could carry on with their lives together. As if needing to speak her thoughts aloud, she grumbled, "I wish my sire would stop growling at Cailean every time he touches me."

Kyla laughed. "He just loves his baby girl."

"Och, you're right. You were right before, too. He'll always see me as a bairn."

They arrived at Kyla's chamber and she pushed the door open, holding it for Sorcha. Inside, there were three gowns with matching kirtles laid out across the bed.

"What's this?" Sorcha asked.

"You've had such a hard time lately, and some of your clothing has been ruined. I would like to give you a gown. Try them on and choose your favorite."

Kyla sat in a chair while Sorcha walked over to the bed, admiring the gowns. "Kyla, your mother is such a talented seamstress. These are beautiful." She picked up a dark green gown and decided to try it on. She probably wouldn't accept the gift, but it would be fun to see how she felt in it.

Kyla helped her with the ribbons, and Sorcha straightened the skirt once it was on. "This is beautiful, Kyla." She twirled around, loving the feeling of the skirt twirling around her. "But 'tis a bit heavy for this time of year."

"Try this one on. The blue one looks more like you." She held it up for Sorcha to see it in the light of the window.

"And the fabric looks lighter." She slipped it on and sighed. "Oh, this even feels wonderful." The undergown was dark blue with a light blue kirtle, tiny beads on the bodice and golden ribbons on the back. "May I wear it for a while? I won't keep it, but 'tis so beautiful, I wish to show it to Cailean."

Kyla sat down again and said, "'Tis my gift to you. 'Tis yours to keep." She smiled, a wicked expression on her face. "Sorcha, we did this as a surprise for Gracie, but I do not want to surprise you completely. Your sire sent for a priest and you're getting married today. I think 'tis a perfect dress for you."

"I am?" Her first thought was to be excited. Finally, she would become Cailean's wife and her sire would stop growling at her. But the next thought was not so exciting. She fell onto the bed.

Kyla sat down beside her. "What's wrong? You do not wish to marry him yet?"

"I do, but I wanted everyone to be here." She couldn't explain, but it just wouldn't be right for her to marry without all of them.

Kyla strode over to the door. Before she opened it, she said, "Your sire took care of everything."

Sorcha didn't know what she meant until she opened the door and saw her mother standing there, a huge smile on her face. Molly, Maggie, Bethia, Jennet, and Brigid pushed around her mother and ran in to hug her, all babbling at once. Tears misted her eyes and she stared at her mother. "Mama, how?"

"Your father sent me a message after you arrived saying we better hurry up and get here if we wished to see you marry. He said he was going to force it soon. Your brother is downstairs with your sire."

Another face popped up over her mother's shoulder. Aunt Brenna said, "May Maddie and I join you? I wish to see the bride before she walks down the staircase."

She looked at her dear aunts and said, "Uncle Alex? Uncle Quade?" They both nodded to her.

"Uncle Alex says he feels well enough to attend. He's excited to see all the clan."

Another head appeared around the corner. "Don't forget us!" Aunt Jennie grinned and slipped into the room, Lily behind her with the twins.

Aunt Maddie said, "Uncle Alex is moving slow, but he's determined to be in the hall for the wedding."

"But how? What about Cailean?"

Kyla said, "This was all part of our plan. Uncle Logan knew everyone was almost here, so we kept Aunt Caralyn out by the gates. She pulled Cailean aside just after they arrived. She and Alan are helping him get ready. Cailean's Uncle Isaac and Uncle Quade are in the great hall now with Jake and Jamie, and Aunt Celestina and Gracie have the food all ready in the kitchens. Everyone is involved in readying the hall for you."

Sorcha plopped onto the bed and cried tears of joy. Her mother pulled her back up. "You cannot sit there. We have to do your hair. Bethia said she would fix it with curls and ribbons."

Sorcha sat in a chair and allowed everyone to fuss over her. She had never been happier to see her family together.

Molly hugged her and whispered, "You must stop crying or Cailean will think you do not wish to marry him. You are so beautiful—without the red eyes."

She laughed and used a linen square to dab her eyes.

She was about to get married.

CHAPTER TWENTY-THREE

⌐

ABOUT TWO HOURS LATER, AFTER everyone had filtered out of Kyla's chamber and down the stairs except for her mother, Sorcha decided she was ready.

"You love him verra much, do you not?" Gwyneth asked.

"I do, Mama. He's a wonderful man."

"Your sire told me the two of you had a long discussion one night."

"We did."

Her mother clasped her hands in hers and said, "You've always been the light in your father's eyes since the day you were born." She swiped at a tear on her face and continued. "You were our first. We took you everywhere with us, and you were such a happy bairn. 'Tis no wonder you're happier when you're running free and off on your own adventure. I knew it would be difficult for your father the day you fell in love, but he is happy with your choice."

"Thank you, Mama."

A loud knock sounded at the door. "Are you ready?"

She chuckled because she'd recognize that voice anywhere. "Come in, Papa."

Her sire came in wearing his leine and his blue dress plaid, his sword shining and strapped to his back for the ceremony. "Papa, you are so handsome."

"Have you changed your mind about Cailean?"

"Nay. You know I love him."

"Then let's get on with this marriage. Come, Gwynie. 'Tis time for our firstborn to move on."

She crossed the room to her father and lifted up on her tiptoes to kiss his cheek. "Thank you, Papa. For everything." She gave him a quick hug and whispered, "You know I'll always love you and Mama."

Her sire lifted his chin and cleared his throat in that gruff way he often did. "There's a man waiting for you, and he's not verra patient. He's pacing worse than I ever did."

She laughed and took his arm. "Take me to my husband."

Her parents walked behind her as she floated down the staircase, her gaze on Cailean at the base of the stairs. She took a moment to glance around at all her family, wishing she had a way to preserve them in her memory just as they were at that moment. No matter, it would be in her heart forever.

She took Cailean's arm and he escorted her over to Father MacKenny. They said their vows, though she remembered little of the ceremony later, only noticing the sensation of her small hand tucked inside Cailean's large, warm one, the Ramsay plaid wrapped around them.

When Father MacKenny said, "Kiss your bride, Cailean," her father let out a large growl to get everyone laughing, and Cailean cupped her face and kissed her tenderly. She gazed into his eyes and knew that she would love this man forever.

◖

While Cailean's relationship with Sorcha's father had improved, he was anxious about their upcoming wedding night. What if Logan insisted on the traditional bedding ceremony and waited for the blood-stained sheets to appear?

Which was exactly why Cailean had set out to find some help amongst the clan after learning of the surprise wedding. Brodie Grant had advised him they'd set up a cottage for their wedding night, but while he'd sworn no one would reveal its location to Sorcha's sire, Cailean was still unconvinced. His brother agreed. Together, they had sought out Loki's help, and Loki and his son Kenzie had come up with the perfect plan. It involved many of the others, all of whom had agreed to help.

At the end of the feast, Jake and Jamie came to the center of the hall and made an announcement.

"In honor of this wonderful celebration, we've decided to try our hand at the Highland Sword Dance, the *Ghillie Callum*. Please join us in the courtyard, where a number of our guards will be participating in the dance. At the end, we will bring the bride into the dance."

Cailean squeezed Sorcha's hand and led her out to the courtyard, the excitement growing in the crowd. They'd not seen it done before, but Jamie and Loki knew of it and had suggested it could be designed exactly to suit their needs.

On their way out, Logan fell in next to them. "I'm verra interested in this dance," he said. "I've heard of it before but never participated. I'll be pleased to watch this eve."

When they were ready, Cailean moved to the center of the crowd and turned to face Jake and Jamie. Together, as the acting lairds, they set Art's sword on the ground in the center of the area. The pipe music from the musicians began to flow freely, and Cailean stepped forward and set his sword over Art's, indicative of the winning of the battle. He then called several other guards forward to dance beside him.

What followed was an intricate pattern of warriors weaving in and around the swords, being certain to neither touch the weapons nor turn their backs to them, indicative of how they would treat any villain. Near the end of the dance, he held his hand out to Sorcha and she joined him, weaving and dancing around the weapons.

The final part of the dance took place with the other guards all raising their swords in a salute to the married couple.

When the musicians finished, Cailean lifted his sword in exultation and a horse was brought to the center of the gathering while the others kept their swords in the air. He sheathed his own sword, jumped onto the horse, and Gavin lifted Sorcha in front of him. He turned the horse around and headed toward the gates, the couple's hands raised in a wave to the crowd.

Logan Ramsay headed toward the horse. "Stop, MacAdam. No one gave you permission to leave with my daughter yet. 'Tis too early for the wedding night, and we must talk before you're allowed to touch her."

All around him, grins and laughter exploded as Logan did his best to stop the couple before they left the crowd. He broke into a run toward the gate but suddenly found himself stopped by a line of Ramsay and Grant warriors, all holding their swords and wearing grins.

"What the hell is this? Are you all going to spear me with your swords?" His look of astonishment fueled the crowd even more.

Cailean slowed his horse, wanting to make sure everything went as planned.

Sorcha whispered, "He'll stop in a moment, Cailean. Do not worry." She squeezed his hand.

"Let her go, Ramsay," Brodie Grant yelled. "She's married and he's a good man."

"Sorcha, do not go out those gates before I talk to him."

Logan again moved toward the gate, but the line closed in around him.

"Och, you think any of you will stab me? You're all part of my *clann*. I don't think so." He moved toward the line in front of him and was just about to walk through it when three people came from behind and grabbed him: Loki, Connor, and Magnus.

"Let me free, you wee bastards." Logan kicked and squirmed.

Loki said, "Go, Kenzie. Tie him up."

Kenzie hurried over with a rope in his hands, his eyes darting back and forth between his sire and his uncle. "Forgive me, Uncle Logan. They're making me do it."

Cailean understood exactly how the lad felt.

At the last moment, someone pushed Kenzie to the side and said, "I'll do it or the poor lass will never have her wedding night."

Logan's eyes widened and he stopped kicking. "Gwynie? Even you?"

She sighed. "Aye, Logan. Leave the young ones be. You'll not lose her."

Cailean brought their horse back over to the melee so his wife could say her good-byes for the night.

"I love you, Papa!" Sorcha shouted over the clamor and the clip-clopping of the horse's hooves across the cobblestones.

Cailean hollered, "I promise we'll return on the morrow."

The pair rode off into the hills of the Highlands, cheers erupting behind them. The only voice that could be heard was one, and only one word echoed out over the land: Logan Ramsay shouting, "MacAdam!"

EPILOGUE

B EARCHUN BROUGHT HIS HORSE TO a halt in front of the gates. The guards said, "State your business."

Bearchun yelled, "I need to speak with Glenn of Buchan."

"I doubt he wishes to see you. You left your assignment."

"Trust me," Bearchun drawled. "I have information he'll wish to hear.

"Wait here." The guard left and returned a few moments later. "He'll see you in his solar."

Bearchun moved inside the gates, dismounted, and handed the care of his horse over to two stable lads. He strode through the courtyard, all eyes on him, and he stared down any who dared look at him.

Once inside the hall, he was escorted into the solar. As soon as they entered, Buchan stood, "I should have you flayed in front of the crowd."

Bearchun retorted, "Do that and you won't hear the most important news you could get all year. Something no one else could tell you. You'd be a fool to lose me now. We left to assist a friend, knowing we could gain more information for you."

"And where is Shaw?"

"Shaw won't be returning. He lost his life to a verra good effort."

Simon de La Porte sat in a chair against the wall, his arms folded across his chest. "What do you want?"

"I want to be in your favored guard, paid coin as your guards from England will be, and I wish to go to London when this is done."

"And how do I know your information is worth it?"

"You don't. But I'm telling you, Buchan, it's the best news you could possibly ask for."

Simon looked at Glenn, who paused for a long moment to stare at the two of them, and then nodded.

"Agreed. What's the news?"

"There's a wedding. Most of the Ramsays are on Grant land for it."

"Which ones?" Glenn's beady eyes lit up.

"Quade and his wife, Logan and his wife, all his children. But the best of all?"

De La Porte said, "We're waiting."

"Alex Grant is back home, and he's unable to fight."

Simon stood, grinning from ear to ear. Glenn of Buchan tossed his head back and laughed and laughed and laughed. When he finally was able to stop, he uttered one word.

"Perfect."

~ THE END ~

NOVELS BY KEIRA MONTCLAIR

DEAR READER,

Thank you for reading Sorcha and Cailean's story. I hope you enjoyed the story of Logan Ramsay losing his firstborn daughter as much as I did. The next book on my list is Kyla's story. You know I have to leave a little tease at the end of each book for the next one, and I'm looking forward to writing this new addition to The Highland Clan. It should be exciting!

I am often asked how many stories I have planned for this series. I have no set number. I'll keep writing for as long as readers continue to want their stories. With all the characters I have added along the way, the possible list would be well over forty stories.

Want to help an author? Tell your friends about your favorite books, and leave a review on Amazon and/or Goodreads. I will be grateful.

To sign up for my newsletter: **www.keiramontclair.com**
My Facebook page: **www.facebook.com/KeiraMontclair**
My Pinterest page: **www.pinterest.com/KeiraMontclair**

Happy reading!

Keira Montclair

ABOUT THE AUTHOR

KEIRA MONTCLAIR IS THE PEN name of an author who lives in Florida with her husband. She loves to write fast-paced, emotional romance, especially with children as secondary characters in her stories.

She has worked as a registered nurse in pediatrics and recovery room nursing. Teaching is another of her loves, and she has taught both high school mathematics and practical nursing.

Now she loves to spend her time writing, but there isn't enough time to write everything she wants! Her Highlander Clan Grant series, comprising of eight standalone novels, is a reader favorite. Her third series, The Highland Clan, set twenty years after the Clan Grant series, focuses on the Grant/Ramsay descendants. She also has a contemporary series set in The Finger Lakes of Western New York.

Her newest series is The Soulmate Chronicles, historical romance with a touch of paranormal. Read on for an excerpt from *Trusting a Highlander...*

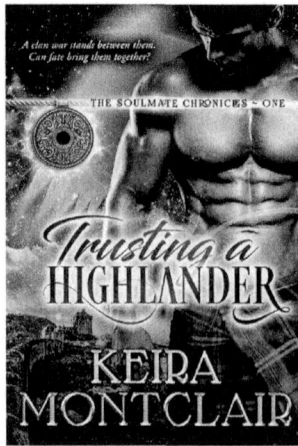

CHAPTER ONE

The Highlands of Scotland, the 15th century

CATHERINE HATED HER HUSBAND.

She sat in her chair—back rigid, hands folded in her lap just so—averting her eyes from the man bellowing in front of her.

"This is all your fault. If you were more of a woman, I would have no trouble performing, but you, you…"

Henry Merrill's face had turned an all-too-familiar shade of scarlet, making his brown eyes and brown hair darker in contrast. Though his features were handsome, he was too cold and cruel to be considered a good-looking man. What would her punishment be this time?

"Answer me. Why?"

"My lord, 'tis our daughter. I worry…"

His hand slammed down on the table, stopping her mid-sentence. "I do not care about her. Isbeil is female. And what are females worth, Catherine?"

She pinched her eyes shut, wishing such an act would make him disappear. She hated him more and more every day.

He loomed over her in the chair, pinching her chin to raise her gaze to his. "What are females worth?"

She stared into his cruel brown eyes.

"Nothing," she whispered.

"You are worth nothing, as is our daughter. Nothing."

Even though her husband lived in Scotland, he'd been born an Englishman—and while he'd been banished to Scotland as a punishment, he still adhered to the ways of his former home. He never missed the chance to mock and belittle the Scots' speech and language, but her sire had sold her to the wealthy scoundrel as soon as he'd offered the right amount of coin.

"I have matters to attend to," the cruel man ground out, dropping his hand so he could return to his task of dressing. "It is your job to make me desire you, and you have failed again. You cannot even complete a task simple enough for a common whore. At this rate, I'll never get the heir that I need."

"Aye, my lord." She kept her gaze on her white hands, clasped together in her lap.

He sat in a chair and barked orders as he lifted his foot and pointed it in her direction. "Once you are finished dressing me, you will go to your spot in front of the hearth in the hall. You will kneel there until I tell you your punishment is over."

She rushed over to get his boot, which she helped pull over his swollen foot. Knowing she would pay for the next thing she would do, she moved ahead with her request as she laced the ties for him, unable to stop herself. "Isbeil is ill, and she is never let out of her room in the cellars. Please allow me to tend to her. I will complete my…"

His hand swung out, catching her square on her cheek with the back of it, the indentation of his ring scratching her tender skin. "I did not give you permission to speak. No, you shall not go to her. You'll do your punishment until I say you are done."

"Aye, my lord." She fought the tears that tried to escape, refusing to show him how he had hurt her. When she finished helping him dress, she followed him down the staircase and over to the hearth, keeping her head down so she would not have to see the looks everyone gave her. Some enjoyed the way he treated her; others felt sympathetic. Either way, it had happened enough times that she knew what to expect.

Catherine stood, as always, and waited for her husband to sift through the crate next to the hearth, searching for whatever form of torture he favored today. He pulled out one of the pieces that had been built according to his instructions. At least he'd chosen the device filled with pebbles. There were more painful options—a pouch he filled with fresh nettles before each use and another device studded with shards he'd collected from the armorer's hut. She prayed it would be kneeling today. Standing on the painful objects made it impossible for her to walk days afterward.

He sat in in front of her and said, "Kneel until I tell you that you are finished. Think about what you've done and mend your ways."

He always blamed her for his inability to maintain an erection after mauling her breasts and her tender skin. He barked orders at her, and she always did as she was told. How could she mend her ways? She had been upset about her daughter, so she'd offered distraction as an excuse, but mostly because she knew of no other. She did her best to stay groomed and clean. What more did he want from her?

In her darkest days, she admitted to herself that perhaps *this* was what he wanted. To see her suffer.

He shook his head, narrowing his gaze at her. "How could I have ever thought you were worth the coin I paid for you? Aye, you are comely and shapely, but you have not given me the sons I require. Is that too much to ask from a wife? Bear me two sons, and I'll give you anything you want."

She knelt carefully, knowing from experience that how she landed on the pebbles would determine how painful her time would be.

"Enough. Kneel!"

She did as instructed and he stalked away from her, cursing as he moved.

In a small way, she was pleased.

No one would bother her, try to tell her what to do, or even speak to her during her punishment, which would give her plenty of time to think.

She needed to plan her escape. She would save her daughter, despite her husband.

☾

Graeme MacGregor stood with his shoulders squared, his chin lifted to the late summer Highlands breeze, his favorite reminder of his sole purpose in life, to protect his lands. As laird of the Mac-Gregor clan, it was his job to lead his clan, honor his ancestors, and fight for Scotland.

Honor his ancestors. That pledge alone forced one other duty upon his broad shoulders, but one he bore proudly.

Revenge. Revenge for the death of his parents and his eldest brother. Memories of the day he'd watched his family die at the hands of Henry Merrill would be ingrained in his mind forever. First his mother, then his eldest brother, then his sire. He'd watched, helpless, as his sire roared and fought, trying to rip free from his captors and save his wife…

And he had listened. He'd heard sounds and words he wished to forget, words that had echoed in his mind every day since.

Henry Merrill would rue the day he'd made an enemy of Graeme MacGregor.

He took in the beauty of the majestic Highland peaks in front of him, letting the sight calm him. Those mountaintops reminded him of the vow he'd made on his sire's grave. His clan would be as glorious as that tallest peak. He was determined to see it happen.

He glanced over his shoulder when the rustling of his brothers reached his ear.

"Graeme, what's your decision?" Conn asked. Conn was two years behind him at nine and ten, and his youngest brother, Rory, was one and ten.

Graeme stared back at the peaks and breathed in the sweet morning air, listening, and finally he felt it. The serenity of the loch this morn and the slight breeze called to him, almost whispering his name in a soft chant. The peaks spoke to him as they often did. This day would be a special one. "We go today. The mountains tell me 'tis our time. Ready yourself and our men. We leave within the hour." The day was just breaking, and he preferred to travel in the early hours of the morn, just after the breaking of dawn. He heard the clap of hands at his declaration, and he knew it was his youngest brother Rory, anxious to move.

He and the MacGregor warriors would travel through the moors and valleys to Merrill land on a scouting mission to uncover more of the information they needed to attack the Merrills and kill their leader. He would strike down Merrill's clan just as Merrill had done to the MacGregors. Once they obtained all the information they needed from their scouting mission, he and his two brothers would plan their careful attack. Then Graeme would ready his two hundred Highland warriors, the force it had taken him years to rebuild and train, for the retaliation he'd vowed to take seven years ago. He'd been a lad of ten and four at the time, and it had taken patience for him to wait until they were ready.

That moment was finally upon them.

He turned to Conn and smiled. "This is to be our day."

His brother Rory asked, "How long have ye had these strange premonitions?"

He headed toward the stables to ready his horse. "Ever since the attack. You may trust that the mountains tell me this is a verra special day."

"In what way? We're not to attack the Merrills today—'tis just our last chance to gather information."

"Aye, and for Tomag to ready the men in the lists. We must practice hard and be ready. Dinnae worry yourself." Tomag was Graeme's second, and he'd assisted him in ensuring the men were trained for the coming fight.

He turned away from his brothers, waving at him to ready their small contingent while he completed a couple of final preparations of his own.

Before they left, he needed to visit their other brother.

Graeme went to see Boyd every day. The two of them had watched Merrill murder their parents and brother that fateful day. Conn and Rory had been inside the keep. The brutal attack in the courtyard had so traumatized Boyd, he'd stayed in his chamber ever since. Moyra, their head housekeeper, was his devoted caretaker.

Prior to this year, Boyd hadn't spoken a word to anyone after the attack, but he had finally emerged from his trauma enough to talk to one person: Graeme. Their conversations centered on one thing—killing the Merrill.

No one else knew about Boyd's progress. Graeme did not dare upset his brother, even by telling Conn and Rory.

The attack had traumatized all who'd witnessed it. Many of the MacGregor warriors had been killed, but some had been out hunting and had not returned until after the tragedy. Henry Merrill and his men had killed at will, cutting down all the warriors they could and slaying some of the clan who worked the land. Others had been left untouched. The only woman who'd been killed was Graeme's mother. Merrill had given no explanation for why he'd spared some and not others—except for Graeme. He'd made sure to tell Graeme why he was sparing *his* life.

He knocked on the door and stepped inside, knowing he would not get a response from Boyd. He found his brother pacing in front of the hearth in his room. "Boyd, is anything wrong?"

He stopped and spun around to face Graeme. "Today?"

Graeme nodded, taking in his brother's slight form, his pale skin. "Aye, today is our last scouting mission. We will finish this within a fortnight." He was so small for a lad of ten and four, but he never left the perceived safety of his chamber. Graeme had tried to convince him to go to the lists, practice working with a sword, but he'd refused. The lad who had once been fearless was now afraid of everything. That alone would have been reason enough for Graeme to seek revenge.

Boyd's eyes lit up and he asked, "Mayhap a sennight?"

"Probably a fortnight." Boyd's face fell, but Graeme knew how to hearten him. "It takes precision to do this right. If we dinnae, we could lose some of our men. Ye know we must be careful."

Boyd took a deep breath and smiled. "Be careful. I miss Mama and Papa."

"We all miss them. Are ye working on your letters? Ye know Mama wanted us all to read. She said 'twas important for the sons of the laird to be able to read the messages brought to them."

He nodded, holding up evidence of his work. "Rory and Moyra work with me every day."

"Good. That pleases me. I may need ye to assist me someday when ye are a bit older."

Boyd nodded, then whispered, "Go. 'Tis a most important day. I feel it, too. I knew ye would come to me with tidings."

Graeme pondered over his statement for just a moment before nodding in acceptance. Boyd knew things sometimes, there was no denying it.

Graeme had turned to leave when his brother stopped him again.

"Do not kill the wee ones."

Graeme jerked his head back to Boyd. "What? Ye do not wish to kill all the Merrills?"

Boyd shook his head.

"Our clan has demanded the blood of all the Merrill clan, women and children alike."

Boyd stared at his feet, his mind churning over something. Graeme could tell by the way he chewed the inside of his cheek that this was a difficult process for him. He'd often wondered what Boyd would have been like without the tragedy in their lives. Would he have been different anyway?

The lad lifted his gaze to Graeme and whispered, "I've learned 'tis wrong. The children have done nothing to us. We should allow them to live. Mayhap the women, too."

"You learned this? Where? How?" This went against everything his clan had demanded, everything he'd promised them. They wanted the Merrill clan to be put to death the same way Graeme's family and the MacGregor warriors had ruthlessly been cut down.

"In my sleep. It came to me then. I cannae explain, I just know 'twould be wrong. Kill the Merrill and his warriors. Leave the others."

Graeme did not know what to say to Boyd. While a small part of him agreed with his brother, he knew what his people wanted. How could he hope to sway them after seven years? "I cannae say ye are wrong. I'll think on it. 'Tis all I can promise, Boyd. Our men, our clan—they're hungry for justice. I must go now. The others are waiting."

"Godspeed. Protect Rory and Conn."

Graeme nodded and left the chamber.

He headed through the courtyard, his mind clouded by these new thoughts from Boyd. He knew not what to make of it. His brother had proven to know things, yet he did not understand how that could come to pass when he stayed in his chamber and spoke to no one other than Graeme. But his gut told him to trust Boyd's premonitions.

The decision did not need to be made this day, and he decided to put it off until after the scouting mission. He wanted—nay, demanded—precision for their final attack.

As soon as he arrived at the stables, the smell of horse calmed his blood. He took a deep breath and stepped inside.

The first rule for any great warrior was to care for your animal—in return, they would take care of you. Before they left, he would find a sweet treat for the beast and give him a thorough rub down, talk to him so he knew to be battle ready. He stopped at the treat barrel near the door, grabbing a few for his favorite beasts.

As he passed down the line of stalls, he stopped at his beloved mare's stall, put one end of a carrot between his teeth and held it for the bronze beauty. The horse greeted him with a nicker and trotted over to him, nuzzling his neck before she carefully bit down on the carrot and retreated, eager to finish her treat. Her antics made him chuckle. She was a fine animal, and with his stallion, she'd mothered two colts he adored. He called to her and she returned to his side so he could pat her neck before he headed down to the largest stall at the end, the one reserved for his pride and joy, Starlight.

He heard the swish of Starlight's tail before he entered his friend's stall. Starlight preened just a bit when Graeme entered, tossing his head with a whinny as a greeting to his handler. He pawed the ground with his front hoof as he often did in anticipation of his morning treat, a sweet apple that he preferred cut into two pieces. Graeme held the fruit and sliced it in half with his dirk before offering the first piece to the beast, who grabbed it and gobbled it down as if it was the most succulent meal ever. Starlight's bright eyes found Graeme's as he patiently awaited the second half. This one he chewed a bit slower while Graeme petted him and rubbed down his coat, talking sweetly to his horse as he always did to ready him for the challenging journey ahead.

He saddled the beast and brought him outside, taking another deep breath of the Highlands air to remind him of his purpose.

Once the others had all assembled outside, Conn asked, "Any special instructions?"

Before replying, Graeme surveyed his ten warriors—satisfied to see they appeared as ready for this mission as he was. "Nay. We proceed as planned. Conn, ye will take a contingency to the back of the castle to make sure ye know the landmarks and best places to climb the curtain wall, and Rory—" he nodded to his youngest brother, "—you and two men will continue to search for the hidden opening to the tunnel beneath the keep. We know there is a complicated maze there, and we must find it. I, along with Tomag and two others, will observe Merrill's schedule and try to determine the number of warriors he has at present. Any questions?"

No one replied, their serious expressions telling him his men wanted this almost as much as he did. "The reign of the Merrill will end in less than a fortnight. We make our final plans after this excursion."

His warriors responded the same as they always did, chants of "MacGregor, MacGregor" filling the area. The loud, booming voices of his men drew other people out of their homes, and their voices joined in with mantras of their own.

"Kill the Merrills, kill the Merrills!" Their voices rose and the excitement of the crowd peaked. "Kill them all. Time to die!"

The chants were usually the same. Something niggled at the back of his mind—Boyd's words. Conn had told him the same thing many times. *Kill only the warriors. They are the ones who killed our family, our clan.*

Graeme led the others down the path that ran between their cottages, listening to the fervor of their voices. The warriors who had missed the tragedy because they'd been hunting had been overcome with guilt over the event. They wanted all the Merrills dead. He had felt the same way after witnessing the horrors of that day, but something now told him it was wrong. He couldn't say what—no different than Boyd. Had he and his brother shared the same dream? Something told him to spare the women, the children, the elderly. Would the people truly accept such a command from their laird?

He could not guess. The entire experience had been traumatic. Some cottages had been burned to the ground. The clanmates who'd survived had rebuilt their huts, but rebuilding his group of warriors had been more difficult. Some families had left the clan, fearing they'd face another attack with few warriors left to defend them.

But he *had* rebuilt. Their numbers were high again, and he was confident the MacGregors would prevail over the Merrills. It had been a long, arduous journey for them, but he had to believe they would become a prosperous clan again.

As they moved through the outer bailey, the few lasses who had stayed with his clan came out, casting coy looks his way. He knew what they wanted—*him.*

Graeme had not had time to focus on a woman. He was single-minded in his goal to regain the power his clan had possessed before the attack—to make the Merrill pay for what he'd done. He had no time to wed or court a lass, though many said his clan needed a mistress. Someday he would find a woman who interested him enough to court her, but not yet.

As Graeme and his lads made their way to the end of the path, he let out the MacGregor war whoop and spurred his horse into a gallop. They could be as loud as they wished while still on MacGregor land, but once they crossed into Merrill land, his men would turn silent. The beast responded with a snort and a charge that made Graeme grin. Even Starlight was eager for their mission.

☾

TRUSTING A HIGHLANDER is available in ebook, paperback, and audio.

Printed in Great Britain
by Amazon